Crossing the Lines

TALES FROM ROCK HAVEN
BOOK 1

Crossing *the* Lines

Peter Stipe

MERIPOINT BOOKS | Williamsburg, Virginia

Series Name: Tales from Rock Haven: Book 1
Title: Crossing the Lines
Author: Peter Stipe
Cover Photograph: Peter Stipe

Paperback ISBN: 978-1-960808-17-2

First Edition

Printed in the United States of America
Williamsburg, Virginia

Hoefler Text: 11 pt

To teachers and educators at all levels, from K-12
and beyond.

Your work makes the world a better place.

PROLOGUE

LUCAS KNOX RAN AT DAWN as he always had ever since college. Routine got him through his days and weeks. He left Jennifer asleep in their dark bedroom, tiptoed past his little girls' room, careful not to disturb them. Then out onto the front porch, into the cool dampness and the slanting spring sunlight. He ran up the hill on Depot Street from his house to the train station on Washington Street. Early morning commuters stood waiting for the early train to Boston. Some of them nodded to him as he ran by. He was a well-known institution in Rock Haven. His route and his passing at sunrise were as predictable as the arrival of their train every morning, right on time. Many of the train riders knew him personally. He was their children's math teacher, a respected educator and minor local celebrity because of the success of the track teams he coached.

Lucas took a turn down the hill off Washington Street and ran along the edge of the marina. The sunrise silence was broken only by the quiet clinking of the rigging on the moored sailboats and the echoes of his footsteps off the granite walls of the pier. The harbor at dawn was still, the water glassy, light reflecting off the incoming tide and from the windows of the upscale seafood restaurants, The Harbor House and others, where the town's wealthier residents and the sailing crowd liked to dine. Lucas and Jennifer ate at the Harbor House on their anniversary every year.

One more turn took him uphill away from the marina, past the granite-based sign at the entrance to the quiet streets of Harbor View Heights. Streets here were empty at this early hour. The residents of the big houses in The Heights, as the neighborhood was commonly called, had no need to be up and out at dawn. They would arrive at their jobs later in the day, on their own schedules.

Lucas cruised along the wide streets that circled inside Harbor View Heights, past the groomed lawns separating each house. For a moment, he thought about the few students from this neighborhood who attended the public high school.

Many parents from The Heights sent their children away to attend tony private schools. He thought of Jessie and wondered why she was in the public high school. She lived somewhere in this prestigious neighborhood.

Many of the athletes he'd coached over the years had a hard edge, an insecurity that drove their desperate need to win. A need rooted in their families' tough lives. They were the sons and daughters of the hard-working blue-collar workers and fishermen who lived down the hill, unaccustomed to the easy lives of wealth and privilege of the households he now ran past. But Jessie came from here. Her family must have money. She lacked for nothing. Nonetheless, she was undeniably the most gifted athlete he'd ever coached. He wondered what fueled her competitive fire, where her edge came from.

He thought of Gabriel, who also came from The Heights. His soft life and his family's expectations that he would succeed had turned him in a different direction. Lucas had him in math class. Gabriel was not an athlete, and because he lacked any such distinction, many of his classmates ignored him. He was always in trouble in school, and, except in art class, was always on the brink of failing many of his classes. His teachers agreed he was capable of academic success. His unwillingness to meet his family's expectations pushed him to rebellion, pursuing his own goals in his own way. It was widely known in school and around town that he was funneling drugs to students and to the town as a whole. His pocket always had cash, earned by his dealing, not derived from his parents' wealth.

How could two such different students as Jessie and Gabriel have emerged from the same background in The Heights? It was a question with no clear answer. It intrigued Lucas. It bothered him not to have an answer.

Lucas turned downhill, passing the Harbor View Heights sign again. His standard early morning route now took him through a neighborhood the locals called the inner harbor. Here, the houses were smaller, but well-kept with lawns carefully tended and mowed by the residents, not by the landscaping companies that took care of the homes in The Heights.

Many of the school's celebrities lived somewhere in this cramped neighborhood. There was the Goncalves family, whose son Joe had already earned a college scholarship for baseball. The Arnolds lived here, too. Violet Arnold was, next to Jessie, the track team's biggest star. Her brother Isaac was Joe Goncalves' best friend and teammate. The cars and pickups parked along the streets here were older and sometimes rusted.

This neighborhood was awake and stirring, people already out, heading to their jobs in the fish processing plant on the pier at the end of the inner harbor or off to their fishing boats. The weather-beaten look and the sour, low-tide smells of the processing plant and the fishing fleet were isolated here, cut off from the upscale marina by a rocky point of land, a bluff that hid the inner harbor from the marina and the sailboats.

A park, Herring Head, sat on the point, overlooking the sailboats at the marina on one side and the inner harbor and the fish processing plant on the other. Lucas followed the perimeter road looping the park, passing the swings and the playground where he and Jennifer liked to bring their little girls late in the afternoon when he got home from track practice.

Lucas exited the tidy park and returned to his small house, caught halfway between the wealth of the marina and The Heights, and the blue-collar world of the inner harbor. He cruised to a stop exactly on time. Thirty-five minutes for five miles. It allowed him almost an hour to shower and get ready for his day of teaching and coaching.

Jennifer was awake and tending to the children's breakfast when he opened the front door.

Life is good, he thought. This is the way I always hoped things would turn out.

CHAPTER ONE

Jessie

JESSIE BRANDT WAITED for the start of her high jump competition. Her competitors had begun jumping at lower heights, four feet four, then four feet six inches, and had worked up to five-feet. Her last two opponents had finished their competition, knocking the bar off, failing to clear that height. The high jump official, Jonas Brown, a volunteer official from the high school's English department, walked to Jessie and asked, "Are you ready? What height would you like to begin with?"

"Set the bar at five-foot-four."

Jonas raised the bar crossbar four inches higher than all the other girls had attempted, six inches higher than anyone else had cleared. He settled the bar on the standards placed on either end of the knee-deep foam rubber pad lining the pit. Now, with no competitors left, Jessie needed only to clear this, her opening height to win the day's competition. All the other events in the meet had been completed.

She straightened her blonde ponytail and was ready. Standing still as a statue, she stared down the crossbar, acutely aware that everyone at the meet had gathered behind her to watch her jump. Each breath she took was visible in the slight rising and falling of her taut abdomen. Her top was rolled and tucked into her bra to ensure it wouldn't flap and dislodge the bar as she jumped. Tanned skin seemed stretched as tight as shrink wrap over her flat abdominal muscles.

For a moment, her fingertips twitched. Then she began, running with long bounding strides, seeming unnaturally tall, her knees high, her fists pumping up. She settled lower for the last three quick steps, giving the impression as she approached the bar of running uphill. Then abruptly, her left foot smacked down, the sound of the impact as loud as a rifle shot. Her right knee reached wide for the far side standard, her right arm reached up and out over the crossbar, and she soared, her back above the bar. At the peak of the jump, stretched out flat, back to the bar, she gave a sudden upward jerk of her pelvis, lifting her hips, leaving a wide gap between her body and the bar. Then she settled her hands in her lap and coolly pulled her knees to her shoulders. A flick of her heels and she was clear. She fell, landing, rolling on her back to her shoulders on the soft pads.

The surrounding crowd of students, athletes, and coaches exploded with cheers and applause. Casually, as though she didn't hear the crowd and leaving the impression that what she had done was an everyday event, which it was, she rolled to her hands and knees and backed off the pads.

Coach Lucas Knox smiled and checked off her jump on his clipboard. By winning the event, Jessie added five points to his team's wide winning total.

"Move it to five-foot-six," Jessie instructed the official. Jonas did what she told him to do, raising the bar.

Again, she stood, staring at the bar. The crowd fell silent again. Again, she ran, bounding, her knees high. Again, she settled and exploded, sailing, flying high above the bar. Again, she rolled from the pit, ignoring the cheering crowd.

Lucas Knox stepped up to his friend Jonas and, standing next to Jessie, interceded, suggesting, "Let's try five-foot-eight." He turned to Jessie, "You're on today. First attempt clearances on these heights. Let's go for the record."

"Sure," she said as she walked back to her starting mark.

Jonas raised the bar and measured it to ensure an accurate height.

The crowd went silent again, sensing that this new height would be a significant moment. Her personal best and a school and league record.

Again, she stood, staring at the bar. Her fingers twitched. Then slowly, looking straight ahead, she walked to the bar, reached up, and knocked it off. "I'm done," she told Jonas Brown. She walked away.

"Are you sure?" he called after her.

"Yep. I won. There's no sense going on."

Lucas went to her and wrapped his arm around her shoulder. "This is the last event of the day," he said. "You've done five-eight in practice. You had it going on today. Why stop?"

"I'm tired. I won the hurdles, anchored the relay, and won the triple jump. Why go on?"

"It's the nature of the high jump. It's one of the only events in sport where even the winner fails at the end. You jump until you can't go any higher. The winner eventually knocks off the bar."

She turned, facing her coach. "Not me. I won't fail. Never. I win. Always. And you don't decide how high I'll jump. That's my decision. Yes, I'll go five eight. Probably five ten. Six feet is possible. Maybe at the State Meet, but not here. Not today. I won't ever let myself fail. I'll never lose."

She walked away, gathering her warm-ups as she went.

Lucas turned to Jonas and shook his head. "She's special. I don't know how good she can be. Neither does she. But I wish she'd push the edge when she can."

Jonas laughed quietly, as though he was sharing a personal joke with his close friend. "Oh, she'll push the edge. Maybe like she said, not today, and maybe in other ways, but she'll find the edge when she's ready."

"I hope you're right."

Chapter Two

Joe

Across the outfield fence that bordered the track, Joe Goncalves stood on the pitcher's mound. He stopped and turned to watch Jessie's jump. When she walked away, Joe turned back to the plate and found himself face-to-face with Harvey Lancaster, his coach. Waiting alongside the coach was Isaac Arnold, the catcher.

Harvey tapped Joe on the chest to get his attention. "Get your head back in the game, Joe. Don't let your girlfriend distract you from all the way over there on the track. We have two outs still to go. You can see Jessie once the game's over. But focus on what's happening here. Let's end this thing. Right here. Right now. We win, we're league champs again. The team is counting on you. Let's go." Harvey clapped him on the shoulder and walked back to his dugout.

"You heard him," Isaac added. "And he's right, of course. Two batters to go. You've got a complete game if you get these last two batters. Let's end this and go home."

"I'm ready. Let's do it." Joe scuffed the dirt in front of the rubber.

Isaac set his hard helmet over his short afro. "Slider," he said quietly to Joe, as he turned and trotted back to the plate.

Joe stood towering on the height of the mound, a tall, commanding figure. His hand seemed disproportionately large, like the hand of David in Michelangelo's iconic statue. His fingers engulfed the baseball like it was a cue ball.

The batter cowered, waiting, knowing he was overmatched.

Joe rocked back, his arms over his head, then he uncoiled, striding toward the plate, giving a quick flick of his long fingers as he released the ball. The ball hissed like a snake, heading right at the batter. The batter leaned back to dodge away and watched as the ball suddenly dipped and cut, hitting Isaac's glove with a crack.

"Strike three," shouted the umpire.

Isaac flipped the ball back to Joe. Joe turned and instructed his infielders. "Be ready. I'm going to serve the next guy a ground ball."

The final batter dug in, determined not to strike out.

Isaac gave the sign. "Low fastball."

Joe rocked, the same stretch mimicking what he had done when he threw the slider. Then he fired. The ball hissed again, and the batter swung.

Clink. The sound of the metal bat chipping the top edge of the ball. It rolled on two soft hops to the second baseman, who scooped it and tossed to first.

Game over! The team rushed around Joe to celebrate their championship, hugging him, clapping his wide shoulders. He basked quietly in the moment.

CHAPTER THREE

Jessie and Joe

Two school buses in the parking lot slowly filled with disconsolate teams: the losing baseball team on one bus, and the defeated boys and girls track teams on the other, ready for the long ride back to their schools. The victorious Rock Haven girls and boys track teams mixed with a happy crowd of parents and spectators as they crossed the field to the school. The baseball team would come across the field later, lagging, spending a few moments celebrating their championship in their dugout, receiving a few final words of inspiration from Coach Lancaster.

Lucas Knox walked among his athletes with Jonas Brown. They said little. Lucas always felt an emotional letdown, win or lose, once a meet was over. He had little to say at this moment. Brown was an old friend of Lucas. He understood and let Lucas take his own time.

Gabriel Sloan hung at the back of the crowd of spectators. Before the girls entered the school, he cut through the crowd and stopped Jessie.

"Hey, Jessie," he tugged her elbow. "I got some great photos of you at the meet today. Want to see?"

She stopped and turned, confronting the scrawny boy in front of her. He pushed his long bangs away from his glasses and turned his camera so she could see the digital pictures. She was driving off a hurdle, powering on to the next one. Hanging in mid-air in the midst of her triple jump. Taking the baton at the start of her relay leg. "Here's the best one," said Gabriel. The picture showed her floating high above the crossbar, stretched out on her back with her legs spread, ready to pull past the bar.

"Nice," Jessie said. "Can you email those to me?"

"Sure. I'll send them to the local paper too, and the school paper, of course. But, could I ask you a favor?"

"Of course, Gabe. What?"

"These are digital. But the best photography is still done with regular film and is developed in a darkroom. A photographer has more control of the picture when he develops it that way. I'd like to shoot a few of you like that, on film, when you're not running and jumping."

"Why?"

"There are photography contests, and I believe I could win with some really good photos of you."

"You want me to pose for you?"

"Sure. Would you?"

"If I'm going to be your model... what's in it for me?"

"I can make it worth your while." He opened a black leather shoulder bag filled with film canisters, lenses, and other photographic equipment, and allowed her to see some loose joints in a plastic baggie at the bottom.

"You've got my email. Send me the track pictures, and we can talk." Jessie turned back to her friends and teammates. Gabe faded into the crowd heading for the parking lot.

Joe, Isaac, and the baseball team arrived. Joe scooped Jessie up, holding her tight, her feet dangling. "We won. We're league champs."

"Us too. But our league championship meet is a week away."

"We need to celebrate."

"Oh, we will." She gave his hand a quick squeeze.

"What did that little clown Gabe want?"

"He shot some pictures of me at the meet today. He's going to send them to me."

CHAPTER FOUR

Jessie

Years earlier, when Jessie was six and in first grade, Patricia Brandt had a late morning, unexpected business meeting cancellation. Suddenly finding free time, she drove to her husband, Gary's, office, hoping to meet him and steal an hour for lunch. Linda, his administrative assistant, told her, "Oh, Mrs. Brandt. Gary's out somewhere with a client right now. Was he expecting you?"

"No, I just thought I'd drop by and see if he was free for lunch."

"You might try calling him."

Back at her car, Patricia dialed Gary. A woman answered. "Hello?"

"Hi," Patricia replied, puzzled. "Who is this? Is Gary there?"

"This is Susan. Gary's somewhere around here. Let me see if I can track him down. Can I tell him who's calling? Are you calling from work?"

"This is his wife, Patricia."

The line went dead.

She dialed again, but there was no answer.

When Gary got home, Patricia asked him, "Who's Susan? I tried to meet you for lunch, but some woman calling herself Susan picked up when I called."

"Oh, that was my new admin. I was down the hall in a meeting."

"Gary, I had just been in your office. I was outside in the parking lot. Your administrative assistant, Linda, told me you were out."

It wasn't the first time Patricia had caught Gary in a lie or with another woman. She was determined that it would be the last. She filed for divorce. He tried to blame her, claiming she must be having an affair if she wanted a divorce. It didn't work.

Why, Patricia wondered, when a man screws up, does he always assume the wife must also be having an affair? Why do they always put the blame on the woman? Why don't they ever assume the responsibility themselves?

Patricia tried to make sense of it. It didn't matter. She found herself months later, financially secure with alimony and child support. Still, she was a single parent trying to raise a headstrong seven-year-old girl by herself.

She was determined to become self-sufficient; never again dependent on a man for an income or support. Patricia found paths over the coming years to build her own career, starting with work in local sales support for a pharmaceutical company. When Jessie entered middle school and showed she was able to fend for herself after school, Patricia accepted an outside sales position with some local travel, but no overnight trips. Whatever it took to close a deal, she would make sure it happened. Two years later, she accepted a regional sales position and began flying to clients up and down the East Coast. The pay, the commissions, and the rewards were excellent.

She worried constantly about her time away from Jessie, but she watched as Jessie became a strong, self-reliant woman.

Jessie's independence is making her stronger, Patricia rationalized. Maybe that's why she's so good academically as well as athletically. She seems to have inherited my ambition, my need to win at all costs. She does appear angry at times. Does she understand what her father did to me? She was so little when it all happened, and her father's never around now. She must know he cheated on me with other women. She's probably still angry at her father for what he did to me; to both of us, really. I get angry, too, at times. But I've found ways to overcome that. She will too. Everything will be fine. I just wish we could talk about things. We're in this together.

*****

Jessie arrived home after the track meet, still sweating slightly from the early summer heat. Patricia sat on a barstool at the kitchen island, appraising her daughter. Jessie sat across the marble countertop from her mom. Dirty dinner dishes sat in front of them.

"How did you do at the meet today?" Patricia asked.

"Good. I won three events and the relay."

"Wonderful. Listen. I've got sales calls scheduled in Pennsylvania on Monday, Tuesday, and Wednesday. I'll be flying off to Pittsburgh Sunday afternoon. Will you be okay taking care of everything by yourself for three days plus Sunday night?"

"I should. I've been taking care of myself all the other times you've been away on business."

"I know. I feel awful about this. It's been years since your dad left us. I feel guilty every time I have to leave town on business, leaving you alone."

"Don't. I'll be fine." Jessie got up, gave her mom a reassuring hug, and went up to her room. She turned on her computer and opened the email with the photos from Gabriel.

He's okay, I guess, but he's such a loser, she thought. Dealing drugs, scuffing around with the artist crowd. Failing all his classes. But I like the photos he took of me. He is good with photography, I guess, even if with nothing else. I wonder what the deal is with him asking me to pose for him.

I could do it. But I can't let people in school see me hanging around with a loser like him. Maybe modeling is in my future. People seem to think I'm pretty enough for a career as a model. Gabe seems to think so. I don't know. But I enjoy that even a fringe type like him is hung up on me. He wants to pay me off with weed. I don't care about that. But I guess I could pose for him and see where it goes from there.

*****

Gabriel found a message from Jessie waiting for him when he returned to his room after dinner.

> *luv the pics thx*

> *sooo what's this abt me posing 4 u* 😏

He texted back:

> *yea for a photography contest*

> *you in?*

> *just say when*

Jessie read his response and thought for a moment. She didn't want the whole school to see her posing for someone like Gabe. It would ruin her status as the coolest girl in school to be seen doing anything with someone like him. She replied, tapping quickly on her phone:

> *sure*

> *sunday nite*

> *my house @ 7*

She was interrupted by a new text that popped up from Joe:

> *Hey girl*

> *beach & food sat afternoon?*

> *sunday's a no go, got family stuff all day*

Perfect, Jessie thought.

> *works*

> *cu after practice*

Gabriel's response appeared:

> *c u sunday 7 @ your house*

Gabriel pulled up the picture of her flying above the high jump bar. He zoomed in on it, fascinated by the way her legs were spread, her thighs open. He zoomed in some more.

*****

Jessie switched off her email and set to work, catching up on her reading for her English class. There was a lot more to her than simply being a track star and the most beautiful girl in school. She was also in the top ten in her class and proud of it. She worked hard for all her successes.

Gabe was typical of most of her classmates. Everyone in school watched her every move. She basked in their attention. There wasn't a challenge she couldn't win, an accomplishment she couldn't achieve. Nothing could stop her. So, she believed. Still beneath it all, she was still a vulnerable eighteen-year-old girl seeking answers and affirmation from her fellow students, her boyfriend, her teachers, and most of all, her mom.

CHAPTER FIVE

Lucas Knox

After dinner, Lucas sat down at his computer on the kitchen table in his small house on Depot Street. He and Jennifer had fed the babies and put them down for the night. Now it was his time to go to work. He pulled up the template he used to record his team's performances and entered the results, not just the team score, but each girl's individual performance in each of their events. He noted the spectacular results from Jessie and Violet Arnold. Combined, the two girls had won seven events: Jessie, the hurdles, the high jump, the triple jump; and Violet, only a junior, the long jump, the hundred, and two hundred meters. They had combined with two other sprinters to win the four-by-one-hundred-meter relay. They alone would make his team a contender in both the league championship meet in two weeks and the state meet later in the month.

With the results of the meet collated, he went to work, grading his math students' homework and tests. It was ten o'clock when he crawled into bed, setting the alarm for five thirty so he could get his morning run in before the start of the next school day.

*****

Lucas Knox had studied mathematics and run on the track team at the University of Massachusetts in Amherst in the Connecticut River Valley. As he saw the world, both math and track were related. He liked the logic, the predictability of mathematics. It generated finite answers. Two plus two always equaled four, and that's how it was with every equation. To Lucas, track and field was the same.

Clean, clear, and predictable. Proper training and technique yielded the best results.

As an eight-hundred-meter runner, he trained with the distance runners in the fall cross-country season and then worked as a long sprinter the rest of the year. He learned that the precise techniques needed by sprinters and jumpers, once mastered, paid dividends in dramatic performance improvements. He appreciated that those improvements were so measurable, logged to the hundredth of a second or a millimeter of height or distance. The clean, exact nature of track and field meshed with the logic he loved in math.

He realized early during his college days that he could merge these two loves if he became a high school math teacher and track coach. Midway through his senior year, with his teacher certification pending, he was offered that opportunity in the small town of Rock Haven on the coast north of Boston. It was perfect! His girlfriend, Jennifer, was from a small suburb north of Boston. When they were married, a job in Rock Haven would bring her close to her family. His family was from western Massachusetts, close enough to visit, and far enough away to allow him privacy. That distance from his upbringing was fine, welcomed even, as it afforded him the chance to become his own man. His family was supportive of the move.

Jennifer was a psychology major. Her plans after college were unclear. There were few careers that demanded the talents of a psych major. She and Lucas were engaged by the end of their junior year. They were married the summer they graduated and moved to the small house behind the train station on a dead-end street in Rock Haven, the purchase financed by Jennifer's parents.

Jennifer went to work part-time in a retail shop on Washington Street. Lucas started teaching and coaching. Then she became pregnant, and the challenges of life took over their time.

*****

It was lunchtime in the teachers' cafeteria. Lucas sat with Jonas and a few of the other teachers.

"Quite a meet yesterday. Did Jessie break the high jump record?" one teacher asked.

Lucas smiled. "No. She will. There will be another day. But we won. That's what matters."

"How did Violet do?"

"She won her events, too. And she's looking good for the state meet."

"The boys' team did well?"

"Yes. Not as dominant as the girls, but we don't have any boys like Jessie or Violet."

"With Violet coming back next year, there's no end in sight. Your teams will win forever."

"I expect so," said Jonas.

"I hope so," added Lucas, cautious as always.

"And we clinched the league championship yesterday," interjected Coach Lancaster. "Baseball and track both are headed for wins on a statewide level. Rock Haven and the whole school should be proud of what our kids have done this year."

Mr. Tibbetts, the art teacher, interrupted. "Why is it always 'let's talk about the athletes'? Our play did well in the state drama festival during the winter, and we had a bunch of artists who were recognized in the Boston Globe art contest earlier this year. We've got great musicians here, too. But it's always all about the athletes."

Jonas replied, "I think the school knows about the arts people as well. I certainly know about the drama club since I teach English and helped with the play. But if the athletes get recognition, that's not a problem. We should celebrate the successes of all our students."

Lucas chimed in. "Why can't people enjoy sports and the arts too? Too many people seem to think they're exclusive. It cuts both ways. Some people believe that if you're a man, you should love sports. They seem to think it's not manly to care about music or art. And if you're a woman, you should like the arts and not really care about sports. Why can't people enjoy both? I love music. And I coach track. Come on, Tibbetts, go to a game or come watch a track meet. You might enjoy it."

Tibbetts sulked, drawing smirks from a few of the teachers but support from others. "I just think the artists should get equal recognition," he mumbled as he headed out the door.

Lucas spoke up. "I go to the plays and concerts. Do you go to any of the sports events?"

"No," Tibbetts replied primly, tipping his chin up. "I don't waste my time with semi-literate, so-called students, whose only claim to fame is their ability to run fast or throw a baseball."

"You should," said Jonas.

Coach Lancaster shook his head and walked out of the teachers' room, heading back to the gym.

CHAPTER SIX

Jessie and Joe

After their Saturday morning practices, Jessie drove her silver Miata with Joe's long body folded into the passenger seat. The top was down. Bathed in a cool breeze and sunshine, they parked at the beach lot and put the top up. Blown sand drifted over the edges of the asphalt, filling the cracks, creating white lines on the black tarmac. She opened the trunk, removed her beach bag, and handed it to Joe. Jessie carefully positioned herself on Joe's right, taking his hand—he carried her bag in his left hand, his pitching hand. Together they walked down the boardwalk, across the dunes, onto the deep sand of the beach. There, they kicked off their flip flops, tossing them in the beach bag, and turned right.

"Where do you want to go?" he asked, scanning the beach in front of them. "There are Isaac and Violet and everyone else."

She surveyed the beach dotted with families and saw Violet with her brother Isaac, and several other friends and teammates. She waved, and their friends waved back.

"They know we're here. That's good enough. There're too many people here. I want to be alone with you. Let's walk down the beach and find a quiet spot for ourselves, somewhere in the dunes."

Joe nodded and let her lead. After two years together, it was the way Jessie had established the habits of their relationship. Even during football and basketball season, all Joe dreamed about was Jessie and baseball. The first time they made love, it was really Jessie who

25

initiated it. Jessie had led the way all the other times as well. Joe was okay with that.

When they were far from the crowds gathered near the beach entrance from the parking lot, Jessie stopped and turned, looking back. They were alone. She walked away from the surf and found a spot low between two dunes. She took her bag back from Joe, set it down, and pulled out a faded old blanket. She spread it with Joe's help and sat in the middle.

"This is a perfect spot," she said.

Joe looked around. "We can't even see the ocean."

"No, but we're alone. We can work on our tans here." She peeled off the T-shirt she had changed into after track practice. She was braless beneath and sat in front of Joe, wearing just her shorts.

He smiled and sat down quickly, pulling off his shirt as well. Jessie ran her fingertips over his thick chest muscles and pulled him to her, grabbing his wide arms as she slowly lay back on the sand.

When they had finished, they rested together on the blanket, nude and breathing heavily beneath the hot sun.

"Unbelievable," Joe mumbled. "An hour ago, we were at school, you running on the track, me finishing up my practice playing catch with Isaac. Now here we are, making love on the beach."

"Everyone in school probably wishes they were us," Jessie said, grinning and rolling over to face Joe.

"If only they knew," Joe said.

"I'm glad they don't. They all probably imagine this is how it is with us, but this is just for you and me."

"Is this our celebration for winning league championships?" Joe asked.

"No. This is just celebrating a warm sunny day at the beach. We both have last period free on Tuesday, right? Study hall. And since both our grades are good, we're free to go where we want."

"Right. So where do we want to go?"

"I'll park over at the supermarket behind the school. Then, we can sneak over there, take my car, and go somewhere to do this again and celebrate our championships. We can still get back to school in time for practice."

"Uh, we're free to go anywhere, but I don't think we're supposed to leave school."

"Don't be silly. Nobody will know."

"Then, we'll go to my house. My parents will both be at work."

Jessie smiled. She had planned to take him to her house since her mom was out of town. But if he wanted to do it at his house, that was fine.

CHAPTER SEVEN

Patricia Brandt left for the airport early Sunday afternoon. Jessie fixed herself a dinner of leftover chicken and a salad, and ate alone in the quiet house. Then she waited for Gabriel to arrive.

He came to the door promptly at seven, carrying his black leather photography bag.

"Come on in." She held the door for him, allowing him to brush past her. "Where do you want me to pose for you?"

"Is there some place here that really captures your personality? I'd like to try to work that into your portrait."

Jessie looked around, surveying the living room. It was filled with her mother's carefully selected furniture, wide sofas, coffee tables, end tables, and armchairs, all of it expensive, in shades of beige and white. It looked like the photographs in fashionable interior design magazines, but it wasn't Jessie. She considered the kitchen for a moment. No. "How about my bedroom?" she offered.

Gabriel smiled, appreciating the possibilities implicit in her suggestion. "Sure."

She led him up the stairs to her room. He opened his bag and took out a large black camera and a flash. He erected a tripod and set up the flash, attaching it to his camera.

"Now what?" Jessie asked.

"Make yourself comfortable. When you pose in a way that seems natural and captures your essence, I'll shoot a picture."

Jessie sat on a chair and mugged at the camera. "Like this? I want to do it right."

"No. Act natural. You're naturally beautiful, so just be yourself, and I'll shoot when I see you find your natural look."

Jessie relaxed and shifted to sitting on the edge of her bed. She looked down, her blonde hair falling forward alongside her face. Gabriel snapped a photo of her profile through the waves of pale hair. "Nice, nice!" he said. He reached over and took her hair, tucking it behind her ear.

"Wait," Jessie said. "You want me to look natural. Would this help?" She crossed her arms and pulled her tank top off.

This should get him. Unless he's gay, I can make him do anything I want.

Gabriel froze, stunned by the sudden exposure of the body he had dreamed about for so long. It took him a moment to mutter. "That's good. Really good."

He shot more pictures. Again, he reached for her, smoothing her hair. His hand brushed against her bare breast. Jessie lay back on her bed. "You've seen enough already, so why stop now?" She pulled her knees up and reached down, sliding her shorts off, edging them past her heels.

Gabriel shot more pictures as she rolled on the bed. Then he stopped, knelt next to her, and put his camera down. "This is really good," he said, trying to sound assertive and take command of his situation.

She pulled him onto the bed next to her.

Jessie spoke, her voice hoarse. "It really turns me on when you're shooting pictures like this and looking at me like this." She reached for him. He was helpless. That power she held over him was her biggest thrill. It was over in seconds.

Gabriel lay back. "Joe doesn't have to know about this, does he?"

"Of course not. Why would I tell him?"

"I don't know. To make him jealous?"

Jessie thought for a moment. That would be interesting to have the biggest star in school and the biggest loser fighting over me. But, no, for that to happen, everyone would have to know I did it with this little jerk.

She grinned and tapped Gabe on his bare chest. "I doubt he'd believe it if I did tell him. Why? Are you afraid he'd beat you up?"

"A little bit."

"No. Nobody in school can know about this but you and me. This has to stay our little secret. Okay?"

"Sure. But listen. Shooting you on film like this, I can't show you digital previews of the pictures like I did with the track meet photos on my other camera."

"That's good. It means you can't load these on the internet."

"I wouldn't do that. But do you want to see what I got?"

"Of course."

"Okay. Do you know where the darkroom is in school? Next to the art rooms on the second floor?"

"No, but I'll find it."

"Can you get away third period tomorrow morning?" He had been tracking her schedule for weeks. He knew the answer, but he asked to make her believe it was her decision.

"Yes. I have a study hall that period, so I'm free."

"Meet me there. I'll wait for you in the hall. I'll take you to the darkroom with me and develop them there, so you can see if any of them are good enough for the contest. We'll select the best ones together. You can veto any you don't like."

"As long as I'm not recognizable for who I am, that's fine."

"Third period tomorrow, at the darkroom."

"Okay. Now you have to get dressed and go."

Gabriel had gotten more than he had dreamed possible. He dressed and left.

Chapter Eight

Jessie

He's such a little loser, Jessie mused after Gabe left. Little scrawny body. Not exactly good-looking. And he's always in trouble with dealing weed and flunking everything. But he's a diversion. He couldn't be more different than Joe. I'll never have sex with him again, but it was fun hanging around with him and teasing him with my body. And I might be featured in an art show? Cool! As long as nobody knows I posed for him.

With Gabe gone, Jessie picked up her English reading. The book bored her, and her mind wandered back to her weekend. Saturday, hidden in the dunes with Joe. And now, alone in her bedroom with Gabe. I've had sex now with the hottest guy in school and with the bottom of the social ladder. All in barely more than twenty-four hours. That's the Yin and the Yang of the guys in school. I flirt for a moment, and they're mine. If I can have both of them, I can probably have any guy I want. I doubt any other girl in school can say that!

*****

Jessie met Gabriel outside the darkroom moments after the beginning of third period. The room was rarely used in this age of digital photography. Mr. Tibbetts and Gabe were the only ones who had a key to the narrow, antiquated space, hardly more than a closet. It assured Gabe of privacy with Jessie and his photos. He flipped a switch as they went in, lighting the room with a dim red glow. He had already prepared negatives of the photos he had taken of her, and now he began printing them in black and white, watching her body slowly emerge in the fluid, lifting them and hanging them to dry. Jessie promptly rejected any that showed her face or that could possibly hint at her identity. She also rejected the notably explicit nudes, bothered not as much by the nudity as she was concerned that people might connect that she had been nude with Gabe. They finally settled on one.

At first glance, it was barely recognizable as a female body. It looked more like a moonscape, an undulating, wide, hard surface. On the left side of the picture were the edges of what could be two small hills, just the lower edges of her breasts as she reclined. There was a shallow crater in the middle of the plain, her navel, and on the right side of the photo was the rise of her bare thigh from the ridge of her pelvis, like a higher mountain.

"How about this one?" suggested Gabriel.

"Nice. That will do."

He set out to print more copies in black and white while she watched.

"You'll destroy the rest of them?" she asked.

"Of course," he lied. While he waited for the pictures to emerge in the developing tray, his hand strayed to her flat belly, checking the reality of the image in his photo, and slid down, beginning to slip inside the top of her jeans.

She grabbed his wrist and pulled it out, twisting it behind his back. He was startled by her sudden, undeniable strength.

"I thought, after last night..." he stammered.

"No. That was a one-and-done thing. In the moment. And don't you owe me something for posing for you?"

"Sure." He dug to the bottom of a side pocket on his camera bag and pulled out three joints, displaying them fanned out side by side. "Two for posing and one for everything else," he said.

Jessie took two and left the third one in his palm. "We're good," she said.

*****

Near the end of the third period, Lucas walked back to his classroom with Jonas, both carrying paper cups of thin coffee from the teacher's break room. A red light glowed above the door of the darkroom next to the art classroom. As they walked past, they heard voices from behind the door.

The door burst open. Lucas and Jonas saw Jessie with Gabriel in the doorway. Behind them in the dim, darkroom light, he could see a table with trays and a line strung across the room with clips to hold developed photos.

"Jessie," Jonas blurted, surprised to see her in a place like the art department's darkroom, so much out of her element, and with someone like Gabriel. "What's up? Everything okay?"

"I'm free this period. Gabe was just showing me how he develops photos. It's fascinating."

Hearing the voices in the hall outside the art room, Mr. Tibbetts appeared. "What's going on, Gabe?" he asked, knowing Gabe's reputation for trouble and wanting to ensure everything was on the up and up. He also recognized that Gabe was a talented photographer and wanted to enable his talent.

"I was showing Jessie how I develop film," he said.

"Did you get any good pictures that might be worth entering in the contest?" asked Tibbetts.

"Oh, yes. I think so?" Gabe took a colorful woodland landscape out of his bag and showed it to Tibbetts. The moonscape of Jessie's body remained buried in the stack of photos, still deep within the bag. He smiled.

"Very good. Keep it up, Gabe."

Tibbetts returned to his class. Lucas and Jonas continued down the hall with their coffees. To Lucas, nothing seemed to be out of order. It was the way he liked things. He admired Jessie's curiosity, that she was exploring the world of photography and broadening her sphere of friends by hanging out with Gabriel.

Jessie headed for a quiet, empty classroom to study. Gabe turned back to the darkroom with his photos. He paused for a moment, watching as Jessie walked away and tossed the two joints in a trash barrel. For a moment, Gabe considered retrieving them.

Too risky. There are people around. I can't have them seeing me digging around in the trash. And what if a teacher saw me and found me with the joints? Anyway, I've got plenty more. But why would she throw them away? Right after I rewarded her with them for posing?

*****

Late Monday afternoon, Jessie and Violet finished their track work and began their strength training together in the weight room. Spotted by Violet, Jessie stood beneath a heavy barbell resting on a stand. She gripped the bar, lifted, straightened her torso, and walked away from the weight rack, the flat plates of the weights clanking on the ends of the bar. She squatted to a sitting position, then stood, suddenly rising back so she was standing tall, squeezing her glutes, finishing by rising on tiptoes. She repeated the exercise five times, her face red, her cheeks puffed, blowing out through pursed lips each time she rose from the squat. Finished, she backed up and with Violet's help, set the bar back on the rack with a final clank. She sat on a bench, sweating.

Violet stood in front of her, "I still have one more set to do. Let me know when you're ready to spot me."

"Give me a moment and I'll be ready." Jessie leaned forward, sitting with her forearms resting on her thighs, exhausted.

"I saw you at the beach with Joe after practice on Saturday. Why didn't you guys come over with the rest of the crowd? We had most of the usual people there. Isaac with Marie, me, and Barry, the whole crew. We had a great time."

Jessie sat up straighter and wiped the sweat off her face with the sleeve of her T-shirt. Long strings of her pale hair, darkened by perspiration, framed her face. "Joe and I wanted some time alone together. You understand?"

Violet nodded, but her brow furrowed. "Yes, I expect. I see how you two are together sometimes." Violet's smooth, dark face showed concern. A small frown appeared; her brow wrinkled. "You be careful, Jessie. You have everything working for you. A track scholarship to UConn next fall. Great grades. You and Joe, Prom Queen and King. You're the star of the school, and you've got all the money you need. Don't screw it all up by doing something foolish with Joe."

"I'm careful. We know what we're doing. Everything's going to be fine. Don't tell me you and Barry haven't fooled around."

"This isn't about me and Barry," Violet said, referring to her boyfriend, a thin miler on the boys' team. "We're not doing anything we have to worry about."

"Neither are Joe and I," asserted Jessie. "I watch my calendar. I know when it's not safe."

"Sure," Violet said, shaking her head, unconvinced. "Just be careful."

Jessie stood and followed Violet to the bar. Violet stood beneath it, lifting it on her shoulders, balanced by Jessie. She stepped away from the rack and began doing the squats, also rising on her toes at the end of each exercise. Like Jessie, her dark face flushed, her cheeks puffed with each repetition of the exercise, her breath noisy gasps on each exhalation.

When she was done, Jessie guided her back to the rack. Violet set the bar on the rack, and they left the weight room.

"You want a ride home?" Jessie asked as they splashed water on their faces to cool off.

"In that little car of yours? Top down? Sure!"

It seemed to Jessie that the whole world was watching as they pulled through the high school parking lot; the two coolest girls in school, the white girl and the black girl, both star athletes, top students, celebrities, top down in Jessie's shiny Miata. Heads turned as they drove down Washington Street through the center of Rock Haven, Jessie's blonde ponytail, blowing in the breeze, Violet's tight dark curls unmoved. When they arrived at Violet's house, Isaac and Joe were leaning against Joe's rusted and faded pickup.

"There they are. Best of buds. My brother and Joe are always together," Violet said. "It's sad, though. As close as they are, it's all about to end. For years, it's been football in the fall, basketball all winter, and now pitcher and catcher in baseball. It'll be hard on both of them going their different ways next year. Joe's off to play baseball at Clemson, and Isaac will be working at the fish plant starting right after graduation. Their lives will go in very different directions."

"Why doesn't Isaac go to college, too? His grades are good enough to get in somewhere, right?"

"I expect so, but we can't afford it. Maybe it might happen in a year or so. But not right now. Mom got him the job at the plant. So, there he goes."

CHAPTER NINE

Jessie

That evening after dinner Jessie's phone rang. She checked the number and answered. "Hi, Mom."

"Hi, Jessie. How are you doing?"

"Fine. I got home from practice a while ago and ordered a pizza. I'm just finishing it."

"Oh, good. I want to be sure you're eating well while I'm away."

"I'm doing fine. How's your trip going?"

"Good! I'm just wrapping up a meeting with a client. I've signed him up for some new business, so it's been a good trip."

"Oh, that's good. I'm glad."

"Yes. Well, I just wanted to check in. I'll be home for dinner with you tomorrow evening. Okay?"

"Yup. I'll be waiting."

"Great. Maybe we'll go downtown and grab a bite at that little Italian place. What's it called?"

"Leonardo's?"

"Yes. That's the place. Well, I've got to run. See you tomorrow."

In her hotel room in Pittsburgh, Patricia explained the call to her client. "Checking in with my daughter to make sure she's okay. It's the worst part about being away from home so much, leaving her and worrying."

"I understand," her client said. "Speaking of that, I need to get home to my family as well. My wife will have dinner waiting."

He stood and began dressing.

*****

Jessie slouched on the living room couch. She sensed that there was more to her mom's call. Calls to check in with her were rare. Maybe her mom was realizing how alone she had been for the past few years. And maybe she'd become aware that their time together, such as it was, would be ending in a few months when she left for college.

She stared blankly at the artwork on the living room wall.

Maybe I should cut Mom some slack, try to reconnect before I leave for UConn. But why? I don't need her. I can handle anything on my own. I guess she had a hard time when Dad left us. We've both struggled with that. Why did Dad have an affair? Mom's pretty enough. Maybe that's just the way men are. I wonder if she's sleeping with anyone?

It's been weeks since I talked with Dad on the phone. The last time I saw him was that one afternoon right after Christmas.

Why did he turn his back on Mom? And on me? Doesn't he know everything I've done this year? Why wouldn't he want to be a part of all this? Why won't he even come to one of my track meets?

I wonder if he'll come to graduation. Even if he isn't with Mom, he should be there. I'll tell him the next time he calls.

CHAPTER TEN

Jessie and Joe

Since neither had a last-period class, Jessie met Joe in the hall outside the gym. They slipped out the side door next to the gym and ran across an empty practice field into the woods. A short trail brought them out at the back of a supermarket parking lot. Here at the desolate end, the lot was empty except for Jessie's silver Miata, pristine among the dirty remnants of a winter snowbank and one broken-down shopping cart. They climbed in the car quickly and drove to Joe's house. It was quiet as they came in through the kitchen door. His parents and all his neighbors were away at work.

Joe called out, "Hello? Anybody home?" There was no response.

They took the quiet of the house as an all-clear sign and hustled up to his bedroom. Hurrying, since they had less than an hour to get back for practice, they made love on his small bed.

Afterwards, Joe held her and said, "I love you, Jessie. Maybe I've always loved you. You know you're the only girl I've ever done this with. This past year, sneaking off with you to make love has been amazing."

"I love you too, Joe. Yes. This year has been amazing."

Joe leaned back and rolled to look at her, propping on an elbow. "Could I ask you something?"

"Of course. Anything you want." Jessie traced her fingers down his chest to his belly.

"My family is having a party for my graduation on Sunday. Can you come?"

"Sure, but graduation is still a couple of weeks away. Why now?"

"My family is big, lots of aunts and uncles and everything. It's hard to find a time when we can all get together. They're always off fishing and working, but for my family, this is a big deal. We really want to celebrate this. A lot of my relatives never got close to graduating high school, here or back in the Azores. And none of them has gone to college. Starting when they were young, they've all gone to work at the plant or gone out on the fishing boats."

"My mom and dad both went to college. Graduation's nothing special in my family."

"It is in mine. So, can you come next Sunday?"

"I'll be there."

Joe got up and went into the bathroom. Jessie reached over the edge of the narrow bed, found her purse, and took out her perfume. She sprayed just a bit on his pillow and down under the blanket on the sheets.

There, she thought. He'll pick up my scent and remember me when he goes to sleep tonight.

Content, she lay back thinking. Three times in four days. With two different guys. How cool is this?

Then she dressed quickly, ready for track practice.

If I keep up like this, she suddenly thought, I should probably get on the pill. I don't want to get pregnant. No. It won't happen. I probably don't have to worry. Things always work out for me. And I don't want to talk to Mom about it. She'd probably make me go to her OBGYN doctor. She doesn't need to know. I've got this. I know what I'm doing.

They left the house and dashed back to school in her Miata, pulling into the school parking lot in plenty of time for their practices.

Chapter Eleven

Joe

Coach Lancaster pulled Joe aside at the end of practice. "Have you got a moment, Joe?"

Joe nodded, "Of course, Coach." He frowned suddenly, worrying. Had Coach seen him running off with Jessie before the end of the school day? Or driving back into the parking lot at the end of school? Did Coach know? Was he in trouble?

Lancaster draped his arm around Joe's wide shoulder, a fatherly gesture of support and maybe affection. "There's a gentleman here who wants to talk with you."

A lean, tanned, crew-cut, middle-aged man sat alone in the third row of the stands next to the baseball field. Coach and Joe climbed the stairs and walked to him. Joe walked gingerly, his cleats slipping on the aluminum stairs, clicking on the walkway.

Coach Lancaster did the introductions. "Mr. Wilson, this is Joe Goncalves. And Joe, this is Frank Wilson. He's a scout for the St. Louis. Cardinals' organization."

Wilson stood and shook Joe's hand. "Call me Frank. Joe, I've been to a few of your games this year. And I've been following your stats. The Cardinals are very interested in a young talent like you."

"Thanks." Joe was excited, but he didn't know what to say. He struggled to keep his face impassive, to show no emotion.

Wilson had seen this before with other young ballplayers. He took the lead with the conversation. "We want you to consider joining the Cardinals organization right after graduation. We'd have you go to one of our minor league teams out in the Midwest. It wouldn't be great money daily at the start, but we can offer you a bonus to join, and with your arm, you'd likely progress rapidly up the ladder. You could be in triple A ball by the end of the summer, next year at the latest, and in the majors, two or maybe three years from now."

Joe's legs felt weak. He sat down next to Wilson. Coach Lancaster still stood. "I've signed a letter to play for Clemson next year," Joe said.

"I know that. I've done my homework. But we're offering you five hundred thousand dollars in bonus money the day after you graduate. Clemson can't do that for you."

Joe smiled, thrilled. The money he was being offered far exceeded what he knew his parents earned together in a year, maybe more than they'd earned and saved over their entire lifetimes. He felt dizzy for a moment but recovered. "Listen. I need to talk to my parents about this. Can I have a few days to think it over?"

"Of course. Take your time. And take care of that arm of yours. It's golden. Call me when you're ready."

They stood. Wilson shook Joe's hand, slipped him a business card, and walked from the stands to the parking lot. Coach Lancaster wrapped his arm over Joe's shoulder again. "This is really something, isn't it? That's big money. We still have State Championship to worry about, but your future's all set."

"But I've committed to Clemson. I've given them my word. That means something, doesn't it?"

"Yes, it does. You can always go to college in a few years. Take the money and become an MLB star."

"I need to talk to my parents. College is something I've always wanted. Pro ball, too. I need to think this out."

"Yes, you do. Go home and talk it over with your parents. It's a big decision. Take your time. And don't let this distract from tomorrow's game either. Keep your focus day-to-day, game-to-game."

As they crossed the field to the school, they watched Wilson drive out of the parking lot in a Lexus.

The next day, Rock Haven baseball won and moved on to the State Finals. Joe struck out ten, walked none, and allowed only two hits, no runs. Isaac Arnold got three hits, including one that drove in the winning runs for Rock Haven. Frank Wilson sat in the stands behind home plate with a notebook and a radar gun.

CHAPTER TWELVE

Jessie

Jessie remembered Lucas's tip on running the hurdles.

"Think of it as a dance where everybody in the race has to set their feet in exactly the right spots, never too close nor too far away from the next hurdle. All the runners run their own races, but they're setting their feet in the same places in each of their lanes, so their bodies are in the best position to attack all ten hurdles. The winner is the one who can do that dance with the quickest feet," he explained.

The dance would be hard today, facing a gusty headwind, here, at the State Meet. Having each qualified for the final, the eight fastest girls in the state lined up, shaking their legs to stay loose.

The starter gave his command, "On your marks."

They knelt in unison, side-by-side, dropping their feet back into the starting blocks.

On the starter's second command, "Set," they all rose, leaning forward over their hands, in line, symmetric.

They were released by the pistol shot.

Jessie and one other girl were away, instantly clear of the other hurdlers, their strides and hurdling synchronized. A sudden gust hit them head-on, and Jessie powered ahead, fighting the wind and leading. Approaching the ninth hurdle, the wind pushed the challenger back only an inch, but it was enough. Her steps were off. She clipped the hurdle and stumbled slightly approaching the tenth, final hurdle. Jessie muscled on, skimmed over the final hurdle, dug hard for her final few strides, and won.

She coasted to a stop, turned, hands on her hips, and walked back down her lane. Her challenger was still in her lane, slumped, hands on knees, breathing deeply, her head down.

Reaching over to her as she passed by, Jessie tapped her shoulder, "Nice race," she said. "Tough wind." The challenger nodded but didn't look up.

With the results confirmed by the finish line officials, Jessie walked away, ignoring the rest of the hurdlers. She jogged back across the field to the high jump area, changed into her jumping shoes, and checked in with the jump official. "The hurdles are done. I'm back. What did I miss?"

"We're about to start at five-six," the official told her. "Only you and two other girls are still jumping." Jessie found her mark and signaled to the official that she was ready.

He gave a quick wave of acknowledgement. "Brandt is up," he called.

Her approach was well-rehearsed through countless jumps in practice. She began, running with long bounding strides, settling lower for her last three quick steps. Then, abruptly, her left foot smacked down, and she soared, her back above the bar. At the peak of the jump, lying flat, back to the bar, she gave a sudden upward jerk of her pelvis, lifting her hips, leaving a wide gap between her body and the bar. A flick of her heels and she was clear. She fell, landing, rolling on her back to her shoulders on the foam pads.

It was the same as her jumps back home in Rock Haven. She climbed off the pads, walked back to her warm-ups, and lay back, arms above her head, resting, barely noticing her competitors as they jumped and failed at the height she had sailed over. When the last girl was eliminated, Jessie sat up, then stood and walked to the official. "Raise the bar to five-eight."

He did. When she was ready, Jessie ran again and lifted, barely brushing the bar at the peak of her jump. The crossbar sat wiggling, shaking on the standards. Jessie watched it, cautiously not moving on the foam pit. After a tense moment, the bar settled, staying in place. Jessie rolled from the pit and walked back to the official. "Five-nine."

"You've already won. Do you want to go for the state record?"

"No. I said, 'five-nine.'"

"The best ever, the state record isn't much more. Are you sure you only want five-nine?"

She looked him in the eyes, her blue eyes, hard, like those of an assassin, her stare chilling. "I said, 'five-nine.'"

The official turned away and set to work, raising the bar, measuring, and confirming the height. She cleared it on her second attempt.

"I'm done," she said, walking away, leaving the official alone with the empty pit and his clipboard. He shook his head.

Jessie had two wins in the State Meet within minutes. Violet won her two sprints. The relay team lost, finishing in a close second place, even with Jessie leading off and Violet running the anchor leg.

CHAPTER THIRTEEN

Walking from the bus across the parking lot to the stadium for the State Championship game, Joe saw the Cardinal scout's dark Lexus gleaming in the bright sun. In the best-of-three series to win the state title, Rock Haven had won the first game, with Joe playing first base, resting his arm. He rested again, and they lost the next game. It all came down to this one last game. Joe was primed and ready to win it all today. The opposing team also started their star pitcher.

Warming up, Joe checked again on the Cardinals scout sitting in the front row, watching him. Joe gave a quick wave, and the scout returned a small nod. "Yeah, he's here," growled Coach Lancaster. "Focus on what you're doing and ignore him."

"Who's that?" asked Isaac after Coach left.

"He's a scout from the Cardinals. I met him a couple of days ago. They want me to go pro this summer."

"Cool. But what about Clemson?"

"I don't know."

Joe was on his game. Five innings passed, and nobody reached base. Rock Haven, even with runners on in every inning, couldn't score. Joe walked a batter in the sixth, then struck out the next two batters to end the inning. The game was tied, shutouts on both sides.

In the seventh inning, the leadoff batter dug in, determined to start a game-winning rally. Joe stared him down. With two strikes on him, the batter swung at a rising fastball. And connected. The ball sailed, a tiny white dot lifting against a bright sky. It cleared the outfield fence by twenty feet.

Joe turned back to the plate, angry, ready to get a new ball and attack the next hitter. The home run hitter still stood in the batter's box, staring in amazement out to where the ball had landed.

"Run, you little bastard!" Joe shouted. "Don't stand there showing me up. Start running." The batter dropped his bat and started jogging around the bases, taking his time. Joe fumed on the mound, not watching the batter.

Isaac walked to the mound, joined by Coach Lancaster.

"Did you see that?" Joe fussed. "He was just standing there, waiting for everyone to cheer for him. The little bastard."

Isaac spoke first. "I don't think he believed he could hit it that hard. I heard him say, 'Oh, my god!' as he watched it go."

"I'm hitting the next guy. Teach'em all a lesson."

Coach Lancaster wrapped an arm around Joe's shoulder. "No, you can't let them see it shook you. You don't want to reward them with a base runner, and maybe get thrown out of the game by the umpire as well. Your best revenge is to shut them down cold the rest of the way. Take a deep breath and then pitch. Go get 'em."

When Lancaster was gone, Isaac gave his final instruction. "You're angry. I hardly ever hear you swear. Take that anger and direct it through the baseball. Let's mow them down the rest of the way. We'll get you the run back in our half of the inning."

That was the game. Rock Haven lost one to nothing. The winners danced in the middle of the field, showering their coach and the home run hitter from the ice bucket. Joe turned his back and walked with Isaac back to the bus.

"Heck of a game, Joe." Joe looked up and found himself face-to-face with the scout. "Frank Wilson, from the Cardinals," he reminded Joe.

"Yeah, I remember you. I saw you in the stands before the game. This is Isaac Arnold, my catcher."

"Good to meet you, Isaac. Your pitcher here had a great game today."

"Not good enough. We lost," said Joe.

"It happens. It's a funny game. A big guy like their hitter swings hard, and sometimes he gets lucky and hits the ball right on the screws. Nothing you can do about it."

"We should have gotten him a couple of runs," said Isaac.

"You did what you could. You got a couple of hits today, right, Isaac?"

"Yes. But we couldn't score."

"Like I said, it happens. Stay in touch, Joe. Give me a call. Have you talked things over with your parents?"

"Yeah, we've talked. I'm still sorting things out with their help."

"You've got my card with my number. I can wait for your decision." The scout walked away.

"College, Joe," counseled Isaac. "I still think you should go to Clemson."

CHAPTER FOURTEEN

Joe

Joao Goncalves left the Azores to come to America as a young man, bringing his wife Anna and his three young boys, Joao Jr., Gualter, and Hermano. Life was better in the United States, people said. There was more opportunity, a better chance.

He had been a fisherman in the Azores, and people had told him there was a community of Portuguese fishermen, from Cape Verde, the Azores, and Portugal, already established in a little town up the coast north of Boston, Rock Haven. Joao settled there with old friends from home and took a job in the familiar world he found on the fishing boats.

A few years later, when they were old enough, each of the boys dropped out of school and also went to work on the boats. The whole family became citizens. They attended a Catholic church, filled with mostly Portuguese, though there were a few Italian and some Irish parishioners. The Priest was French Canadian.

It was an insular, tight community of Portuguese fishermen, working on the fishing boats and in the big fish processing plant, packing and canning the catch. The Italians owned the boats and the packing plant. The boys all married Portuguese girls they had met at church and around town. They lived near each other, within blocks of the harbor. Compared to the sparse life they had left behind in the Azores, Rock Haven was heaven.

Joao Jr. met Helena at a church dance and married her when they were eighteen. He dropped out of high school and went to work to support his new bride, going out on the boats with his father and brothers; Helena worked as a packer in the plant. Six years after they were married, they had a baby boy, Joao III. He would be their only child.

They called him Joe to make him fit into American life. As a young boy, Joe was already the biggest kid in his class. He was a star in Little League at just eight years old. He was a good boy, listening to his mom and dad, absorbing their lessons and those of Grandpa, Joao Sr. He was obedient, always doing what he was told. Most of Rock Haven knew Joe Goncalves was destined to become something special. Now, Joe was a high school senior, and instant wealth or college awaited him.

Chapter Fifteen

Jessie and Joe

Jessie dressed in white shorts, a dark blue top, and white sandals. Her golden hair was pulled back and clasped behind her head. Oversized beige sunglasses completed her outfit. She exuded chic and felt totally cool when she checked herself in her bedroom mirror. She didn't know who she would see at Joe's cookout, but whoever was there couldn't miss her. She checked herself in the mirror one final time and smiled. Perfect!

"You look like you're dressed for a picnic," said Patricia, assessing her daughter as they passed each other in the kitchen.

"I am. Joe's family is having a graduation party for him this afternoon. I'm dropping by."

"Joe Goncalves? The baseball pitcher? Your prom date? Why do you persist in seeing him? Sure, he's a big, good-looking guy, but his family are fishermen, right? I know you and he are friends, but you could do better than a Portuguese fisherman for a boyfriend."

"Mom! We've been over and over this." Jessie rolled her eyes and sighed loudly. Her tone of voice grew from her exasperation. "He's a good guy. I like him and he's going to Clemson next year with a full scholarship."

"For baseball. Does he have a brain or just a lot of brawn? And a future? You'll find a good boy from a good family down at UConn next year. Or I expect there's even a respectable boy from a good family right here in The Heights."

"Mom! I like Joe."

"Find a good man and marry him. Don't make the mistake I made with your father. There is a good man out there for you. You can have anyone you want. Don't settle for a guy like Joe Goncalves."

"Oh, Mom. Give me a break! I like Joe." Jessie turned and left rather than staying to prolong a fight they had been having off and on for more than a year.

*****

The street was lined with old cars and pickups for a block on both sides. Jessie parked her Miata on the street near Joe's house, around the corner, half a block away. Sleek and shiny, it stood out among the tarnished vehicles nearby. Slipping past the cars filling his driveway, she opened the chain-link gate into his backyard. The yard was jammed with strangers. Unfamiliar music, not Latin but not rock, was playing. Jessie couldn't understand the lyrics. Two grills sat side-by-side: one, the lid closed, smelled like it was cooking fish, the other was loaded with thick, blackened sausages. A cluster of burly, dark-haired men surrounded the two grills. Joe was with them.

Jessie went to him. Seeing her, Joe pulled her to him, his arm around her waist. "Hey, Jessie. This is my family. This is my dad, Joao; my grandpa, Joao senior, and this is my uncle Gualter and my other uncle Hermano. And this is my girlfriend, Jessie." Joe proudly pushed her forward, showing her off to the men in his family.

Jessie was accustomed to being the center of attention and having men stare at her, but this was unsettling. She felt out of her element. One of the old men seemed to be leering. "It's so nice to meet you all," she said, her voice tense. Then she whispered to Joe, "Are any of the other kids here?"

"Yeah. Isaac and Violet are over there, in the back, up against the fence with Barry and Marie."

62

"I think I'll go see them." She slid from Joe and the group of men and searched the yard, looking for her friends.

"Okay, I'll be over in a few minutes," Joe called after her as he turned back to the men in his family.

As Jessie pushed through the crowd, a short woman, her hair dyed a dark blonde, stopped her. "Hello! I'm Helena, Joe's mom. And you're Jessie, his girlfriend?"

"Yes."

"Joe's always talking about you. It's Jessie this, and Jessie that. I'm sorry I missed you on prom night, but I had to work. I've seen the pictures."

Suddenly, Helena pulled Jessie to her, hugging her. Jessie pulled back from the unexpected embrace, feeling Helena's warm breath on her neck, uncomfortable with the unfamiliar touch from this stranger.

 Helena stepped back, assessing the tall blonde girl in front of her. "I like your perfume," she said. "Where have I smelled that scent before?"

Jessie smiled weakly, puzzled by Helena's comment. It sounded like a compliment, but Helena wasn't smiling. "Thank you. It's nice to meet you," Jessie replied.

At last, she made it through the crowd across the back yard to the chain-link fence where she squeezed in next to Isaac with his girlfriend Marie, a petite, dark, Portuguese girl. Violet hung on the lean frame of Barry, her boyfriend, a miler on the boys' track team.

"Sheesh," Jessie said. "What a mob. I don't know anyone here but you guys. I feel like a fish out of water."

Violet reassured her best friend. "They're all Joe's family and their friends. Relax."

"They're good people," said Isaac. "I know a few of them from working on the fishing boats in the summer and down at the plant with my mom."

Marie added, "My parents are here too. It's like everyone from the boats and the plant took the day off to party."

"I don't know if I belong here," said Jessie.

Violet hugged her. "Of course, you belong here. You're Joe's girlfriend. Relax. Like Isaac said, they're all good people."

Back by the grills, Joe listened as the men in his family offered their advice.

"Take the money," said Hermano. "That's a fortune. And you'll make a lot more when you make it to the majors."

"I've never made anything close to that kind of money," added Gualter. "I've worked my whole life out on the boats. Ever since I was younger than you. Hard work, every day, all year long, in all kinds of weather. And what do I have to show for it? Rough hands and a sore back, and next to nothing in the bank. Take the money. There's no question what you should do. This is your chance to do better than the rest of us."

Joe's father remained tight-lipped, listening to his brothers. Finally, he spoke, "Nobody in this family has ever gone to college." Sweeping his arm to include everyone in the crowded yard, he continued. "None of us ever even graduated from school back in the Azores, not even when we came here. And college? Not even a possibility. I'm so proud of you having this opportunity to go to college at Clemson. But we're looking at life-changing money. Maybe ask the scout, this Frank Wilson, if you could go to college in the off-season."

Joe shook his head. "I could ask, Dad, but I don't think it'll work. I'll be playing ball or working out with the Cardinals in the fall and spring, as well as summer. And if I don't play for Clemson, I don't know if they would let me go to school there."

Joao Senior stepped to the middle of the group, commanding their attention, standing between his three sons and Joe. He looked his grandson in the eyes.

"Listen to me. I'm the head of this family, so what I say matters. Everybody's got an opinion. And let me tell you something to watch out for, young Joe. Whenever any one of us starts to be successful, everyone else in our community is always trying to pull them back down. It's like they think one person's success makes everyone else look bad. They don't have any right to be telling you what to do when they're not even part of our family. A lot of the advice you get won't be good advice. Listen to them politely, but then ignore them. Some people may say you're all full of yourself because you can play baseball and you're a star. They'll say you should stay home and go out with us on the fishing boats. Don't listen to any of them. Go to Clemson or go play pro baseball. Either one. It's up to you. Don't let anyone tell you differently."

The three sons and Joe listened. The men stood holding their sweating beer bottles, nodding and acknowledging what their father had to say. Joao Senior continued, his voice husky from years of cigarettes. "We're your family. What we think is what matters. Not what anyone else has to say to you. And between the four of us, we can't make up our minds. 'Take the money' or 'Go to college'!" Joao Senior gave a dismissive wave of both his hands to his sons. "In the end, the decision is up to you, Joe. My opinion is this. Go to college. A college education will set you up for success for the rest of your life. You won't be playing baseball forever. Not for the Cardinals, not for Clemson. But if you decide to go to college, that education will be there for you for years to come."

Joe nodded. "Thanks, Poppa. I'm still trying to make up my mind. It'll be hard to say no to five hundred thousand dollars, but I've committed to Clemson, and you're right. A college education would be a good thing to have. I've given my word to Clemson. My word matters, right? I've made a commitment. I have to do the right thing. I agree with you, Poppa. I'm thinking I'll still be going to Clemson. I have to stand by my word, right?"

Joao Sr. added, "Maybe more money would be out there after you go to college. You don't ever know."

"Bah!" Hermano waved his hand dismissively at Joe.

"You're a fool, Joe," added Gualter. "And that girl. She's pretty, and she's hot, but why can't you find yourself a nice Portuguese girlfriend? Is that girl even Catholic?"

"Leave Jessie out of this," cautioned Joe, pointing his finger at Gualter to stress his words. "She's special. I really like her. There's nothing wrong with her just because she's not Portuguese."

"Bah!" repeated Hermano, knocking back the last of his beer.

CHAPTER SIXTEEN

Only five Rock Haven track athletes were still at practice, preparing for the New England Championships: Jessie, Violet, and Bob, a hulking, slope-shouldered boy who threw the discus. Nobody else from Rock Haven had qualified to continue the championship season, except the relay team comprised of Jessie, Violet, and two other sprinters.

Lucas had finished coaching the discus thrower through his workout. He, Violet, and the other two relay runners waited. Jessie was uncharacteristically late to practice. She arrived, offered no apology, and began stretching. "I'm ready, let's go," she finally announced.

"We'll run our usual long acceleration sprints to warm up," said Lucas. "Then we'll run through the relay a few times to ensure we're hitting the baton passes at full speed."

Now Lucas watched as Jessie and Violet ran the long sprints, leading the two other relay runners, coasting around the turn, then accelerating to full speed down the straightaway. Jessie seemed listless, allowing Violet to blow away from her on most of the drills.

"C'mon, Jessie! Run like you mean it," shouted Lucas. "Don't just drift along behind Violet. Let's go!"

"Get off my back!" Jessie barked.

Lucas was used to Jessie's temperamental words. It was part of the emotion, almost anger, that fueled her and made her competitive.

But this was different. This appeared to be a real issue. He paused and walked to her. "What's the matter? Are you hurt?" he asked quietly.

"No. Just leave me alone." She walked away, down the track toward Violet to get ready for the next sprint.

"You okay?" Violet asked softly as she walked beside her best friend. Gently, she reached over, her fingertips touching the back of Jessie's hand.

"I'm fine." Jessie pulled her hand away. "Just shut up and run."

Rounding the turn, they quickened their walk, broke into a jog, and then into a full run as the lanes straightened. They built more speed as they circled the next turn and accelerated full out into the straightaway. Halfway down the straight, Jessie veered to the right, out of her lane, off the track, out through a gate. She jogged alone back to the school, still wearing her spikes.

Lucas walked to Violet. "The workout's almost over, but this isn't like Jessie. She usually wants to do more than I ask of her. What's going on?"

"I don't know. She'll tell me when she's ready. Not until then. Everything has to be on her terms. You know how she is." Violet picked up Jessie's flat running shoes to bring them to her whenever Jessie reached out to her. With Jessie gone, practice was finished for the day. They hadn't practiced their baton passes.

*****

Jessie sat alone on a bench at the end of Herring Head Park. Behind her were the empty swing set and the small playground. In front of her was the harbor, the marina on her right, and the fishing docks below her to the left. The smell of the fish processing plant rose to her.

I'm late. I can't be. I'm not pregnant. I won't allow myself to be pregnant. Maybe Violet was right, and I should have been more careful. Maybe I should have been on the pill. I see the other girls in school who get pregnant. They all have abortions and everything. They're all careless losers. Everybody talks about them. But they're not like me. Or, I'm not like them. Am I? I don't want people talking about me the way they talk about those other girls.

But I'm late. I'm never late. I feel fine, but I'm late. So, I finally broke down and bought a test. And the test I took confirms it. I'm pregnant. What can I do? I don't know what to do. Oh God, I hate what's happening to me! I'm not in control of my own body. I should be, but I'm not. How could I be pregnant? All Joe and I did was have sex. And only when it was a time that was supposed to be safe. This can't be happening to me.

She looked down on the loading dock behind the fish plant, seeing trash and debris near the dumpster. Inhaling to try and clear her head, all she smelled was dead fish. This place is disgusting. This whole town is hell on earth. Maybe I should just leave, run away from all this. No, that wouldn't fix anything. I'd still be pregnant. What can I do? Focus! There has to be an answer, a solution.

After several minutes, she took her phone and dialed Violet. "Hi, Violet. I want to apologize for being such a bitch at practice today."

"That's okay. We all have our good and bad days. Today's a bad day for you?"

"Yeah. I've got some stuff going on I have to deal with."

"Where are you? Do you want to talk?"

"I'm out at the end of Herring Head on a bench. Yeah, talking might be good."

"I'll be right there."

Violet cut through the kitchen, telling her mother, "I'll be back in a couple of minutes."

"Hurry back. It's almost supper time." Evelyn Arnold watched with concern as her daughter left.

"What's up?" asked Isaac as Violet passed.

"Jessie needs me." The screened door banged shut behind her.

Chapter Seventeen

Violet and Isaac, and the Arnold family

Sam Arnold joined the Navy right after high school. Jobs were hard to find for a young Black man in Boston in those days, and military service was a paycheck. He met Evelyn while he was stationed in San Diego, married her in one impulsive weekend, and brought her home to Boston when his service ended. He had been trained as a mechanic while in the Navy and found work in the fish processing plant in Rock Haven, helping keep the machinery running. Evelyn had taken a year of accounting at a junior college in California. She landed a job in payroll at the plant. They were one of the first non-immigrant families to settle in the inner harbor. Most of the folks in The Heights only saw their black skin and figured the inner harbor was where they belonged.

Sam had been raised by a single mom. He wanted better for his two children. He hoped to give them a stable, two-parent home and ensure they learned good values. That and a good education, another opportunity he had missed as a child. He and Evelyn made sure to share dinner with Isaac and Violet every evening. Beginning when the children were in first grade, Sam and Evelyn asked the children about their day at school and went over their homework with them. They were thrilled by the successes, both academic and athletic, of their children. The Arnold parents hoped both Isaac and Violet would go to college and have better lives than their own. Reality set in when they realized that, regardless of their children's high school successes, the cost of tuition left college out of reach.

Dinner was the Arnold's special family time, when everyone shared the successes and challenges of their day with the whole close-knit family. For Violet to rush off just before dinner was unexpected, but it pointed to a serious crisis that needed to be attended to. Evelyn and Isaac looked at each other. Neither said a word, but they nodded, accepting the reality of Violet's actions and what they implied.

Sam nodded, his face grim. "Whatever it is with Jessie, Violet needs to be there right now. Let's eat."

Chapter Eighteen

Jessie and Violet

Violet took the short walk from her house up the hill to the bluff. She found Jessie on the bench, head down, her tall frame slumped, her elbows on her knees. Violet sat beside her. "What's going on?"

Jessie looked down at the dirt where the grass was worn away beneath the bench. She looked back up, out to the harbor, thinking. I should own this, I guess. I should tell Violet. But I don't want her judging me. I have nowhere else to turn.

"I'm late. I think I might be pregnant. I took the test. The test confirmed it."

Violet leaned over, pulling Jessie to her. For a moment, Jessie's shoulders shook. Then her whole body shuddered, as though she was terrified of something she'd seen. "Are you sure?" asked Violet. "You say you've taken a test?"

Jessie fought to stop shaking, but her voice still quavered, almost pleading. "Yes. No. I couldn't walk into a pharmacy here in Rock Haven and buy a test. Everyone in town would know in ten minutes. So, I drove out a couple of towns away last night and bought a test. I didn't want to see it if the test said I was. So, at first, I didn't take the test. But I took the test this afternoon, right before practice, and it says I'm pregnant."

"You're sure?" Violet asked again.

Jessie's voice was pleading, begging for help. "Yes! I don't know what to do. I'm always in control of everything: with my body, with my whole life. But this is out of my control, and I don't like that. I don't want to be pregnant either. I can't be."

"Does Joe know?"

"No. I can't tell him."

"If you're pregnant, he has to know. He's the father."

Jessie's mind raced. What if he isn't? Gabe. No! It can't be Gabe. That nagging thought worried Jessie as well. But that was a problem she'd confront later, not now with Violet.

"Have you told your mom?"

"No."

"You need to. I expect she can help you sort through this. I mean, you've got me. You can count on that. But you need to tell Joe. And you need your mom right now."

"I know. I will."

Behind them, they heard the voices of small children running onto the playground. They turned and saw Lucas with Jennifer and their little girls.

"Oh, God," said Jessie. "This is all I need. I really don't want to talk to Coach right now."

Seeing his two stars, Lucas came over. "Hey! How are you two? What's up?"

Violet stood, shielding Jessie. "We're fine, Coach Knox. Just talking things over. Thinking about New England's next weekend."

Lucas looked down at Jessie. She looked away, watching the progress of a late-arriving fishing boat powering around the point. He sensed he wasn't wanted as a part of this conversation and backed off, leaving his two stars. "Okay, good. I'll get back to my family. See you both tomorrow."

Once Coach Knox was gone, Jessie stood. Violet hugged her and held on. "Tell Joe," Violet whispered. "And talk to your mom. She can help. If you need me, I'm always here for you, too. Call me."

Lucas went back to Jennifer and sat watching his girls play on the swings.

"What's that all about?" asked Jennifer.

"I don't know. Jessie's got something on her mind. But Violet seems to have it under control. I don't need to be involved. I'll let them work it out. I'll get to the bottom of it tomorrow."

He took Jennifer's hand and began to smile. The sun was low, the water shining in the harbor. Clouds on the horizon were glowing as the sun set behind the town. His little girls were happily at play in front of him. "Life is perfect," he declared. "My little girls are playing here in the park at sunset. My team had a great season. Those two grown-up girls over there were just about unbeatable. So, here I am with you watching my girls. This is all exactly the way things ought to be."

*****

Violet was late for dinner. Her family, sensing she had more important things to handle with Jessie, had eaten without her. They held Violet's dinner for her and let it go.

As Violet ate her dinner alone in the kitchen, Isaac joined her.

"What's going on? Can I help?"

"Not really. There's a situation. Not mine, really, but a problem."

"You went to talk with Jessie. It's her problem?"

"Yes. If I tell you, you have to keep it to yourself. She wouldn't want this being spread all over school." Violet couldn't cope with this alone. She had to get it out of her mind and share it with Isaac. She needed her big brother's support.

"Okay. I can keep a secret."

"She's pregnant. Joe doesn't know yet. So don't call him. She's going to tell him, probably tomorrow, when she sees him."

"God! She has it all, and she goes and messes up like this?"

"I know. It's real trouble. I wish I could do something for her more than just listen."

"Do what you can for her. That's what friends are for."

Isaac mulled everything over while he took care of his last remaining class assignments. This late in the year, there was little academic work left. Mostly, the senior's energy was devoted to preparing for the graduation ceremony. Still, he couldn't focus on anything as mundane as school, not with this revelation. Finally, distracted and bothered, he texted Marie.

> *hey u up?*
>
> *yeah can't sleep either—what's up?*
>
> *need to tell u something but u can't say anything ok?*
>
> *👀 ok spill*
>
> *my friend might be pregnant*
>
> *wait who??*
>
> *can't say*
>
> *it's totally joe + jessie right*

why u think that??

lol everyone knows they've been like... doing stuff. definitely not violet + barry. or us. we're careful

yeah... but joe doesn't even know yet. she's telling him tmrw idk what to do

nothing not our business

yeah just... keep it quiet ok? nobody else knows

promise. lips sealed

Marie kept it to herself. For almost half an hour. Then she texted her best friend, Amanda, a pretty cheerleader who lived in the Heights. Marie needed to get it off her chest, and talking to her girlfriend was the only way to do that.

Chapter Nineteen

When Jessie got home from Herring Head, she found her mom sitting at the granite island in the kitchen. A plate of food, freshly served and steaming, sat in front of her.

"Oh, good! You're home," said Patricia. "I'm just sitting down for dinner. There's meatball stroganoff and noodles on the stove. Help yourself and join me. Would you like a glass of wine? The bottle's in the chiller. I've got something I'd like to talk about with you. Big news."

"No wine. I need to talk to you, too, Mom."

Patricia started right in while Jessie served herself dinner. "I have these sales trips all over the Northeast and Mid-Atlantic region, right?"

"Yes."

Patricia continued, excitement lighting her face, her words racing. "One of my business associates out there on the road, his name is Michael. We really get along well. He called this afternoon and asked me to marry him, and I said yes!" Patricia beamed.

Jessie sat down and began to pick at her dinner. "Michael? Which one is he? Albany? Philly? Pittsburgh? Do you have boyfriends in all those towns?"

"No! I have friends in those cities, business associates and customers, just business relationships, you know. Michael's different. Michael works out of D.C. He's my boss, the Mid-Atlantic regional sales manager, really successful, and he just finalized his divorce. I'll be heading there late next week on business, and we'll confirm our plans then. I'm so excited! After a dozen years alone, living the life of a single career woman..."

"And after you work out the details with Michael? Then what?" Jessie pushed the food around on her plate, distracted by her own situation.

"We haven't planned that far ahead yet. Maybe a fall wedding? Would you be my maid of honor? Whatever happens, you'll go to UConn next fall, and maybe I'll sell this house and we'll move to DC. We still have to sort out a few things."

"Congratulations, Mom," Jessie mumbled. Her face was blank.

"You don't seem excited for me. You're okay with all this? I know it's a big change. Moving and everything. But it's been years since your dad left us. It's time."

"Yeah, I'm fine with it. I'm done with this stupid little town."

"Oh, good." Patricia stood and hugged her daughter. "I'm glad you're on board. And you said you needed to talk to me, too?"

"Yeah."

Patricia sat back down and waited. "Well?"

Jessie paused, gathering strength to share her situation with her mom. Patricia waited, suddenly attuned to the anxiety she saw in Jessie.

"I'm late. I think I might be pregnant." Jessie finally let go and cried silently, tears flooding from her eyes. In that moment, the brazen teenage girl who had all the answers vanished, and a needy child emerged, desperate for her mother.

Patricia stood and hugged Jessie again, quickly, trying to show support as she processed Jessie's predicament. Finally, her face betrayed real anger as the awful truth of Jessie's situation came to her. Patricia pushed away from Jessie. "Oh, Jessie. With that Portuguese boy? No, no! Oh, dear. Are you sure?"

"I'm never late, Mom, and I'm more than a week late right now. So, I took a test and I'm pregnant."

"No! You can't be pregnant! What were you thinking? Why would you do this to me? To us. Why weren't you on the pill, for God's sake?"

"I'm not on the pill because I didn't think I would get pregnant. I don't know. I might have had to talk with you about it and meet your doctor for that anyway."

"You could have come and talked with me about this. Just the way you're doing now."

"You were never around for me to do that. I have to talk to you about it now. I have no choice. And now it's a little late for the pill."

"Don't blame me for your mistake," Patricia shouted. "And if you were going to sleep around, why with Joe Goncalves?"

"Mom! I'm not sleeping around. And Joe's my boyfriend."

Patricia sat back, fighting for control. Her hand rested on Jessie's forearm as she tried to show support, but her grip began to tighten. "Damn!" She let go of Jessie's arm and slammed her palm down on the granite. "You have everything laid out in front of you. Graduation. College. The future was right there waiting for you to take it. How could you mess up like this?"

"Mom. Yes, I screwed up, but it's too late now for debating right and wrong decisions. I need you to help me figure out what to do next."

"We'll take care of this," Patricia stated. "You can't let this get in the way of everything you have planned. I'll take you to see my doctor. Nobody will know. He can take care of it for you."

"What do you mean, take care of this? Having a baby wouldn't be that bad, right? Maybe there's nothing to take care of." Jessie watched, waiting for her mom's reaction. Pushing her mom's buttons was what she'd always done. Now, even though she needed her mom, Jessie fell back into that habit.

"Are you nuts? No, you're not having this baby! You have college. You have your whole life ahead of you. You don't need to be raising a baby from some poor Portuguese fisherman. He's not really even white, is he? I only met him once, on prom night. Is he even a citizen?"

"Would it be any better if it were a rich white boy's baby?" For a moment, Jessie thought of Gabe. God, don't let it be Gabe's baby.

"No. This isn't really a racial thing. It's a problem either way. But your boyfriend is Joe Goncalves, a fisherman's kid, for God's sake. You don't have much of a future with a boy like that. You'll end up living in some shack down by the harbor when you could do so much better. I'll call my doctor tomorrow. We'll set an appointment for later this week, before graduation, and take care of it. I'll be right there with you through the whole thing."

Distressed as she was, it gave Jessie a sense of renewed control to see her mom flare as she explained the situation. Jessie goaded her mom again. "Don't tell me you never had sex when you were young. Mom. Why did you and Dad split up anyway? And don't tell me you and this new guy, Michael, have never done it. How many others are there?"

Patricia fought back, defensively, her hands on her hips. "This isn't about me and your dad. Or about me and Michael. And how many men I might have been with is none of your business. The issue is what we're going to do about you and your baby."

"Maybe I should keep my baby," Jessie repeated, enjoying her mom's distress.

"No! Absolutely not! An abortion's the best way out of this mess. It's the only way. Take care of this and then move on with your life like nothing happened. And we'll get you on the pill. Just be more careful with your next boyfriend."

"Joe is my boyfriend. Don't tell me what to do."

Patricia stood, turned away from the counter and her daughter, crossed the kitchen, and dropped her plate clattering in the sink. Angrily, she walked out on the deck with her glass of wine.

Jessie ate her dinner alone in the kitchen, chewing slowly, watching her mom's back through the glass door. I need you right now, Mom. I don't know what to do. Come back inside and help me. Tell me what to do. Not an abortion, but what is the answer? I promise not to fight you right now. I need you, Mom.

Patricia stood with her wine, next to the railing, looking across the dark lawn to the still water of the pool.

"Damn!" she said quietly to herself.

Chapter Twenty

The next morning, the school cafeteria went silent when Jessie walked in, a half hour before classes were to start. Everyone seemed to be staring at her. That, she was accustomed to; her classmates always seemed to watch everything she did. She usually enjoyed being the focus of their attention. But this was different. Someone giggled. She saw Joe and cut through the crowded rows of tables to get to him. He looked stern, almost angry, his dark young face creased with new lines.

"What's going on?" he asked, leaning in and turning her by the elbow so they had a bit of privacy in the crowded room.

"I don't know. Why is everybody staring? We need to get some alone time and talk."

"I guess we do. Are you pregnant?" his voice was contained and quiet, but anger showed on his face.

"Why would you say that?" Jessie asked. She stood defiantly, shoulders thrown back, scanning the faces of her classmates.

"It's all over the school. I saw it online first thing this morning. I tried to call you, but you didn't pick up. Then I figured it was better to talk it out face-to-face."

Jessie looked back at Joe, but she avoided eye contact and said nothing. Her face turned pale. Suddenly, her jaw clenched.

"Well, are you pregnant?" Joe demanded again, his voice rising, almost shouting. His anger overcame his need to keep the conversation between just him and Jessie. The crowded cafeteria was silent, all the students rapt, straining to hear every word. "This is important. What I do depends on if you are or aren't."

"What would you do if I were?" Jessie replied defiantly. She spun suddenly to confront Joe and met his half-shut dark eyes.

"The right thing. I'd marry you and raise the baby with you."

"Oh, Joe. You don't have to do that." She softened, placing a soothing hand on his arm.

"Are you pregnant? Yes, or no?" he asked again, shaking off her hand.

"Maybe. Yes. I took the test. Yes, I'm pregnant."

Jessie's confirmation set off a mix of laughter, applause, and catcalls.

"Way to go, Joe!"

"Knocking up the hottest girl in school? Awesome man!"

Joe turned and faced his followers, his look silencing them instantly. Then he turned back to Jessie, searching for the best way to handle his pregnant girlfriend.

Gabriel strode to the middle of the crowded room. His diminutive frame was dwarfed as he stood next to Joe. "What makes you think the baby's yours, Joe?"

Gabe's statement was met with laughter. "Who else?" someone shouted. "Good job, Joe!"

Gabe, raising his voice to be sure everyone heard, carefully stated, "It might be mine."

"Gabe! No!" Jessie screamed.

"What? Nobody believes it could be mine?" Gabe reached into his ever-present photography bag. Having seen the late-night rumors online, he'd come prepared. He pulled out a thick stack of photos and tossed them, sliding, splayed like playing cards on a cafeteria table. There, in black and white with a sharp focus were more than ten photos, unmistakably of Jessie: the artistic moonscape of her belly, one of her nude, sitting up in a coquettish pose, one hand tossing her hair, and one of her lying back on a bed, smiling with her arms thrown wide and her legs spread.

"Gabe!" Jessie tried to snatch the pictures off the table, but it was too late. Most of the people in the cafeteria hadn't been able to see them. But enough had, and word spread quickly throughout the jammed room. Gabe scooped them and tucked them back in his bag. His case was made. The damage was done.

Joe wrapped a protective arm around Jessie. "Gabe, you little shit! I don't know how you got those pictures. I don't really care. Jessie's my girl, and you can go to hell."

"Not if the baby's mine," Gabe bragged.

Suddenly, the cafeteria divided itself into two camps, crowding at tables and in the aisles on opposite sides of the room. Behind Joe were his baseball teammates, including Isaac, of course, right at his elbow. Most of the boys on his side were athletes, strong young men, black, white, and Portuguese, who worked as fishermen, hauling nets and lobster pots when they weren't in school. On the other side, behind Gabe, were the rich, white kids from The Heights, indolent, lounging against the wall, sprawling nonchalantly at the tables.

Jessie stood in the middle, between the two factions, with Violet at her side. Violet leaned to her friend and whispered, "You better be sure about this? You told me you took the test, right?"

"What the fuck, Violet. How does everyone know? I only told you."

"I only told Isaac. It got out and around somehow. I'm sorry."

One of the fishermen called out, "Kick his ass, Joe! We're right behind you."

"Privileged rich kids. It's payback time!"

A Portuguese girl shouted, "I doubt Gabe could get it up. Even with Jessie looking like that."

Joe ignored his friends' taunts, but he stood, arms crossed, his immense physical presence moving Gabe back against a table, even though he wasn't touched. The fishermen crowded closer.

*****

The noise from the chaos in the cafeteria came through the kitchen to the Teacher's Room.

Lucas Knox and Jonas were sitting around a table, drinking coffee. Coach Lancaster and Tibbetts stood nearby. They were marking off the final days of the school year. They were all tired.

A first-year social studies teacher, Tom Butler, assigned the unenviable duty of morning cafeteria supervision, burst through the Teacher's Room door. "I need back-up," he shouted as though he were a policeman facing a riot. "There's trouble in the cafeteria. I think there's a fight brewing."

With a surge of energy, Lancaster, Lucas, and Jonas jumped up, leaving their coffees, and ran after Butler around the corner into the cafeteria. Tibbetts trailed.

At first sight of the teachers, the divided cafeteria quieted.

Joe defused the moment. "Whatever. Gabe, you're not worth the bother. Just bringing those pictures here, you're a disgrace."

He brushed past Gabe, his elbow nudging Gabe's chest, leaving him sitting on the table where he'd displayed his photos. Then he strode

88

out the cafeteria door toward the parking lot, calling over his shoulder. "Jessie, come on out here! We need to talk."

After a moment of hesitation, Jessie rushed after him, banging out the door, chasing him across the sunbaked parking lot.

With Joe and Jessie gone and the teachers in the cafeteria, things returned to normal. A low murmur of conversation continued.

Lucas pulled Violet aside. "What happened?"

"Jessie's pregnant. Joe's the father. But Gabe had pictures of her and said he might be the father."

"Oh, God! How's Jessie doing?"

"She's confused. Doesn't know what to do."

"Of course she's confused. She's pregnant, which alone is enough to upset any girl. And she's got the New England Championship on Saturday and graduation on Sunday. She's got a lot to handle all at the same time. The meet and the graduation are important. But none of that matters in light of all this."

"Yeah? So....? We need to help her. What can we do?"

"Stand by her and offer our support? I'm just a teacher and her coach. What else can we do?"

"I'll have her come see you. When's your free period?"

"Four."

"Me too. I'll bring her to your classroom."

Tibbetts cut over to Gabe. "You seem to be in the middle of all this. What happened?"

"Jessie's pregnant. I might be the father. But everyone thinks it has to be Joe."

"How could it be you?"

"We had one night. She posed for me. Nude. She wanted it with me even though she likes Joe." Gabe settled his hand on Tibbett's shoulder. He leaned up to his teacher, taking him into his confidence. "We're both men. You know how it goes."

Tibbetts pulled back, reassuming command of his student. "Gabe, be careful. You've finally got so much working out for you, going in the right direction. After all your past struggles. You're going to graduate. You're in that photography contest. You're all set for college in the fall. Don't set yourself up for trouble with some girl. She's not worth it. You've had some bad times in the past. Don't fall back into that pattern."

"I'm not. All I did was sleep with a pretty girl. Can you really blame me?"

Tibbetts patted Gabe on the back. "Hang in there. You'll get past this moment." He followed Lancaster, Lucas, and Jonas back to the teacher's room.

*****

"Well, there you go," said Tibbetts as he came through the door. "Just what you have to expect of these athletes. Always screwing around. Everything's always physical with people like them. All brawn and no brain."

Lucas fired back. "Your little protégé Gabe seems to be involved, too."

"Oh, I doubt it's his baby. I see Joe and Jessie carrying on. And now they have to pay the price. I expected you two would be thrilled," Tibbetts said, indicating Lancaster and Lucas. "The two best athletes in the state having a baby together? Imagine what that will

90

mean for your teams when you get to coach their kid in a few years. That's how it works with breeding race horses."

"Jeez. Tibbetts!" Lucas could hardly contain his own anger. Red in the face, he shouted, "We have a couple of students with a problem, and this is your attitude?"

Tibbetts sat at a table with his coffee, smug and satisfied. Fuming, Lancaster walked out, heading back to his office next to the gym. Lucas left with Jonas, heading for his home room and his first period class.

CHAPTER TWENTY-ONE

Lucas

As they walked, Jonas patted his friend's shoulder. "Let me know if I can help."

Lucas stopped. The hallway was quiet. Most of the students were already in their homerooms after the chaos in the cafeteria. "Jonas, can I ask you for some advice? You've been a teacher for a long time, and I always seem to turn to you when things get dicey."

"Of course. You want to know how to handle this morning's situation?"

"Yes. Violet's going to bring Jessie by my room fourth period. I don't know what to tell her. How can she run in the New England's if she's pregnant? I don't want her or the baby getting hurt. What do I tell her?" Lucas said.

"Okay. Well. I can't say I've ever had to deal with something like this," Jonas said, stopping and turning to face Lucas in the deserted hallway. The teachers had to be brief with this essential conversation and get to their home rooms as well.

Speaking quietly, Jonas continued. "I see three directions you can take. None is ideal. First, you could say nothing, do nothing. Let her run in the meet. How do you feel about that?"

Lucas replied, "I wish she could run, but I don't want her having a problem with the pregnancy. What if she loses the baby?"

"Exactly. You and the school would be liable. So that's not a good option. You have to say something to her. So, here's your second option. You tell her she's out of the track meet because she's pregnant and you're concerned for her well-being."

"Yeah, that's what I was thinking I'd do. But then she or her mom sues me and the school for denying her the opportunity to compete just because she's pregnant," Lucas said.

"Right, so that's also not a good option. But you have to talk this through with her. Here's option three. You tell her she can compete, but only if she gets a doctor's note saying it's okay. That way, the burden and liability are on the doctor, not you or the school. And if she gets the note, you'd still need to be very careful with her, watching her for any signs of distress."

"It's not ideal. But that could work. And if she doesn't get the note, she's out. It's up to Jessie and her mom to get the note to compete."

"Right. So, when you meet her, take the meeting to the front office. Make sure you have Principal Adams with you. Not just Violet," Jonas said.

"Good. It's not a perfect plan. Nothing is ideal. But it's as good a plan as any. Thanks, Jonas."

"I'll be there for you, Lucas, thinking of you fourth period. Good luck with this. Let me know how it goes."

Lucas called Principal Adams and set up the meeting.

Chapter Twenty-two

Jessie and Joe

Jessie left the awful scene in the cafeteria, chased Joe to his pickup, and climbed into the passenger seat next to him. He was on his phone. He held up a finger, signaling her to wait.

"Yes, Mr. Wilson. Joe Goncalves. I've decided to take your offer. How do we proceed?"

Jessie heard only muffled talking as Wilson spoke to Joe.

"Fine. Yes, graduation is Sunday. I'll track down a lawyer with my family and meet with you first thing on Monday. When would I get that signing bonus?"

"Perfect. I'll meet with you at my house on Monday morning at nine. You have the address?"

Joe ended the call and turned to face Jessie. "Well. Fill me in. I don't want to depend on nothing more than rumors on the internet. I don't trust what they're saying. What's really going on?"

"I'm late. You know I'm never late. I'm pretty sure I'm pregnant."

Joe nodded, absorbing her words. He said nothing, but he took her hand in the confined space of the truck.

"Pretty sure? You said you did a pregnancy test, right? I mean, I love you. I want to be with you and take care of you, whatever is going on. But I need to know the truth."

"Yes. I'm sure. I took a pregnancy test."

"You'd better be sure," he said, dropping her hand, suddenly angry. "Everything hangs on this. I'm giving up a lot to take care of you and my baby."

They sat in silence, sorting their individual thoughts.

"It's *our* baby," Jessie stressed.

"That's another thing. What was all that with Gabe?" Joe asked, his face darkening suddenly.

"He asked me to pose for him to shoot pictures for some art contest. It was a mistake posing for him. I don't care about Gabe and his dumb pictures. He was supposed to get rid of all but one artsy shot he's going to enter in his contest. That's all there is to that. He's a fool."

"You were naked in his pictures. Did you sleep with him?"

"Yes. I thought it would be cool for me to pose for him to get some artsy nude photos. So, to that question, yes, I was posing nude. Did I have sex with him? Seriously? A loser like him? What do you think?"

Joe nodded, accepting her ambiguous answer as a denial. Then he frowned and slammed the steering wheel with the palm of his hand. After a moment, he continued, struggling for control, his voice choking back his anger. "That's no good. What were you thinking? You can't be doing that with other guys. Gabe or anyone. You're my girl. And if you're pregnant, we need to stay together to work through this. This nonsense has got to stop!"

Joe seethed.

Jessie sat in silence, watching him, suddenly frightened.

After a moment, Joe began to gather himself. He pulled his hand back from the steering wheel, but his face was still flushed and dark.

"I love you, Jessie. You're my girl. You can't be doing things like that."

"Who was that on the phone?" Jessie asked, hoping to change the subject.

"The scout for the St. Louis Cardinals. Remember, I told you they were making me an offer? I just agreed to play pro ball."

"What about Clemson?"

"I called them earlier this morning. Before I saw you. I told them no. It was a decision I had to make anyway. Knowing you might be pregnant, it seemed right. You telling me you're pregnant confirmed that this is the right way to go."

"Why? You didn't know for sure if I was pregnant when you turned down Clemson."

"The whole situation made me rethink everything. Even if you weren't pregnant, this might be the way to go. Now that I know you are pregnant, the answer is obvious. Five hundred thousand dollars in bonus money for signing, and more to come when I start playing pro ball. All that will take care of you and our baby."

"What if I fix this? What if I don't have the baby?"

"An abortion? You can't do that!"

"Why not? My mom thinks I should. She says a baby would get in the way of all my plans for the future. Anyway, it's my body. It's my choice." Jessie recited the mantra she'd heard on a Pro-Choice podcast. "It's not my mom's decision or yours. I can do whatever I want to do with my body."

Smugly, Jessie was now watching Joe. Sure, Joe, she thought to herself. Squirm a little. It's not just the pregnancy now. It's about my decision to have an abortion. Defying Mom got her upset. And now

I go the other way, and Joe's worked up. It takes their minds off my pregnancy as long as I deny them their way. It is my decision. I'm in control of at least this small piece of this mess.

Joe picked his words carefully, watching Jessie closely. "You're pregnant. We messed up together with that. So, we'll work through it as a team. It's our baby. You said that earlier. We're in this together. But I'm the father, so I'm involved in what we decide to do. We share this responsibility. No, I don't want you to have an abortion. That's not what my faith says is right." He paused, again considering Jessie sitting quietly next to him. "But it is your choice. I'll support you either way. What do you really want to do?"

"I don't really want an abortion either. If I'm pregnant, we're having a baby." Even as she said it, Jessie felt a hint of happiness. "Yes! We're having a baby. I'll tell my mom tonight that I won't have an abortion."

Joe hugged her. "Then we have to get married. It's the only way to deal with this. I'm not one of those guys who gets a girl pregnant and walks away. So, we'll get married! Right after graduation. We'll raise our baby together. That's why I'm taking the Cardinal's offer."

"Oh, Joe. I don't know. Having a baby together, yes. But getting married is such a big step. I don't know if I really want that right now. You know I love you, but is that the best way to handle this? You should go to South Carolina for college in the fall, or play pro ball for St. Louis. Either way, I'll be off to UConn. We don't have to get married."

Joe shook his head, frustrated. "I thought about this all night, after I saw everything on the internet. I hardly slept. I have to do the right thing. That's the way I am, the way I was raised. So, I'm going pro with the Cardinals. I'll play baseball and provide for you and our baby. No, I won't be going to Clemson. I can meet you in Connecticut in the fall when the baseball season is over. We'll get married as soon as possible, and live together and raise our baby together."

Jessie weighed her options. "You seem to think you've got my life all figured out for me. I don't know. I'll do what makes the most sense for me. But right now, I'm confused. I don't know what to do. And I always know exactly what to do. Not with this. I can't do this; make that decision right here, right now. I like that you want to marry me. But I'm not sure. I don't know. Give me time to sort this all out."

Joe slumped over the steering wheel, angry, red in the face, and frustrated. He said nothing. He rested his forehead on his thick forearms.

"We'll talk later, Joe." Jessie got out of the truck, quietly closed the door, and walked alone back to face the disaster that was waiting for her in school.

CHAPTER TWENTY-THREE

Lucas sat behind his square, dull-gray steel teacher's desk, waiting for his star athletes to arrive. Moments after the start of fourth period, Violet led Jessie through the door. Jessie pushed past Lucas' desk and took a seat in the front row, sliding down, almost recumbent beneath the curled arm of the student desktop. Her long legs filled the space between the front row of the student desks and Lucas's bulky desk. Violet stepped over Jessie's legs, moved down the aisle, and sat behind her friend, leaning forward, attentive.

Lucas stood, went to the door, and said, "I'm not comfortable having this conversation alone with the two of you here in my classroom. Let's take it down to the main office."

He led his two stars back out to the hall.

"Where are you taking us?" asked Jessie, anxious as she trailed her coach down the hall. "Why?"

"The main office, or maybe the guidance office. Maybe we should get your guidance counselor involved. That would be Mrs. Gould, right? It might be good to have a woman with us. For you. For me, too."

"No. Mrs. Gould is too proper. She wouldn't understand. She'd judge me. She thinks I'm the perfect girl. Too many people know I'm pregnant already. So, no. Leave her out of this."

"Okay. I've already given Principal Adams the heads up. She's expecting us."

"What? Why her?" Jessie fumed. "Why does she need to know about this? Why does everybody have to get into this?"

They paused in the lobby, outside the doors to the main office. Students and teachers passed by, entering and leaving the office. The office was busy with graduation just days away.

Lucas turned Jessie to face him. "Listen to me. Mrs. Adams already knows. After the events in the cafeteria this morning, the whole school knows. Mrs. Adams and I both want to be sure we do the right things with you. I'm concerned about your health and the welfare of your baby. We have to talk about this. Okay?"

Jessie shook her head 'no', but followed Lucas in.

Lucas, Jessie, and Violet sat across from Mrs. Adams. The principal closed her office door behind them and returned to her desk.

 She sat, leaned forward, elbows on the desk, and nodded to Lucas to begin.

"Now, take a deep breath. Then fill me in, Jessie," Lucas started. "Let me know what's really going on."

Jessie stared straight ahead, not looking at her coach or Mrs. Adams. "I think I'm pregnant. I missed my period. And Joe and I..." She stopped.

Lucas paused and raised his hands, allowing his star jumper to take her time.

Mrs. Adams interceded, sparing Lucas for the moment. "Okay. I have a few questions. How far along are you? Have you seen a doctor yet? You've told your mom? What does she think about this?"

"No. I don't know how far along. Maybe a couple of weeks, maybe a month? I don't know. And before you ask, yes, I took the test. I'm definitely pregnant. I haven't seen a doctor yet, but my mom's going to make me an appointment with her gynecologist today. I told Mom last night."

Violet nodded and tapped Jessie on the shoulder. When Jessie turned, Violet smiled at her friend and gave a thumbs up, pleased that she had talked with her mom. That helped Jessie for a moment, and she returned a faint smile.

"Okay." Lucas struggled with what to say next. "This isn't easy for me to talk about with you. As a man, and as your teacher and coach. Let me think for a moment. I'm not sure where the line is that I shouldn't cross with discussing this sort of thing with a girl. I don't know what's okay to say and what's not." He looked to Principal Adams for support.

Adams nodded. "This is difficult for all of us, Jessie. We just want to do what's right for you. Go on, Lucas."

Staring straight ahead, Lucas added, "Maybe I shouldn't get involved at all, but you're an athlete I've worked with for four years. I care about you and your well-being, and I want to help you."

Violet interceded, saving her coach from his predicament. "You've told your mom. And now Joe knows. That's a good start."

Jessie nodded, saying nothing. Why can't they all just leave me alone, she thought.

Lucas continued. "When did you say you'll see your mom's doctor?"

"I don't know. She's going to call him to make an appointment today. Why do you ask? Does it matter?"

"Yes. It absolutely matters. I've heard of track athletes, women, who continued light training for the first few months they're pregnant," Lucas stated. "But that's not the same as all-out, hard competition in the high jump and hurdles. Those can be brutal events; leaping six feet in the air and crashing down on the pads. Sprinting a hundred meters in thirteen seconds, jumping ten barriers. When you see the doctor, ask him if it's okay to keep jumping and hurdling."

"What if the doctor says 'no'?"

Lucas sighed, hands out, palms up. "Then you're out of the New Englands. I want you to compete. You could win two events, maybe three with the relay. But I'm sorry. You can't take the chance that you or the baby gets hurt. It's in the doctor's hands. We had to have this talk, and I have to tell you this. Unless the doctor says it's okay, you're out of the meet. I can't have it on my conscience if either you or the baby is hurt. I can't have the school or me being liable if anything happens to you."

"What will the coaches at UConn think when they see I didn't go to the New England Championship?"

"If they ask me, I'll say you had an injury and couldn't compete. Violet will still be going," Lucas said, turning to his other star. "If the doctor says no, Jessie, you can come along, ride to the meet with us, and watch."

Lucas said nothing more, but he wondered silently to himself. If she is pregnant, what will she tell the UConn coaches when she arrives on campus in September, four or five months pregnant? Let's not worry right now, what they might think if she doesn't compete on Saturday. Let's deal with the present challenge today and not worry about September.

"But not jump? Not run the hurdles? Like you said, I could win both events." Jessie's face was red, her fists clenched. "I'm the best in New England."

"If the doctor says it's okay, yes, you'll be able to compete. If not, no. I'm sorry."

Jessie flared suddenly and bolted from the principal's office into the main office. She rushed down the hall, slamming a door behind her. Coach Knox looked at Violet.

"You want to go get her?" he asked.

"No. You know how she is. It wouldn't do any good to chase her down. She'll come back when she's ready."

The door opened, and Jessie came back, contrite. "Sorry. I'm just a bit on edge. I shouldn't have done that. Yes, I want to go to the meet on Saturday. And, if the doctor says it's okay for me to compete, I'll let you know."

"I'll need a note from the doctor."

Jessie gave an exasperated sigh. "Sure. Whatever."

"Okay. You and Violet can go now," said Principal Adams.

The girls left, and Lucas slumped in his chair, sweating. "God help us. Why can't they just compete and not bring all this drama into it?"

Adams stood. Lucas did as well. Adams patted Lucas's shoulder briefly. "You did well with this, my friend. It's up to her now. If she doesn't get that note, she's taken herself out of the meet. She gets the doctor's note, then she's assumed the risk, along with the doctor. Let me know what she does next."

CHAPTER TWENTY-FOUR

Violet and Isaac

Violet sat on the tailgate of their father's lovingly polished Ford truck parked on the street in front of their house. Isaac leaned on the fender next to her, his wide shoulders slumped. Behind them, music played quietly inside the house. Old, classic jazz, Oscar Peterson, *Summertime*. Except for the faint music, it was quiet outside.

Violet shifted to face her brother. "C'mon, Isaac. What happened? I told you about Jessie and Joe and asked you to keep it to yourself. Next thing I know, it's all over school."

"I know. I messed up. I'm sorry. I texted Marie. I needed to talk about it with someone, and I didn't want to be the one to tell Joe. Marie let it out, and you know how rumors spread."

"But this wasn't a rumor. All hell broke loose this morning. Jessie's really upset."

"Yeah. I know," Isaac shifted foot to foot, anxious to appease his sister. "So's Joe. I'll back him up with whatever he decides to do. Right now, I think he's decided to marry Jessie and go pro rather than going to college."

"That would be a mistake. He should go to college. I don't know what he and Jessie should do. That's their business to decide."

"I agree, but I can't change his mind. That's the way he is. Both he and Jessie can be really headstrong. Maybe that's why they're both such great athletes. Joe and I talked a lot this afternoon. He's pretty determined. It's what makes him such a competitor, but it can also make him stubborn. He says he loves Jessie and marrying her is the right thing to do since she's pregnant."

"And I'm doing everything I can to help Jessie. But she won't listen to me or to Coach Knox or anybody. She does whatever she wants. All she can say is that she wants to run and jump in the New Englands. Here she is pregnant, and running in the New Englands is all that seems to matter to her."

"So. I can't get through to Joe. And Jessie won't listen to you. And here we are up to our ears in all their drama."

"In the end, I guess we have to let them figure it out for themselves. Be there for them and let them make their own decisions, even if they're making mistakes."

Isaac nodded. "They made a mistake getting pregnant. We can't fix that."

"Did you talk to Marie about starting all the rumors?"

"Yeah, we had a fight about it. She doesn't think she made a mistake. Says all she told was one of her friends."

Violet took control, lecturing her big brother. "If we hear any more news from Joe or Jessie, we have to keep it between us. We can't help them if this happens again."

"I agree. I can't trust Marie anymore with things like this. I made a mistake telling her. I can sort things out with Marie over time. But you and me, we need to stick together, Little Sister. Do you still trust me?"

Violet contemplated Isaac's apology, then hopped down from the tailgate and hugged him. "Yes. We've been through worse. I know you didn't mean for all this to happen. It's really Joe and Jessie's problem, not ours."

Chapter Twenty-five

Down the hill near the fish plant, Joe sat on his back patio with his parents. A blue bug light zapped, keeping the mosquitoes away. Dusk was settling in, the sky glowing peach above the harbor. It would have been a beautiful evening except for the discussion Joe had to have with his parents.

"Mom, Dad," he began, shifting forward on his chair. "I've got a lot of news to share with you. I've made my decision. I'm going to play for the Cardinals and turn down the scholarship to Clemson."

Joao and Helena sat silently, shocked by his news. After a moment, Joao spoke, his voice a quiet, controlled growl, "I thought you'd settled on Clemson. Why the change of mind?"

 "It's complicated," Joe began. "You know my girlfriend, Jessie?"

"Yes," nodded Joao. Helena reached for her husband's hand, but sat tight-lipped.

"I think I got her pregnant. So, I'll need that bonus money to support her and our baby."

Helena snapped. "You *think* you got her pregnant? Well, did you? Or didn't you?"

Joe's tight-lipped face confirmed that Jessie was pregnant. He said nothing, just nodded slightly.

Helena ranted, red in the face. "I knew it! That little bitch. She's no good, Joe. Leave her be. Walk away and let her deal with it."

"She's my girl, Momma. We love each other. I have to do the right thing. I'm not going to be the kind of guy who gets a girl pregnant and turns his back on her. That's not who I am. That's not how you raised me."

"She's an evil little bitch. I knew it! I smelled her perfume on your pillowcase when I did the laundry a week or so ago. Now she's screwed up your whole future."

"Ma, we're in love. This isn't a bad thing that's happened."

Joao reached over and put his hand on Helena's shoulder, attempting to settle her. She pulled away, stood, and began pacing, continuing to fume as Joao spoke to Joe. "Joe, I thought I was okay with whatever you decided, whether to go to college or to the pros. But now that you've made up your mind, I realize I really was hoping you'd go to college. Can you rethink this? Can't you support the girl and the baby while you play at Clemson?"

"I don't know. I don't think so. I don't see how. But five hundred thousand dollars can set me and Jessie up nicely."

"So would a college education. That bonus money won't last forever. Go to college. You have a scholarship. If I have to, I can dig into our savings. I'll do whatever I need to do to help you get through this."

"It's too late, Dad. I called Clemson this morning and told them I was going pro. And I called Mr. Wilson, the Cardinal scout, this morning too. He's coming to meet me here at the house at nine on Monday morning to sign me. He said I should have an agent or a lawyer here on Monday to look over the contract."

Helena interrupted, stopping her pacing, turning to face Joe, her finger pointing. "She's no good, Joe. That little bitch. She's rich. Maybe she'll get an abortion. Wherever you play baseball next year doesn't matter to me as long as she's out of our lives. Walk away from her. Let her deal with her problem."

"C'mon, Ma. You know abortion's wrong. It's a sin. Jessie's pregnant, and it's up to me to support her and our baby. Look at it this way. I'll be rich after Monday morning, and you'll be a grandmama in a few months."

"Huh!" Helena muttered. "The little bitch."

Joao took charge. "I'll support you however I can with this. To say I'm disappointed that you won't be the first one in our family to go to college... yes, there's that. But if you're sure this is the way to go, I'll call Peter Gomes and have him here Monday morning. He's always handled all our legal affairs."

Helena looked worried, turning from her son to confront her husband. "Does Peter Gomes know anything about baseball contracts?"

"He's a good lawyer. He helped us with the bank mortgage and all the paperwork when we bought this house. He'll do a good job for us. He always has."

"The money will fix things for Jessie and me," Joe added. "And we'll get married too."

"She's no good, that girl," Helena continued to rage. "Don't marry her. I forbid it!"

"Ma?!" Joe begged, hands out, pleading. "You know I love her. You'll love her too, once you get to know her."

"No. Never!"

"When do you want to get married?" asked Joao.

"Soon. Everyone already seems to know she's pregnant. But it would be good to get married quickly, before she's showing. That way, the baby's birthday and our anniversary would be close together. In a few years, nobody would know what really happened. Maybe we could get married in a couple of weeks? I'll go talk to Father Tourigny this week."

Helena vented the last of her anger. "That little whore. She's probably gotten herself pregnant to make you marry her to get at your money."

She stood and crashed through the screened storm door into the kitchen, slamming it behind her.

Joe laughed nervously and called after her, "Momma, you said it a moment ago. She's rich. Her family's wealthy. She's got plenty of money already. She's not after my money."

"Then she should support the baby and you, while you go to college," Helena shouted from the kitchen.

Joe got the last word. "I've already made my decision. I'm going to marry Jessie and play for the Cardinals. Look at it this way. I've got a great job opportunity to play professional baseball. I've got a beautiful girlfriend. And I'm going to be a father. What's not to like? It's all good."

Joao patted his boy's hand. "We'll sort this all out. Piece by piece. One day at a time. First, the baseball contract, then the girl and the baby, maybe a wedding. Talk to Father Tourigny. I'll get Peter Gomes here Monday morning to take a look at your contract, and we'll play it out from there. Let me deal with your mother."

CHAPTER TWENTY-SIX

Lucas Knox sat with Jennifer at their kitchen table. They had put their little girls to bed and finally had some time alone together to talk while they ate dinner. Jennifer served salad into bowls. Baked chicken and pre-packaged stuffing were steamed on their plates.

"How's the end of the school year going?" she asked.

"The usual in most regards. Everyone's just counting down the days. The Seniors are preparing for graduation on Sunday. But not everything is going as smoothly as I wish it were. You know me and how I like things to be. How I like everything to happen according to the plan, without a hitch. No headaches and no hassles."

Jennifer put down the salad tongs. "I knew something was on your mind. You've not been yourself this evening. Distracted by every little thing. What's wrong? What's going on?"

"Jessie Brandt, my star high jumper?"

"Yes."

"She might be pregnant. She and her boyfriend apparently.... Anyway, if she's pregnant, she'll probably miss the New Englands. I want her to be able to compete; she could win both her events. But I can't let her go if she's pregnant, can I? I told her she needs to bring me a doctor's note saying it's okay. But I worry about her and her health. How can she high jump and run the hurdles if she's pregnant?" Lucas waited, hoping Jennifer would say it would be okay for Jessie to compete, and knowing she wouldn't.

Jennifer shook her head. "I don't know. I don't think she should, even with the doctor's note. We both know what can happen. That's a shame. You've told me how good she is. What about Violet?"

"Violet's fine, and she could also win. But without Jessie, we'll have to skip the relay, too. So that takes out Violet and two other girls. Jessie can still come along to watch on Saturday, even if she can't jump. I doubt she'll come if she can't compete. The hard part is that I don't know what to say to help Jessie. I'm her coach, and there are boundaries. Poorly defined, but things I can't or shouldn't say and do. I hate the ambiguity. But as her coach, I have to be looking out for her health and well-being. I don't want her to get hurt. Or her baby. And her mother's not always there for her. I've never even seen her mom at a meet, coming to watch how good her daughter is. She doesn't really have an adult in her life she can turn to at a time like this."

"Would it help if I talked to her? Woman to woman?"

"Thanks. No, I don't think so. She doesn't really know you. I asked if she wanted to involve her guidance counselor, a woman, and she said 'no'. And, she was angry that I included Susan Adams, the principal, in our meeting. I wanted to have a woman there with us. She's going to have to talk to her mom. Let's leave it there."

Lucas continued, "I didn't want to get pulled into any of this in the first place. It's so much easier when it's just coaching kids on how to run and jump, and throw. Training and competition? That's what I know how to coach. None of this other nonsense. I hate being in this position right now. I have to leave well enough alone, but I'm so invested in her, both as her coach and as her teacher. I don't know what to do, but I can't keep her out of the meet. Not if she brings me a doctor's note."

Jennifer leaned across the table and held Lucas's hand. "I expect it's never going to be that easy. Kids will make mistakes. Let's hope our little ones never have trouble like this."

Upstairs, Sophie and Emma slept peacefully, snuggled in their bunk beds with their stuffed animals. Lucas looked in on them on his way to bed. It terrified him to think of what their futures might hold. At least as their parents, he and Jennifer had better opportunities to help them with their problems than he had with his athletes.

CHAPTER TWENTY-SEVEN

Jessie

Shortly after seven on Friday morning, Jessie reclined on a narrow table in Dr. Goodman's office, her heels cradled in cold metal stirrups. Her hospital gown gapped in the back. Slick paper crinkled beneath her. Patricia sat in a chair next to Jessie's shoulder.

Dr. Goodman stood from his position on a stool between Jessie's knees, peeled off rubber gloves, and looked her in the eyes. "Yes, you're pregnant. Everything seems to be fine. I only gave you a quick exam, but we'll give you a full check-up in a couple of weeks to make sure both you and the baby are healthy. We'll have your blood test results back shortly."

"How far along is she?" asked Patricia.

"I don't know. Jessie, when was your last period?"

"Last week of April." Jessie's voice was a flat monotone. It was terrible to have this stranger, a man, poking about between her legs and asking her such personal questions. But this is where she found herself in the unfamiliar, odd world of pregnancy. She steeled herself and thought, I just have to get through this so I can go to the New Englands on Saturday.

Dr. Goodman nodded. His face showed no emotion. "So, you would have conceived possibly early to mid-May. That means you're about four, maybe as much as six weeks along. I'll know better when I'm able to give you a complete checkup in a couple of more weeks."

For Jessie, this was good news. That rules out Gabriel as the father. "I thought Joe and I would be safe. We never went all the way when it was the time of the month where I could get pregnant."

"That's fine, and it may be true," answered the doctor. "But you're still young. And you're a lean athlete. Young people with lean bodies don't necessarily have a regular cycle. Your mom says you're on the track team. Do you work out particularly hard at track practice?"

"Yes," Jessie answered proudly. "I work as hard as any athlete I know. Harder than most. Why?"

"That physical stress also can throw off your body's regular rhythm."

"We want to get her on the pill," interjected Patricia.

"I can give her a prescription, but she can't start it until after the pregnancy and birth."

Patricia pushed ahead with her agenda. "We want an abortion as soon as possible."

"No, Mom!" Her brow furrowed, she spoke with determination for the first time since they arrived at the doctor's office. "I thought about it all night and most of the past few days. I want to marry Joe and move on with my life. I'm certain about that. It's about the only thing I'm sure about right now."

Dr. Goodman sat at Jessie's feet, facing the feuding mother and daughter. It was difficult being caught between the two women, but he'd been through this before. He knew how to proceed. "Jessie, how old are you?"

"Eighteen. Why?"

"That makes you an adult. It's your choice, Jessie. Patricia, I respect your wishes for your daughter, but it's her decision whether or not to keep the baby. Not mine and not yours, Mrs. Brandt. Jessie, you need to give this decision a lot of thought and discuss this with the baby's father, too. Neither I nor your mom can make this decision for you, but you need to really think things through. We have a few more weeks before you have to make your final decision."

Patricia stood, her face grim, her mouth set. "Dr. Goodman, I expected you to back me on this. Jessie, if you keep the baby and marry Joe, it ends any chance you have for college, for running at UConn, for any sort of a life."

"I'll have a life with Joe and with our baby. That's what we want."

Dr. Goodman waited for his two patients to settle their dispute. A hard silence filled the room.

Finally, Jessie spoke. "There is one thing I do need from you today, Dr. Goodman."

"Of course. What is it?"

"I have a track meet on Saturday, but my coach says I'll need a note from you saying it's okay for me to run."

"Sure. Running shouldn't be a problem this early in your pregnancy. In fact, staying active and fit is good for both you and your baby." He took out a prescription pad and scribbled quickly. "Jessie Brandt is cleared to run track." He signed the note and handed it to Jessie.

"I do want to schedule you for follow-up visits once a month going forward to check on you and your baby."

"What about the abortion?" insisted Patricia. "We have an appointment for you to do that next Monday."

"Your daughter doesn't want the abortion." Dr. Goodman's tone carried authority and finality. "Jessie, make an appointment on your way out for a checkup in a couple of weeks, sometime around the middle of July and again in August."

Patricia gave up. Her daughter was determined to have this baby. Dr. Goodman was no help. There was nothing she could do. At least for the moment. She would give it some thought and figure out a way to go with her stubborn daughter.

Dr. Goodman turned and opened the door. "You can get dressed, Jessie. And I'll see you again in a few weeks." He walked out, leaving Jessie and Patricia to sort out their differences.

Patricia and Jessie rode home together; Patricia at the wheel, Jessie slumped in the passenger seat. The car was filled with a tense silence. When they got to the house, Jessie ran to her Miata and drove away without a word to Patricia. She was late for school.

*****

As soon as she arrived, Jessie carried the note triumphantly, waving it as she entered Coach Knox's classroom. Clumps of sophomores were starting to gather for the first-period math class. They backed away, giving the celebrity athlete, the pregnant senior, her space with her coach. "I got the doctor's note, Coach. So, am I back in the New Englands?"

Lucas looked over the note. "Sure." His voice betrayed his concerns, but he had promised his star she could compete if she got a doctor's note, and she had complied with his request. "We'll have a short practice this afternoon. Run through the relay passes, prep your high jump approach, and maybe run just a couple of times over the first three hurdles. You've been unable to practice for almost a week, so you may be a bit rusty. At this point, this is all we can do to be ready for tomorrow's meet."

"I'll be there this afternoon. And I'll be set for tomorrow!" Jessie walked away with a quick, triumphant fist pump in the air, having won this small victory. She headed to the auditorium for the final graduation rehearsal with her classmates.

120

*****

Mid-morning, Lucas took Jessie's note to Tom Stephens, the Athletic Director and head football coach. "Jessie got a note from her doctor clearing her for the meet tomorrow." He handed the note to Stephens.

Stephens looked over the note. "How do you feel about this?"

"I'm a bit worried. But if the doctor says she's fine…"

"Yes. Legally, we're covered if anything should happen. Just keep an eye on her. If she has any problem at all, pull her from the meet."

"Absolutely."

On his way back to his classroom, Lucas looked into Principal Adams' office. "She got the note. She's going to the meet tomorrow. I'm worried, but I'll keep an eye on her and pull her back if I see a problem."

"That's good. Let me know how she does. Thanks for keeping me informed."

Lucas quietly let Jonas know when they were at lunch.

He told Jennifer that night after they put their girls to bed.

"I hope she's okay. I don't want her getting hurt. Or the baby. I worry what it would be like if she lost the baby and it was somehow my fault for letting her compete. I can't carry that on my conscience."

"God willing, it won't happen," Jennifer said, shifting close to him on the sofa. "She's taken on that responsibility with her doctor and her mom. You've done what you can. Take good care of her tomorrow at the meet. I hope she does well and doesn't have anything go wrong."

121

Chapter Twenty-eight

Jessie and Violet

Waiting for the start of the New England High School Track Championship, the small Rock Haven contingent of athletes, Bob with his discus, Jessie, Violet, and the other relay runners, waited on a blanket in the shade underneath the grandstand. Hot sun steamed the immense college stadium, reflecting off the press box windows and empty seats. The heat challenged the top athletes in the region to compete at their best. It was cooler, but still humid in the shade where the Rock Haven athletes rested.

The three-ring circus typical of a major track meet went on despite the heat. When they weren't competing, the athletes moved slowly, clinging to the shade as much as possible, conserving their energy. Most carried bottles of water to their competition areas. Runners entered in upcoming races waited corralled in pens, roped off with bright, pennant-laced cords near their starting lines, stretching and jogging in place, baking in the sun while they waited, anxious to be called to the starting line. Announcements blared, summoning athletes for events and listing results. Races streamed by on the track, the runners' intent. The field event competitors sat on the infield, waiting for their turns in their events. When they were called, jumpers and throwers gave short, explosive bursts of action, sometimes accompanied by animal-like shouts.

Lucas saw that Jessie had lost her edge in the hurdles. It didn't surprise him. The distractions of the past days and the missed practices had left her without her usual balance, quickness, and grace. Her dance through the barriers was off. She won her trial heat but not without a struggle, chopping her steps and flailing her arms to sustain her rhythm as she cleared each hurdle. She powered over the last three, barely ahead of the other competitors. Still, that victory moved her to the final against seven other girls.

What is wrong with me, Jessie wondered. Get it together. I should be able to crush these other girls. I'm the best hurdler here.

She struggled again in the preliminary heat of the relay. The four-by-one-hundred relay requires precisely timed handoffs, with the outgoing runner hitting top speed just as the arriving runner catches up in the middle of the short passing zone. Ideally, the incoming runner should stretch forward for the hand of the outgoing runner, who reaches back, still racing ahead. Both should be running at full speed when they make the pass. The first runner slaps the baton into the next runner's palm as though hammering a nail. The pass must be completed before the end of the zone. A team is disqualified if the pass occurs outside the zone.

Running the first leg, Jessie hugged the inside of the curve in her lane and took the lead, bursting past all the other runners in their lanes. Lack of recent practice threw off the timing between Jessie and Annie, the second Rock Haven runner. Annie left her mark too early and slowed almost to a stop as she crowded the end of the passing zone. Jessie found herself suddenly alongside her teammate, facing Annie, handing her the baton as though she were handing off a football. All the other teams burst past while Annie and Jessie completed the awkward exchange at a standstill. Annie took the baton, turned, and started sprinting again, but the Rock Haven lead had been lost.

Lucas threw his arms up in disgust. It was an event his team of girls could have won.

"Go! Go!" Jessie screamed after her teammate, but it was too late. The Rock Haven team failed to qualify for the final.

Briefly, cooling off back in the shade with her teammates, Jessie bitched, "Annie left her mark too early. It's her fault we lost the relay."

Annie fought back. "You were late coming into the zone. Maybe if you showed up for practice…"

Lucas started to speak, but thought better of it and kept quiet. Violet interceded. "We screwed up as a team. It's over. Let's forget it and move on." None of Jessie's other teammates said a word.

Jessie walked away, heading for the high jump. Lucas walked with her. "Put the relay behind you. Focus on the jump. Start at five-four today," he advised. "You haven't jumped for a few days."

"Why waste the energy? I can clear five-four in my sleep. It's hot. Why not start at five-six?"

"The lower height will get you back in the groove. Lock in your approach for the higher jumps. The missed practices can't be helped now, but starting at five-four will only be one jump. It won't tire you out. It's where you should start."

"Sure, Coach." Jessie fumed inside, but said nothing out loud. *What does Coach know about the high jump anyway? He was never a high jumper. I'll do what he says, but really? I had to fight through it in the hurdles heats, and then Annie messed everything up for me in the relay. This isn't the way I thought today would go. What's wrong?*

She started at five-four. Though her approach was awkward, lacking her usual gazelle-like bounds, Jessie sailed over the bar easily.

Atypically, Jessie knocked the bar off on her first attempt at five-six, catching the fiberglass bar with her heels, pulling it beneath her into the foam pit. It bent beneath the small of her back as she landed on it, the ends whipping the air on either side of her. Lucas looked away, concerned for Jessie and her baby, but when he looked back, he saw Jessie roll out of the pit and toss the bar aside, angrily.

She cleared the height on her second attempt.

Only three girls cleared five-foot-seven: along with Jessie, there was a tall, muscular Black girl from Rhode Island, and a lank, willowy, pale girl from Vermont.

All three missed their first two attempts at five-eight. Then the Vermont girl sailed high above the bar, clearing the height with an inch to spare. She climbed from the pit, laughing, waving to her coach in the stands, and smiling angelically. The Rhode Island girl crashed into the bar and was finished.

Jessie had one last attempt to win the competition. Twice, she began her approach and twice she realized her steps were off and circled away from the bar without jumping. Finally, with time running out for her to attempt the jump, she approached again and jumped. She cleared the bar, but as she had done at five-six, she caught it with her heels. The bar flew, flapping away, rattling as it hit the ground next to the pit.

Jessie pounded the pit once with her fist, rolled to her feet, and began walking away. The winning girl from Vermont rushed to her, "Good jumping today. You're an amazing competitor."

"Thanks," Jessie shook the Vermont girl's offered hand, noting as she did that the girl's hands were rough. She must be a farm girl to have hands like that, Jessie assumed.

Jessie walked faster, but the Vermont girl wouldn't leave her alone. "Are you going to college next year?"

"Yes. UConn."

"Wonderful. I'll be at the University of Vermont. I'll probably see you at some meets next winter."

"I expect. Now, I've got to go. The hurdles final is coming up." Jessie broke away and jogged across the field. *Screw the high jump. Screw this farm girl. It's over. I've got to win the hurdles. It's my last chance. My only chance for a win.*

The Vermont girl watched Jessie's retreat and shook her head, wondering why her fellow competitor wouldn't talk with her.

The hurdles final was a battle. Jessie led early, diving over the first few hurdles, determined to win after her failure in the high jump. Then, the missed practices caught up with her again. She tired near the end of the race, and her steps were off. As in the earlier heat, she began flailing her arms to stay balanced and lost ground to her competition. The girl she had edged in the Massachusetts State Meet pulled even with Jessie as they cleared the last hurdle. Desperate, Jessie muscled away and dove for the finish, head down. The finish line string snapped, wrapping around Jessie's torso, trailing behind her as she slowed. Jessie stood and brushed the string away like it was a cobweb. She had won by a tenth of a second.

Finally! I should have won three events today. At least I got this one. Annie screwed me out of the relay, and that Vermont farm girl had the jump of her life. All I've got is this one win.

With the meet over, the Rock Haven athletes, flushed and sweating, piled into the school van for the ride home. Lucas tried to encourage his young team. "All in all, a good day. Two second places for Violet in the hundred and two hundred, A first for Jessie in the hurdles, and second in the high jump. And Bob got sixth in the discus. People certainly know about Rock Haven track and field now!"

"Best day I've ever had!" crowed Bob, waving a red prize ribbon, happy as a kid with a new toy. "I really nailed it on two of my throws."

"We didn't place in the relay," grumbled Jessie. "Annie botched the pass."

"You both did," said Violet. "It happens. Let's not talk about it."

"Maybe if you'd been at practice..." Annie started.

Jessie started to speak, but Lucas cut her off. "Enough. It's over. Put it behind us and move on. We had a good meet."

The ride home to Rock Haven was quiet, with all the athletes lost in their thoughts about the day's events. Lucas parked the van behind the school when they arrived. Tired and sweaty, Violet and Jessie walked from the van to Jessie's car. Jessie took her two medals, displayed in flat, clear plastic boxes, gold for the hurdles, silver for the high jump, and tossed them behind the seat of the Miata with her gym bag.

Violet's two boxes, both with silver medals for the hundred and two hundred, were buried in her gym bag. She would display them on her dresser when she got home.

"I should have come home with three golds," grumbled Jessie. "Annie cost me the relay gold."

Violet stopped and tugged Jessie's arm, turning her so they faced each other. "Listen. I'm your friend, and I have to say this. You need to start accepting responsibility when things don't work out the way you want them to. You and Annie both messed up that pass. That's on you as much as her. You need to shut up, stop blaming her, and own that."

Jessie squared her shoulders and looked Violet straight in the eyes, ready to fight her. Then she saw the hard look in Violet's eyes and caved. "I own my mistakes. I screwed up my approach in the high jump. That's on me. And, yes, I'm pregnant. Joe and I messed that up together. No one's to blame, or maybe we both are. But it's not something I'm used to, having things go wrong. I always win. I always have things falling my way."

Violet softened. "Okay. Just lay off Annie and own your share of that."

"Sure. But I don't know how to do this," Jessie pleaded with Violet. Violet watched in alarm as Jessie choked, starting to cry, her shoulders shaking.

"You don't know what it's like being me," Jessie continued. "I never have days like this. Some farm girl from Vermont, of all places, beat me in the high jump. I could have beaten her. I should have. And the relay? And on top of it all, I have this pregnancy thing to deal with! Violet," Jessie begged, "I don't know what to do." Tears began again in the edges of Jessie's eyes. "It scares me not to know what to do." The tears released and poured down her cheeks.

Violet hugged her friend. "You'll survive all of this. Look at it this way. You just tossed a gold and silver medal in the back of your fancy little sports car. Most people who were at the meet today wish they were you."

Jessie grinned now, a wry smile. "Yeah, like big old Bob, thrilled to get sixth. Five guys beat him, and he's on top of the world." She pulled from Violet's hug and mopped the tears away with the palm of her hand.

Violet laughed and hugged her friend again, a little tighter. "It's all relative to what you expect. Anyway, it's over. We'll sort it out. Give it time. Let's go home."

CHAPTER TWENTY-NINE

Rock Haven

A front passed over Rock Haven during the night, sweeping the damp air and heat out to sea. Lucas ran his usual route at dawn, even though it was a Sunday morning. Graduation would consume this afternoon, the time when he would normally run on the weekend. Refreshed by the change in the weather and pleased that the school year and the track season were finished, he cruised along his familiar route. Now he could relax, and a dawn run was a good way to start his day. It said to him: Life goes on as always. Your students may graduate. The cycle continues. They may experience all sorts of successes and calamities, but you still have your run at dawn. It was a pleasant, soothing run, with a soft breeze blowing in from a fog bank offshore.

The morning warmed, the fog melted, and a bright sky added to the joyous feel of the afternoon. Families of the graduates gathered in the bleachers around the football field, most of them dressed for the important occasion, men wearing ties, women in summer dresses. All wore sunglasses against the glare. The award-winning Rock Haven High School band, dressed in white shirts and black slacks, sat sweating near the low stage erected in one end zone of the football field. The graduates in red caps and gowns milled in the other end zone at the far end of the field, waiting for the ceremony to begin.

Promptly at three o'clock, the band started Pomp and Circumstance. The graduates marched along the track in front of their parents in the stands before turning onto the grass and filling the rows of white folding chairs set out on the field. Some walked with the slow paces they had been taught to use for the processional during the previous days' rehearsals. Most simply ambled in, staying in their lines, but carefully refusing to march in time to the music. Though it wasn't cool to do so, some waved to their parents and friends as they passed the bleachers.

Lucas stood with Jennifer and Jonas, and several other teachers, next to the end of the bleachers by the stage, leaving the seats for the graduates' families. It gave them a fine vantage point to watch the ceremony and keep an eye on their own children, Sophie and Emma, who played with other teachers' children on the grassy field behind the bleachers. From time to time, Jennifer walked over to say something to her girls.

"Jessie did okay yesterday?" Jonas asked.

"Okay. Not great. She won the hurdles and got a second in the high jump. She was off, a bit rusty. She'd missed too many practices this week and, with everything else she's got going on... She did okay, but not great."

"How about Violet?"

"Two second places. Next year will be her year. The relay blew up."

"And Bob? Did he get anything?"

"Sixth! It was a great day for him."

"All good. Now you can relax. Jessie's on her own. Nothing more you can do for her."

"Sure, but I still worry about her. I worry about all my athletes. Most aren't a problem. Jessie's different. She doesn't do anything halfway. Not athletically or with anything in her life. Top student, Prom Queen. With all that, she's always been an accident waiting to happen. And now it has"

"You can't control that," said Jennifer, turning from supervision of their daughters. "It's really up to Jessie to get her life together."

After the opening remarks from the superintendent, the valedictorian and the salutatorian gave short speeches about the importance of the day, giving dictionary definitions of *Graduation* and *Commencement* and *Success*, and quoting from old poets that few in the crowd remembered. Then the lines of graduates progressed across the stage. One by one, each shook hands with the principal, the superintendent, and members of the school board as they received their diplomas.

A few of the graduates from the Heights received polite applause when their names were announced, reminiscent of the clapping a professional golfer receives when they sink a putt. Gabe was among those; his graduation had been in doubt for most of the past four years. That he had made it gave a moment of relief to his teachers as well as his parents.

Several of the graduates from the inner harbor neighborhood heard rousing applause from their parents and friends as they crossed the stage. For many of these children, whose parents had begun work as fishermen in the Azores or Cape Verde as teenagers, these graduates were the first in their families to complete school anywhere and get a diploma. This was a significant accomplishment; a moment worthy of the shouts. Their diplomas would be hung prominently in their homes. Many of these graduates paused halfway across the stage to wave their diplomas in the air and acknowledge their friends and families. The Goncalves family screamed when Joe's moment came.

There was silence when Jessie's turn came. Patricia clapped, but otherwise, the crowd, all of them aware of Jessie's situation, sat mutely. Jessie crossed the stage, staring straight ahead, and returned to her seat in the crowd of other graduates.

It's over. I'm out. I can't wait to leave this dumb little fishing village and move on. What about Joe? And my baby? Should I marry him? Is Mom right? Should I get an abortion? I could end up living here the rest of my life in some shack down in the inner harbor. I want more. But what about my baby?

Afterwards, people gathered in the parking lot, taking pictures. Hugs, handshakes, and kisses were exchanged. Gradually, the crowd dispersed. Lucas and Jennifer gathered Sophie and Emma and went home. It'll be good to have a quiet, relaxing evening with just my girls," he said, opening a bottle of wine in their tiny backyard. Breaded fish, shrimp, and raw scallops, bought at the fish market adjacent to the plant, sat on a platter waiting for the charcoal to be ready. They put the girls to bed and returned to the backyard to finish the wine.

Joe and Isaac headed back to their houses for backyard cookouts, less elaborate celebrations than the huge pre-graduation parties of the past weeks. These were smaller, family-only celebrations, though Harvey Lancaster dropped by both Joe and Isaac's houses briefly to commend his stars on their graduations.

Patricia took Jessie to The Harbor House, the finest seafood restaurant on the marina dock. Their reservation had been made a month in advance. They sat at a quiet table in a corner near the back. "I love this place," Patricia said after she and Jessie were seated. "If Michael ever comes to Boston, I'll bring him here. This would be the perfect table for an intimate romantic dinner, just the two of us."

"And I suppose I'd stay home with a pizza?" Jessie shook her head.

"No, of course not. You would join us. I can't wait for you to meet him, Jessie. He's really nice. Not at all like your father. You'll love him the moment you meet him."

"Sure."

Where was Dad today, thought Jessie. I told him a month ago when graduation was. Even if he didn't sit with Mom, I wish he'd come. Probably off in Boston with his new girlfriend. Too busy for me. Does he even know what I did this year? My success on the track? My acceptance to UConn with a full scholarship? My graduation today? He should have been here. I'm his only child.

"And you'll be my maid of honor next fall. Right?" Patricia asked, bringing Jessie's mind back to the present. Patricia had asked Jessie a few days earlier, but that discussion had gone off track, derailed by the discussion of Jessie's pregnancy.

"Of course. You won't mind having me there six months or so pregnant?"

"We can find a nice dress for you that would hide your condition. Nobody will notice."

"Can I bring a plus one? Or will I be alone?"

Patricia paused, mulling how to respond. Having her daughter, visibly pregnant, as her maid of honor was not something she'd considered. And now Jessie was asking to bring that Portuguese boy with her.

"Are you still thinking of keeping the baby and marrying Joe?"

"Yes, to keeping the baby. I don't know about Joe. I mean, I love him and everything, and he is the baby's father. But that ties me down to him forever. I don't know. I see a lot of marriages that don't last. Maybe most of them. Yours didn't. I don't need to make a mistake like you did by marrying Dad. I have to stop making mistakes like that."

Patricia perked up. It was a hopeful sign that Jessie was considering not marrying that boy, though Jessie's comments about her marriage cut. "That's right," she said. "But a baby is forever, too. There's still time for you to take care of the baby situation. You don't want to be trying to go to college as a single parent."

"Mom, it's my baby. Not yours. You heard Dr. Goodman. I'll see how things go with Joe when he goes off to play baseball this summer, and then I'll decide about him in the fall when I go to college. But I'm keeping my baby."

They sat quietly, subdued for the rest of the celebratory dinner together. Lost in their thoughts.

CHAPTER THIRTY

Joe

Promptly at nine on Monday morning, Frank Wilson stood at the door to the Goncalves' house. He wore a red polo shirt with the Cardinals logo, the closest he ever came to regular business attire. Joe and Joao greeted him and led him into the living room. Peter Gomes and Harvey Lancaster were already there, sitting in chairs they had brought in from the kitchenette table. The room was cramped with too many chairs, people sitting elbow to elbow.

"Would you like a cup of coffee, Mr. Wilson?" asked Helena, standing in the doorway to the kitchen, graciously leaning toward their important visitor. Gomes and Lancaster already had coffee cups sitting next to them on side tables.

"No, thank you," Wilson answered.

Speaking quickly, trying not to appear nervous, Joe made introductions. "Mr. Wilson, these are my parents. And this is Peter Gomes, our... my lawyer. And you already know Coach Lancaster."

"Frank Wilson from the St. Louis Cardinals," said Wilson, circling the crowded room, stepping past everyone's legs, shaking hands. "I've got your contract, Joe," he said, addressing the room as a whole. "I've brought several copies, so everyone can take a look." He handed them to Joao and Gomes, and Joe. He offered one to Helene, but she waved him away and looked on with her husband. Lancaster sat back as an observer.

"There is one issue we need to discuss," Wilson continued. "We're still a few days short of the official 'draft day', when all the teams sign their new players. But you want to become a Cardinal, and we want you. So, we're locking up the deal. We'll give you a small retainer now, half of the bonus, and a set of workouts we'd like you to do to stay game-ready. Then, after the official draft, the week after next, we'll provide the rest of the five hundred thousand signing bonus and fly you out to our minor league team in Peoria. We just have to wait a short while to finalize the deal. Is that okay with everyone?"

Joe nodded.

Peter Gomes spoke up. "Are we breaking any rules by signing before draft day?"

"Not really. It happens all the time. No other teams have noticed what he's done in high school. Nobody can tell Joe he can't sign a professional contract. He just can't start playing until the draft. After he's officially drafted, we'll have him stop in St. Louis for an introduction and a press conference on his way to our minor league affiliate in Peoria, and then he's on his way!"

Joe looked puzzled. "I can't start playing in the majors now? And where's Peoria?"

"We want you to stay fit and ready to play. After the high school season, you could use a few days off anyway to rest your arm. But you'll be playing in less than a month for the Peoria Chiefs, the Cardinals' single-A affiliate. Peoria is in Illinois."

"Single A?" Joe's face showed a mix of anger and disappointment. "Why not a higher level, at least triple A or something?"

"Yes, you start at single A. It's where most of our new guys start. I'll tell you, though. I've watched you all season. With your stuff, you won't be there long. I expect you'll be in Memphis, on our triple A team by August. So, don't get too settled when you get to Peoria."

"Where will he stay out there in Peoria?" asked Helena, always looking out for her boy's safety and interests.

"We have an apartment building a couple of blocks from the stadium. It's a safe neighborhood, a good place for him to be, and he'll be sharing an apartment with a lot of his teammates there."

"Will he need a car?" asked Joao. "Should he drive out instead of flying?"

"We want to fly him through St. Louis for a press conference. I'll be with you all the way to Peoria, Joe. And about the car, it would be a good idea for you to get one. There's a dealer there in Peoria, a big fan who gives our guys a great deal. And you'll have that bonus money by then. The coach in Peoria will set up a meeting with the car guy. Buying a car won't be a problem."

Gomes looked up. He had been flipping through the contract. "The contract is pretty straightforward," he said. "They're going to pay you to play baseball, Joe. And that apartment is part of the deal. It's free as long as you're in Peoria."

"Great!" said Wilson. "Joe, do you have any questions?"

"A couple. Both kind of personal concerns."

"Okay." Wilson leaned forward in his chair, elbows on his knees, focused on Joe. "Go ahead."

"Can my girlfriend join me in Peoria?"

Helena threw her hands up. "Damn! Let her go, Joe."

Wilson remained deadpan, looking past the family feud. He shook his head. "I won't stop you from bringing her with you, but you'd need to get your own apartment unless you'd want her sharing an apartment with you and five other ball players. And I would recommend against bringing her anyway. You'll be focused on playing ball and wouldn't want any distractions. And she'd be alone whenever the team travels to away games. Think about it and let me know what you decide."

"Leave Jessie here in Rock Haven, Joe," said Joao. Joe nodded.

"What else?" asked Wilson.

"My catcher. Isaac Arnold. You've seen him all season. He's a hell of a ballplayer. Can you sign him, too?"

"Yes, he's a good player, and I've seen how you and he relate to each other. I'm not surprised you asked about him. I like that you're looking out for your friend. But, no, we're not ready to sign him. He's not ready for pro ball. We'll keep an eye on him. Where's he playing next year? Is he going to college?"

"He can't afford college. He's going to work in the fish packing plant, probably starting today."

Wilson sat back, looking at Joe, assessing the situation. "You're kidding. A talent like that going to work packing fish?"

"That's his only option. If you hadn't signed me and if Clemson hadn't wanted me, I'd be out on a fishing boat for the rest of my life. It's the way things are."

Wilson nodded. "Okay. I get it. Here's what I can do. We want you to play for the Cardinals. But I really can't take care of all your friends, too. Your catcher, Isaac, is too good to stop playing ball. But I can't sign him. Not yet. Let's see how he can do at the next level. I'll make some calls. There's a summer league down on Cape Cod. The Cape League. I know some guys there who owe me favors. I can get Isaac playing with a team in the Cape League. It's mostly top-level college players. If he can hold his own there, maybe a college scout will see him, and who knows how things will go from there. I'll make some calls. Can I get back to you by the end of the day?"

"That'll work," said Joe.

"Good. Give me Isaac's contact information before I leave this morning, and I'll see what I can do."

Joe looked over his copy of the contract and turned to Peter Gomes. "Does everything look okay?"

"Looks fine to me," said Gomes.

"It's a standard deal," Wilson said. "A bit more money than most, but you're worth it."

Joe signed three copies of the contract, handing one to his dad, the second to Gomes, and the third to Wilson.

Wilson handed him a check. "Here's your first two hundred, fifty thousand. You're a Cardinal!" They shook hands. "I'll let you know about Isaac this afternoon, and I'll be in touch with your flight information to Peoria by way of St. Louis."

*****

Joe opened his front door late that afternoon and found Isaac standing on the porch, grinning with excitement. Isaac's words poured out. "I got pulled out of new employee orientation down at the fish plant about an hour ago. I had a call from Wilson, your Cardinals scout. He had a guy on the call from the Cape Cod League. They couldn't do anything with me until I graduated, but now they want me to play ball for Orleans all summer. They'll set me up with a part-time job on the Cape during the day, and they have a place for me to stay. I'll be playing just about every night. The Cape League is all college players, and if I do well, I might get a scholarship to play for a college somewhere."

141

Joe stepped onto the porch and hugged his best friend. "That's great news, Isaac. I know you'll do well. Maybe that scholarship is out there waiting for you."

Isaac laughed. "Yeah. This is my chance. What will my part-time job down on the Cape pay? It'll probably be about what I would have made at the fish plant. So, maybe today will be the only day I work canning fish. And if a college coach sees me and I get a scholarship... I guess while Wilson was checking you out, he liked my game as well."

"Maybe. I signed the contract with him this morning. I'll be starting in Peoria, Illinois, in a couple of weeks."

"I leave for Orleans tomorrow morning, driving down to the Cape. I have a load of laundry running back at the house, so I'll be ready to pack tonight. I have a game tomorrow night."

"Excellent, Bro. Stay in touch. I'll miss you." They shook hands, ending by pulling each other into another hug.

Chapter Thirty-one

Isaac

At dawn, Sam and Evelyn Arnold stood on the street in front of their house as Isaac loaded three duffel bags into his mom's dingy ten year old SUV. The two smaller bags held most of his clothes; the bigger bag was full of his catchers' gear and two scratched aluminum bats he'd used all season.

"You're sure you won't need the car, Mom?"

"No. I can walk to work. And I can ride with your dad or take his car when I need to go shopping. Violet takes Dad's car when she goes to her summer job. You'll need a car to get to the Cape and to get around while you're down there."

A proud dad, Sam hugged his son, already missing the boy. "You go have a good season down there on the Cape. They're all college boys, but when it's all said and done, they're still ball players, just like you. Nothing more. You can play at their level. Show them who you are. I'll take care of everything here. We'll all be fine. Call if you need anything."

Violet hugged her big brother. "This is your chance. Go get it."

As Isaac was about to get in the car, Joe pulled up in his pickup, stopping in the middle of the street, jumping out, and rushing to catch Isaac before he left. Isaac stopped and waited for his best friend. "What's up?" he called.

"Just wanted to see you before you hit the road, to wish you the best. I know you'll open a few scouts' eyes down there on the Cape. Have a good summer."

They hugged. Then Isaac was in the car, slowly pulling away, waving out the window as he left his boyhood home behind.

Evelyn turned to Joe. "Did you have anything to do with Isaac getting the call from your scout yesterday?"

"Not really. I signed with Mr. Wilson in the morning and told him Isaac wasn't playing ball, now that we've graduated. Wilson took it from there."

"We owe you a thank you. If this gets Isaac a scholarship somewhere, what you've done for him is immense."

Sam nodded. "We can't thank you enough for getting him this chance."

"It's nothing more than what anyone would have done for a friend. I hope it works out."

*****

Isaac drove through Boston's morning rush hour, dragging along on the highway around the city, dodging the intense commuters cutting in and out of the frantic traffic. Traffic lightened as he turned south for Cape Cod. The road to the beaches would be jammed on the weekend, but early on a weekday morning, it moved smoothly; a reverse commute, driving south, away from Boston.

He relaxed, enjoying the freedom of being out, on his own for the first time in his life. He already missed his family and friends, but the adventure of starting his life made him smile. *If I hadn't gotten that call yesterday, I'd be on an assembly line right now back at the plant, skinning fish and packing the filets in cans. Or something. I don't even know what I'd be doing there. I've been out on the* fishing boats. I know that work. But I never worked in the plant. Baseball on the Cape will certainly be better. I need to do well and get a college coach to talk to me. If not, this is just a delay until fall, before I'm right back there at the fish plant.

He cleared the bridge over the canal late in the morning, stopped at a Burger King for a quick lunch, and arrived at the baseball field in Orleans early in the afternoon. It was a well-tended high school field, baking in the afternoon sun.

The manager and a few of the players greeted him. "We had a catcher," said the manager, "but he got hurt and we really need you. Welcome to the Firebirds. Here's a uniform. I hope it fits; it should."

Isaac sat through a brief scouting report on the Falmouth team, the Commodores. It was the team he would face that evening. He jotted notes in a notebook already filled with tips on the high school teams he'd played all spring. A clip held the high school notes together. Fresh pages were ready for his new season. The other players eyed him skeptically. He sensed their thoughts. The new guy. Can he catch? Can he hit? Can he fit in with the rest of us? We've only been together as a team for a couple of weeks, but we're a tight group. Who is this guy?

"You can forget about your aluminum bats," the manager told him, hearing them clanking in his equipment bag. "This is a wooden bat league, just like the majors. Leave those in the trunk of your car."

After the team meeting, his new teammates questioned him. "What's your story?"

"How did we get stuck with you?"

"Can you really play at our level?"

"Where do you go to school?"

Isaac spoke up. "I just graduated high school up north of Boston."

"Okay," the player shook his head, skeptical. "You're fresh out of high school? And, where will you be playing this fall?"

"I don't understand."

"What college will you be playing for?"

"I don't have a college. I'll probably be going to work packing fish back home once this season is over."

"You pack fish? This league is just about all college players. And you're nothing more than a high school ball player. How did you get here?"

"My buddy, my best friend, just signed with the Cardinals. The scout who signed him sent me here."

"Really. Pro ball? Your friend is pretty good?"

"He's the best high school player in Massachusetts. A pitcher. I was his catcher."

"We need a catcher. Can you hit?"

"I can hit."

"We'll see," said one of the players, shaking his head.

"I can hit," Isaac repeated, staring down his doubter.

"Okay. Have a good game tonight." The other player looked down at the dugout dirt, gave a quick smile, almost a smirk, and walked away.

The uniform was a little tight, but Isaac didn't care; he could play wearing it. The manager put him in the last spot in the batting order. After hefting a few different bats, Isaac selected a wooden bat that balanced the same as his aluminum bats. In his first at-bat, he swung awkwardly with the unfamiliar bat and struck out. He saw some of his teammates suppressing laughs. His next at-bat, he hit a quick ground ball, skimming the grass up the middle, but the shortstop cut it off and threw him out.

Now the new bat felt better. On his next trip to the plate, he got a looping single to left field.

In the eighth inning, he lashed a streaking line drive into the gap in left-center field that caught the fence on one bounce. When the play was over, Isaac stood on second base, watching the second of two base runners he'd driven in cross the plate. As the ball was relayed back to the infield, he clapped his hands twice, looked into his dugout, and pointed to the player who had doubted him. The player pointed back to Isaac and clapped.

The skeptical teammate walked back to his car after the game alongside Isaac and caught him by the shoulder. "Okay. You can hit." He clapped him on the back. "Let me show you where you'll be living all summer. My name is Juan."

"I'm Isaac."

CHAPTER THIRTY-TWO

Jessie lolled in the sun on the lawn by her backyard pool. She was alone and lonely. She stared up at the sun through her fashionable sunglasses. It blinded her, and she looked away, seeing spots.

I'm bored. What should I do? Mom has gone to work, not that I would do much with her if she were home anyway. Violet's also at work, serving breakfast and lunch at a diner somewhere in the next town, over on Route One. Joe got Isaac that job in a baseball league down on Cape Cod, and Isaac's left for the Cape. Joe seems to be busy all the time, though I didn't know where he is or what he might be doing. I've called him three times this morning, but he hasn't answered his phone. Everyone seems to be busy. I'm restless. While school was in session, I was always on the go, classes, track practice, Joe. Now, with nothing to do but work on my tan, I have too much time to think about things. All of it scares me, and that's depressing. I've lost control of my life, my body, my friends, everything.

She untied the straps of her bikini top and let them hang. Since she was alone, she considered for a moment lying topless on her towel in the sun, but now that seemed like an awful idea. Showing off my body is what caused all my problems: getting pregnant with Joe, the big flap with Gabe, all of this mess. She retied the strings on her neck below her pulled-up hair, cinching the knot tight.

If this is all I have to do, it's going to be a long summer, she mused. Maybe I should get a summer job? No. I don't want a job. I don't need to work. Maybe I should go to the beach? No, there'd be nobody at the beach. They'll all be working. But I need to do something. Maybe I should get some books and read all summer. Maybe I should join a gym and work out like I did all track season. Can I work out that hard if I'm pregnant? I'll need to be ready for the indoor track season at UConn. Oh my God! Can I even run track this winter if I'm pregnant? Maybe an abortion is the answer. No. I don't want to go through an abortion. What about Joe? He leaves for Illinois in about a week, I think. I should spend time with him before he leaves. Then, when he's gone, what will I do? And do I really want to spend the rest of my life with him? Where is he?

She called Joe for the fourth time, but still got no answer.

A moment later, he called. "What's up? You keep calling me."

"I just wanted to talk. Maybe see you. I'm home alone. Can you come over?"

"I'm in the middle of my workout here at the gym at school. Do you want to come down? Coach got me access to the school to do my lifting."

"It'll be a few minutes before I can get there. I'm out by the pool, and I'd have to get dressed. How long will you be there?"

"I should be done in half an hour. You want to get together somewhere for lunch? I got my bonus money, so I don't have to worry about what it'll cost."

"Sure. Where?"

"I don't know. McDonald's?"

Forty-five minutes later, Jessie parked her silver Miata next to Joe's rusty pickup and joined him in a yellow plastic booth inside McDonald's.

"I'm buying," he said. "What do you want for lunch?"

"A salad. I'm trying to eat healthy because of the baby. I've got my water bottle, so nothing to drink."

Joe got in line. He came back with two bags, one with Jessie's salad, the other with a double quarter-pounder with cheese, large fries, and a chocolate shake. He sat across from her, gave her the salad, and spread his lunch across the table on paper napkins.

"I leave for St. Louis on Monday morning. I officially become a Cardinal when they do the draft this weekend. I go on from there to Peoria, wherever that is. I have the workouts they gave me, lifting and running, and stretching. That's why I was working out this morning."

"That's wonderful. But we need to stay in touch, particularly after you leave. Do you want to come by my house for a while after lunch?"

"I don't know. I've only got a few days left, and I have a few things I need to take care of at home before I go."

"I could make it worth your while if you came over." She smiled, letting her eyes drift half-shut, an invitation. "My mom's at work all day."

Even if I am pregnant, an afternoon in bed with Joe would give me something to do. That could be fun.

"I don't know, Jessie. With the baby and all. I don't want to risk hurting you or the baby."

"It won't hurt anything. C'mon!"

She thought, but didn't say, Right now, I need you, Joe. It's not just about sex. I need you. Come over to spend a bit of time with me.

"How about I take you out to dinner Sunday night, before I leave on Monday? I'll make a reservation at Leonardo's."

"That would be nice. You sure you can't stop over this afternoon?"

"No. I think it would be better if I didn't."

*****

They sat quietly waiting for their meals at Leonardo's on Sunday evening. Neither said much, sitting across from each other, lost in their thoughts. It would be the last night they were together for months to come, and they both knew it. There was so much they both needed to say, but the words weren't coming to either of them.

Jessie continued to mull. I should talk with him about everything. Do I really want to marry him? But why talk about it? It can wait. He leaves tomorrow, and then I won't have to worry about it. At least until the end of summer. And then I'll be off to UConn. I feel like I've trapped myself into the inevitability of marrying him by becoming pregnant. Sorting this out isn't something I'm ready to talk about with Joe. Sorting out problems has never been something I've had to do. I've never had problems until now.

Joe was consumed by worry about leaving Jessie behind in her condition, but knew he needed to do well when he began playing ball in Peoria. "I should have found time to go buy you a ring. It's been crazy, getting ready to go out to Peoria. Maybe I should get you a ring out there and mail it back to you."

"No, Joe. You can give me the ring when you come home at the end of the summer. It'll give us both time to think about marriage. I still don't know if it's the right thing for us to do."

Joe took her hand. "We don't have a choice. You're pregnant. We should get married."

After a long, silent moment at the table, Jessie asked, "You wouldn't answer my calls on Friday? Why? Didn't you want to talk with me?"

"No, I always want to talk with you. I wish I could spend more time with you. But my mind is all about baseball right now. I have to do well when I start with the Cardinals."

They ate the meal in more silence.

After dinner, Joe took Jessie back to her house. Sitting in his truck in her driveway, he said, "You take care of yourself, Jessie. You know I love you. Never forget that while I'm away. Take care of our little baby, too. I'll call every day from Peoria. And I'll see you here or at UConn when my season is over. I wish we had time to get married before I have to leave, but we'll do that as soon as I come home."

"I love you too, Joe. Have a great season. And safe travels. Call me as soon as you get to Peoria."

Jessie kissed him, passionately, her arms around his neck, pulling him to her. Then, abruptly, she jumped out of his truck and rushed into her house.

Late that night, sitting alone in her bedroom, Jessie wondered. Was that the last time I'll ever kiss Joe? The last time we'll ever see each other? He leaves early tomorrow. But I'm carrying his baby. Our baby. I'll see him again when his season's over. What can I do? It's not over. Should I marry him? No. I can't.

Suddenly, that seemed to Jessie to be a certainty. I can't marry Joe, but I can't tell him when he's about to go off to somewhere in Illinois to play baseball. Maybe, once he leaves, things will fall apart on their own. Maybe he'll meet a new girl out there and forget about me. Of course, then I'll have to deal with the baby alone. Is that what I really want? To be raising a baby without a father?

CHAPTER THIRTY-THREE

Joe sat at the gate at Logan Airport in Boston with a carry-on bag filled with two days' clothes and his baseball equipment. The rest of the clothes he would need for the summer were in bags he had checked. Across from him, a uniformed flight attendant sat with a small boy.

"Are you flying to St. Louis?" the boy asked Joe.

"Yes."

The flight attendant interrupted, almost scolding the boy. "Don't bother the man."

Joe smiled. "Oh, he's not a bother. Yes, I'm flying to St. Louis."

"Me, too," said the boy. "I've been visiting my grandparents here. My mom and dad are going to meet me when I get to St. Louis."

"And I'm flying with him to make sure he gets there safe and sound," added the flight attendant, providing distance and security between the boy and the stranger the child had spoken to.

"Are your mom and dad going to meet you when we get there?" the boy asked Joe.

"No. I live here. I'm going there for my new job. I'm going to be playing baseball in the Cardinals' minor league system."

The boy's face lit up with excitement. "Wow! The Cardinals are my favorite team. And you're one of the players?"

"Well, not quite yet. I'll be meeting people in St. Louis right now, but then they're sending me to Peoria to play for the team there until they think I'm ready for the big leagues."

"Can I have your autograph?"

"Sure."

The flight attendant found a pen and a piece of paper and handed them to Joe. "What's your name?" she asked.

"Joe Goncalves."

Joe signed the paper and gave it to the boy. "Thanks, Joe. I hope you make it to the Cardinals soon," the boy said, admiring the signature.

"Me too," said Joe.

"Me too!" interjected the flight attendant. "Play well in Peoria. I'm Melissa. Here's my card and my number. Call me when they bring you up to St. Louis. I'll show you around town."

Joe looked at the card and back up at the smiling flight attendant. "Thanks" was all he said. He stuffed her card into his wallet. But he liked the sunshine in her smile and the sweep of her light brown hair.

This is nice, he thought, but I have Jessie. I don't need a new girlfriend.

When they boarded the plane, the boy and the flight attendant passed through the curtain to the back of the plane. Joe found his seat in first class, a wide, tan, leather seat next to the window. He spent most of the flight watching the Earth roll by outside his window. This wasn't his first flight. He had flown with his family to the Azores twice for family reunions. Both flights had been at night and over the ocean.

This time, he was alone, and it was morning. The day was clear. Joe was fascinated by the new, high altitude perspective on the world, watching towns and occasionally cities pass by beneath him. Halfway through the flight, he realized he was acting like a little kid, gawking out the window. And, this being his first time in first class, he looked around at the luxury. The seasoned business travelers all around him rarely looked out the window. He wondered if the boy in the back of the plane was doing the same thing he was.

After they landed, Joe followed the crowd of travelers through security, looking for the baggage claim area. He was met by Frank Wilson, dressed, as always, in tan slacks and a red, Cardinals' logo polo shirt.

"Mr. Wilson, I didn't know you'd be here."

"Of course. I'm going to make sure everything goes smoothly for you today. I'll be with you 'til we get you to Peoria. Right now, we need to pick up your luggage and get you to the hotel. There's a lunch for you at the stadium after we get you settled at the hotel."

"Oh. Okay. I wasn't sure where I was going to go when I got here."

"That's why I'm here. You can relax and enjoy the day. Tomorrow, when you get to Peoria, that's when you go to work. They'll probably get you right into a game. Let's go pick up your luggage."

As they were leaving baggage claim, the little boy rushed up to Joe. "Good luck, Joe! I'll see you when they put you on the Cardinals' team."

Joe leaned down and shook the boy's hand while two people, probably the boy's parents, stood by and watched, smiling. Across the terminal, he saw the flight attendant also watching him. She waved and smiled. Joe gave a brief wave back.

Two hours later, Wilson escorted Joe into an austere dining room behind the press box at the stadium. Clusters of tables contained three dozen men and women. "The Media", Wilson explained. Joe was seated in the middle of the head table with several men in suits. "The Front Office," Wilson said, introducing each of them. Joe tried, but failed to remember all their names.

A woman introduced herself to Joe, "I'm Lisa, from Cardinals' Media Relations." She went to the center of the head table, leaned across Joe, and spoke into a microphone. "We're here today to welcome our number one prospect, Joe Goncalves. You all have his stats from his high school days, there in the packet I gave you. They're impressive. He'll be going to Peoria tomorrow, but we don't expect him to stay there long. If he does in the Midwest league what he did throughout his high school career, we expect he'll be in Memphis by the end of the summer, and it won't be long before he's pitching right here in St. Louis. Please welcome Joe Goncalves."

The media clapped. Before Joe knew what was happening, Lisa set the microphone on a stand in front of him. Someone put a crisp Cardinals cap, a bit oversized, the bill still stiff and slightly curved, on his head. He realized he was supposed to say something, but he wasn't prepared. Cameras flashed. The reporters continued clapping. Everyone was looking at him. Television cameras pointed at him. It was only a short time since he had gotten off the airplane. He had woken at dawn in Rock Haven, and now he was suddenly here in the center of everything in St. Louis. Frozen with fear.

Wilson, sitting next to Joe, nudged him and whispered, "Just say a few words. The reporters will take it from there."

The applause faded, and Joe surveyed the room, smiling. Finally, thoughtfully, he spoke. "It's great to be here. It's a dream come true for me to be with a major league team. I can't wait to get to Peoria and get started working my way back here to St. Louis."

He looked around the room again, noting that waiters were setting plates with sandwiches in front of all the reporters and also serving the head table, moving the food towards him. "Now, I see it's lunch time. I'm starving. Let's eat!" Food might spare him from having to speak in front of the reporters.

The media woman leaned across him to the microphone. "Do we have any questions for Joe before lunch?" she asked.

The reporters raised their hands and shouted questions. "What's your best pitch, Joe?"

Talking baseball, Joe was more comfortable. "My best pitch? Probably my slider. I have three fastballs, but I grip each differently, so they move differently when they get to the plate. One rises. Batters miss that one a lot, and if they hit it, they pop it up. One fades away from a right-hand hitter and dips in and down on a lefty. My other fastball is straight. I use that to bust the batter inside to keep them off balance. If they're sitting on my fastball, my slider looks the same, but it cuts suddenly, away from the lefties and in on righties. They miss that one a lot. That's why I like my slider."

"Did you win your State Championship?"

"No. We lost. I had a good game. But they just beat us. One to nothing. I've moved on."

"We understand you almost went to Clemson instead of turning pro. What made you decide to join the Cardinals?"

"I have a girlfriend and we want to get married. I'm doing this for her."

The reporters loved Joe and his answers. They peppered him with more questions. Finally, Joe insisted again, "I can see you're all hungry, so let's eat."

That night, Joe toured the clubhouse and met the team before the game. He was startled to see how big some of the players were, particularly the pitchers. Even the other players, though smaller, were taut with weight-trained muscle, their strength evident as they wandered the locker room in tee shirts without their game jerseys. Joe was used to being the biggest athlete on the field. He was intimidated by the thoroughbred athletes he now associated with, some bigger and evidently stronger than him.

During the game, Joe sat with Wilson in the front row, next to the Cardinals' dugout. Partway through the game, Lisa came and spoke with Joe and Wilson. "Come on, Joe, we're going to the press box for a couple of innings." Wilson and Joe followed Lisa up the aisle, through a door, and up an elevator. They emerged behind home plate, high above the field. Then, with the stadium glaring beneath them, the broadcasters interviewed Joe on air between pitches while the game progressed in front of them. It was a repeat of the lunch interview, this time broadcast to Cardinals fans everywhere.

A few miles away, in a house in the suburbs, a small boy watched his new hero with excitement, lighting his face. "I talked with Joe, just this morning, Dad. And now he's on television!"

In a small downtown apartment, Melissa also watched the game and saw the interview. "That's the guy I told you I met on the plane this morning," she explained to her roommates. "He's such a gentleman." She also noticed when Joe mentioned his girlfriend back in Massachusetts.

A highlight of the interview occurred when the broadcaster asked Joe, "What do you think of Busch Stadium? I expect it's a lot more than the high school fields you're accustomed to playing on."

"Yeah, it's big. I'd expected that. Being from Boston, I've been to Fenway a bunch of times. This place is newer. Fenway's nice. A lot of tradition, great fans. But you've got great chili dogs here. Much better than Fenway Franks. I had two of your chili dogs for dinner tonight."

Finally, close to midnight, Wilson drove Joe back to his hotel. "You've had quite a day, Joe. The flight, the press conference at lunch, the game, another interview, this one on air. I know it can be a whirlwind. Get some rest, but set the alarm. I'll meet you for breakfast downstairs at 8:30. We have an eleven o'clock flight to Peoria, and you have a game tomorrow night."

Chapter Thirty-four

Joe and Isaac

Joe sat in the dugout with his new teammates in Peoria.

"Be ready," the manager told him. "Win or lose, I'm bringing you in for an inning late in the game. Head out to the bullpen."

"But I'm a starter." Joe protested.

"Everybody here was a starter in high school. This is now, and you're here. I'll use you as a starter next week, but I want you to get in a game and get your feet wet before I have you start a game. This is the best way to get rid of the nerves, the butterflies."

Joe nodded. "I don't have butterflies," he mumbled under his breath. He went to the bullpen. He'd show them when he got his inning.

The call came at the end of the seventh inning. Joe warmed up and went in for the eighth. Nine pitches later, the inning was over. Two strikeouts and a pop-up.

Sitting in the locker room after the game, Joe spoke to his manager, "When do I get my start?"

"How about Saturday night?" The manager clapped him on the shoulder and walked back into his office.

"I'm ready," Joe said quietly to himself as he sipped beer with his new teammates. He exuded confidence. Nothing could stop him.

*****

On the Cape, Isaac was also enjoying daily success.

The team had set him up with a part-time job in a souvenir shop. He quickly established a routine. Late every afternoon, he left work and rode to the ballpark with his teammates to play another game. He kept hitting, getting one or two hits in every game. His batting average was well above .300. The coach had moved Isaac up in the order to the second spot.

On the bus ride home after a game in Falmouth, his roommate, Juan, a lanky outfielder, slid into the seat next to Isaac. "You said you're going to get a job after the season? You're not going to college?"

"I don't have a scholarship, and my family can't afford it."

"I told my college coach about you. Northeastern. He'll be at tomorrow's game. Show him what you can do."

Isaac nodded, smiled, and wrapped his arm over his teammate's back. "Thanks, Juan. I'll do what I can."

Darren, the shortstop, leaned over the back of the seat in front of Isaac and Juan. "I told my coach about you, too. I play for Vanderbilt. Do you want to go to Vanderbilt?"

"Let me think about it."

Isaac got two more hits the next day. One of the times when he made an out, it was a line drive into the left-center gap that hung up for the outfielder to catch.

Juan pointed out his college coach in the stands, but the coach left with an inning to go.

CHAPTER THIRTY-FIVE

Jessie's mom got home from work at 6:30, Monday evening. They ordered out for dinner, and barbecue was delivered from a place in the next town. Patricia and Jessie sat across from each other at the granite kitchen island, eating their dinner. Patricia had a glass of wine, Jessie, iced tea.

"How was today?" asked Patricia.

"Fine, not much going on."

"Everything's okay? How are you feeling?"

Jessie looked down, then back up at her mom. "Okay, I guess. I don't know how this is supposed to feel. I'll just take it easy this summer and make sure my baby's healthy. I have some books I can read."

"Okay," Patricia nodded. "That seems like a good idea. I'm flying to DC tomorrow morning. I'll be seeing Michael there. And then I have to go to Pittsburgh for a few days, and maybe Philadelphia the rest of the week. I wanted to have a couple of days with you after graduation, so I stayed here rather than traveling. But I need to get back out there now."

"You wanted a couple of days with me? But you were at work all day at your office here."

"Well, I have to earn a living, don't I? I'll see you Friday night late when I get home."

"Will you be home next week?"

"Some. Probably."

"Sure." Jessie nodded. She was used to being alone at home. But now, with the baby on the way, she felt abandoned.

Thoughts filled her mind. I need you, Mom. I need someone, anyone, to be with me. There've always been people around, talking to me, asking about the things I'm doing. Right now, I'm so alone. Violet's always at work. Joe's gone. I've got weeks to kill before I get to start over at UConn. What am I going to do?

Chapter Thirty-six

Jessie and Violet

Intense cramps woke Jessie in the middle of the night. She sat up, looking around the dark, still bedroom, grimacing in pain while clutching her abdomen. She was still alone. After a few moments, her muscles relaxed and she breathed out in relief. Maybe this is part of what it's like being pregnant, she thought. She fell back against her pillow and was soon fast asleep.

Two hours later, with dawn approaching, cramps woke her again, tearing at her, pulsing with every heartbeat. Again, she sat up. She felt wetness, and when she threw back the covers, she saw a small, but spreading blood stain on the sheet.

Her mind was panicky.

Oh my God! What is happening? What should I do? I always know what to do. But not with this. This is new. I've never had anything like this happen before. I need help. I need someone. I need Mom. It's six in the morning; too early to call Mom in Pittsburgh. I'll wait until I know she's up.

The cramping became unbearable, worsening with each minute. Jessie gave in and called her mom. There was no answer; the call went to voicemail. "Mom, I'm having trouble. I'm bleeding and cramping. Please call me."

Jessie got up, cleaned the bed as best she could, and tried to take a shower. She ended the shower sitting on the floor of the tub, in too much pain to stand. A slow trickle of blood crawled to the drain.

Looking at it, Jessie began to cry, her hand at her mouth. I need help. I need my mom. Or someone. Anyone.

When she was able to stand, she turned off the shower, toweled off, and called her mom again.

"Jessie, I just got up and found your message. Are you okay?" Jessie heard legitimate concern in the tone of her mom's voice.

"I don't know, Mom. Awful cramps, and I'm bleeding. I don't know what's going on."

"Okay. Let's stay calm." Even as she said it, Patricia felt herself panic. "Oh, God, Baby. What can we do? It'll take me a couple of hours to get a flight home. You need help right now. I'll catch the first flight home. I should be there early this afternoon. Right now, you need to get to the hospital. Can you drive?"

"I don't know. No."

"Then you need to call 911 or someone to help you. Who can you call? Violet, maybe?"

"Okay."

Patricia heard the terror in her daughter's shaky voice. "Hold on, Baby. I'm on my way. Lie down while you wait for a ride. Take a deep breath and blow it out whenever you feel a cramp. That will help, but you need to get to the hospital."

"Okay. I love you, Mom."

"I love you, too. I'll be there as soon as I can." Patricia sat on her hotel bed, hundreds of miles away from her baby. She fought off her tears and called her airline, rebooking her flight. It was a start, she thought, but she needed to get home. Dear God, let her be okay. I need to get there and be with my baby. I don't want her to be in pain like this. Or die. Or her baby.

Another cramp tore through Jessie's belly right after she hung up with her mom. She dialed Violet.

"Violet. I need your help. Are you busy?"

"I'm about to head into work. I'm supposed to be there at seven. What's up?"

"I think I'm losing the baby. I'm bleeding and there are these awful cramps."

"And your mom's out of town, right? You're alone?"

"Yes. Can you come?" Jessie's voice was pleading.

"I'll be there in ten minutes."

Violet took a deep breath, fighting for control. Then she called her boss at the restaurant and told her she would be late.

Terrified and confused, she pulled her mom aside as she and her dad were about to leave for work at the Fish plant.

Quietly, she explained. "Mom, Jessie just called. She thinks she's losing the baby, and her mom is out of town. She needs me to take her to the hospital. Can I borrow the car this morning?"

"Of course, do you need me to come too?" asked Evelyn, tears suddenly clouding her eyes. For a moment, she sat down at the kitchen table, leaning her head in her hands. "We can take care of Jessie. You and I. We need to."

Violet was startled by her mom's reaction. She stepped up to her and put her hands on her mother's shoulders. Evelyn stood and pulled her daughter to her, holding her tightly for a moment. Then she pulled back, holding her girl at arm's length. She took a deep breath and blew it out. "What can I do?"

"No, there's nothing you can do, Mom. Not much I can do either, but get to her and be with her. I've got this. I'll go pick her up and take her straight to the ER."

"Take the car. You're sure you don't need me to help you? I'm here for you if you do. You know that."

"No. I've got to go now and pick Jessie up. I can do this."

"Your dad and I can walk to the plant for work. But call me. I need to know how Jessie's doing and how you're doing."

Violet found Jessie, dressed in loose sweatpants and a T-shirt, sitting on her front steps waiting for her. She held Jessie with an arm around her waist and helped her to the car. Jessie sprawled in the front seat, almost reclining. Her face was pale. Her eyes weeping. She said nothing.

"I'm taking you to the emergency room," Violet said as she backed down the Brandts' long driveway.

"Okay." Jessie's voice was soft, quiet. She could endure the pain, but not the fear. She reached over as Violet drove and squeezed her friend's forearm. For a moment, she moaned as a cramp hit.

Violet stopped at the emergency entrance and ran in to find help. Explaining Jessie's situation, she led two nurses out to her car. Jessie was transferred to a wheelchair. Violet let the nurses take Jessie and went out to park. She caught up to her moments later, finding Jessie reclining on a bed in the emergency area. She reached over and held Jessie's hand.

After a quick check-up in the emergency bed, Jessie was rolled down halls, up an elevator, and into Maternity. Violet followed. She waited with her until a doctor arrived. Then Violet was ushered by a nurse out of Jessie's room to a waiting area. She gave Jessie's hand a quick squeeze before she left.

“It’s Jessie, right? I’m Dr. Goodman. We met each other a few weeks ago when your mom brought you into my office.” He scanned the notes from the emergency room. “How do you feel?”

“Awful. I’m cramping a lot and bleeding.”

“Let’s take a look and see what’s going on.”

The examination took only moments. “I could do an ultrasound, but it’s clear you’re losing the baby,” Dr. Goodman declared. “The baby can’t survive this early in your pregnancy.”

Jessie began to cry again. Despair filled her voice. “What can I do? What can you do? How can you save my baby?”

“Your body is ending the pregnancy on its own. I’m so sorry.” Dr. Goodman paused, choosing his words thoughtfully. “I can make sure you come through this experience with the least physical discomfort possible and the least risk to you, to your life, and your long-term health.”

He paused again, assessing Jessie’s reaction as she absorbed his words. “The baby can’t survive, Jessie. We want to make sure you’ll be okay.”

Dr. Goodman waited, watching his young patient, giving her time.

“Take care of me.” Jessie’s words squeaked out.

*****

In the waiting area, Violet sat, stunned, afraid for her friend. She called her mom and gave her an update.

Later that morning, a nurse came to the waiting area. “Violet Arnold?” she asked, looking around the room at expectant relatives.

“Yes.” Violet stood.

171

The nurse was startled for a moment. Her blonde patient's friend was a young, black woman. Clearly, they had little in common. It didn't matter. "Your friend is asking for you."

Violet was led into Jessie's room by the nurse. Jessie sat upright in the narrow hospital bed in a hospital gown. She was pale, with shadows around her eyes, her hair tangled. When she saw Violet, she broke into tears.

"I lost my baby." Jessie's voice croaked.

Down the hall, they heard a baby cry in another maternity room.

Violet held her friend, rocking her slowly while they wept together.

Gathering her strength, Jessie called her mom, letting her know where she was.

*****

Patricia arrived early that afternoon, rushing into Jessie's room, tears in her eyes. She hugged Jessie, pulling her close. She stroked her hair and kissed her. "Are you okay?"

"No."

"Oh, Jessie. When you called and said you were in the hospital... how are you feeling?"

"Awful. I lost the baby, Momma." Again, Jessie started to cry quietly, but it was as though her eyes had run dry. Her body shook, but there were no more tears. "I tried to wait for you to get here. But my body said no. The baby's gone. Where were you, Momma?"

"Pittsburgh. I canceled my appointments as soon as I hung up the phone with you this morning. I got the first flight back to Boston and got here as soon as I could."

Patricia sank onto the chair where Violet had been sitting. Jessie reached for her mom and held on, squeezing her hand. Her voice sounded like that of the little girl she had been not so many years ago. "I'm glad you're here. I really need you, Momma."

"I'm thankful you're okay, even if you lost the baby. Your health is what matters. You're okay, right?"

Violet stood at the foot of the bed, watching the drama unfold.

"Dr. Goodman says I'll be fine. But the baby's gone." Jessie clung to her mom's hand, pulling her mother's love close. Again, Patricia leaned over, holding her daughter close, clinging to her, stroking her hair.

"Dr. Goodman is taking good care of you?"

"Yes, he's been wonderful. He wants to keep me here overnight to make sure I'm okay."

Through the door, they watched a young man walk by in the hall, practically swaggering, grinning. Next to him, a smiling woman was being pushed in a wheelchair by a nurse. A blanketed baby was bundled on the woman's lap. Foil pink and yellow balloons floated on pastel ribbons above the new family.

Jessie, Patricia, and Violet looked away. Patricia turned to Violet. "Have you been here the whole time?"

"Yes, since driving her in this morning."

"Oh. Thank you for looking after her."

"No problem. You've got her from here, right? I'm heading home for dinner." Then she turned to Jessie. "I'll call you tomorrow morning, Jessie. And I'll come by to see you tomorrow afternoon after I get off work. Whether you're here or at home, I'll find you. Okay?"

She leaned down and hugged Jessie.

Jessie held on, pulling Violet to her. "Thank you."

*****

Violet cut her breakfast shift short the next morning and skipped her lunch shift so she could meet Jessie and Patricia at the hospital. Her boss understood when Violet told her what was happening.

"They're getting ready to let me out," said Jessie. "There's a lot of paperwork, I guess. I just want to go home."

"How are you feeling?" asked Violet.

"Lost. I've always been in control of my body, of everything really. But now I realize, maybe I never really was. Maybe I was just fooling myself, believing I had control. Maybe I never had anything under control. Right now, I'm not sure what to do. I don't know how I feel about any of this. I've always been able to take care of everything without anyone's help. I can't seem to do that anymore. Not with this, anyway. I'm so glad you came for me yesterday morning. I don't know what I would have done if you hadn't been there for me. But now my baby's gone."

Patricia took her daughter's hand and held it. She realized she'd been doing that a lot since she came home from Pittsburgh.

A woman, wearing a blazer, came in, checked notes on her clipboard, and approached the bedside. "Are you Jessie Brandt?" she asked, her voice compassionate, her soft eyes meeting Jessie's eyes.

"Yes."

"I'm Susan Hillman, a counselor here at the hospital. Would you like to talk about what's happened?"

"No. Not with you. I don't even know you."

"Would you like me to have a chaplain drop by to see you? They're still getting everything ready to discharge you, but I'm here to assist with anything you need before you go. I understand all the emotions you must be experiencing right now after the loss of your baby. We're here to help."

"No. I have my mom and my best friend here. I'm all set."

"Okay." The counselor took two business cards out, giving one to Jessie, the other to Patricia. "I'm here if you need me. Call me anytime." She left.

"Have you called Joe?" Violet asked.

"No. What can I say to him? I can't just say, 'I lost our baby.'" Jessie's voice cracked. It was all she could do to get the words out.

"He needs to know," asserted Violet.

"I know," Jessie said with resignation.

Patricia interceded. "Where is he? I would have thought he would be here with you. At a time like this."

"He's out west somewhere playing baseball for the Cardinals. I don't want to bother him."

Patricia spoke, a touch of anger in her voice. "He needs to come back and be with you. If he loved you and if he knew you'd lost the baby, he'd be here with you. If he truly cared, he'd be here."

"I don't want to distract him when he's playing baseball and trying to move up from the minors to the Cardinals. What could I say to him?"

"He needs to know," repeated Violet. "It's his baby too. Tell him what happened."

"Okay. Okay. I'll call him." Jessie threw up her hands in frustration.

Violet had seen the gesture before. She knew it was time to back off.

Chapter Thirty-seven

Jessie and Joe

Jessie made the call an hour later during the delay while she was waiting to be discharged. Patricia and Violet left the room to give her the privacy she demanded while she spoke with Joe.

"Joe, hi. I have some," she hesitated a moment, then continued, "news to share with you."

"Okay," Joe replied. 'News' didn't sound like something good, but he needed to know why Jessie was calling. They had only spoken twice since he flew to the Midwest. Most of his calls to her went to voicemail and she never called him. "Okay," he repeated, "What's going on?"

"Something happened. I don't know what, but I lost the baby."

"Did you have an abortion?" Joe spat the words out.

"No, I just lost the baby. A miscarriage. I'm calling from the hospital. It was just one of those things, the doctor says. Sometimes, pregnancies just don't work out right. Why would you assume I'd had an abortion?"

"You talked about it."

Jessie flushed for a moment. She was too tired to fight. Too drained. She said nothing.

Joe heard her sigh in exasperation. He softened. "How are you feeling? Are you okay? If the baby's gone, that's not good, but are you in trouble?"

"I'll be fine, I guess. I'll be going home in a bit. The doctor says I'll be okay in a few weeks, physically. But I'm pretty messed up emotionally right now. I really wanted our little baby and now she's gone."

"Do you need me to come home?"

"No. I want you to make it out there with the Cardinals. Violet is here with me, and so is my mom. Just stay in touch with me."

"Okay. If you need me, I'll be there. I'll catch the first flight home if you say you need me. Do what you have to do to get better. And we can move on together from this. We can make a new baby when we're married at the end of the summer after my season is over."

"Sure. I love you, Joe."

"I love you too, Jessie. Get better."

CHAPTER THIRTY-EIGHT

Jessie and Violet and Patricia

Jessie relaxed after the difficult call.

Momentarily alone in the hospital room, she was able to think without the distraction of Violet and her mom.

Do I still want to get married now that I've lost the baby? There's no need to now. I'll be running for UConn in a couple of months. College track's not a problem, now that I'm not pregnant. God, I've lost the baby. But do I really want to be married? To Joe? I'll sort that out later. Right now, all I can think about is my baby girl. She's gone. I need to work on finding a way to get past this. I don't know what to do. Where do I start?

*****

Late that night, with Jessie back at home, Patricia looked in on her daughter as she slept.

Jessie lay on her back, her eyes open in the dark. She looked up at her mom. "I lost my baby girl, Momma. Two days ago, she was still here. Now she's gone." Tears flooded from her eyes.

"You don't know it was a little girl, do you?"

"It was a little girl. I'm sure of it. And just like that, she's gone."

Patricia lay down next to her daughter, pulled her close, and held her soothingly. No words could change what had happened to her daughter. All she could do was hold her close. The hug gave comfort to both of them.

CHAPTER THIRTY-NINE

In Peoria, Joe fretted and wondered if he should leave the team and fly home. If I just abandon my team here in Peoria so suddenly, I doubt anyone would understand. It might end my career with the Cardinals. But I need to get home to Jessie. I can't appear weak. I can't let the team know that I'm in trouble. Should I call Wilson? Would he understand? No. Not an option. Maybe I'll call my parents after the game? Maybe Isaac? I'll decide what to do after the game. Right now, I have to go to work.

There was no one on his new team with whom he felt he could discuss Jessie's miscarriage. He didn't expect to stay in Peoria long, and he hadn't become close friends with the manager or any of his teammates. He had a game that evening and was scheduled to start. Jessie's call had come just as he was about to leave for the stadium. It gnawed at him. It was a distraction, but so much more. What he needed to do was push thoughts of Jessie away and focus on the game. He needed to get to the ballpark.

He tried to shut Jessie and the baby out of his mind while he pitched. His mind was blank, thinking pitch to pitch, of nothing but taking down each batter, one by one, each after the next. His anger at losing his baby, his frustration at being unable to help Jessie, his loneliness all coalesced into an intense game. The opposing team scratched out three hits and no runs. He pitched a complete game.

After the game, icing his arm, he let down his guard, and the feelings about Jessie and the baby raced back, overwhelming him. He almost cried, choking for just a moment. He leaned forward in the training room, his elbow on a table, his hand on his forehead, shielding his eyes. His manager noticed and stood beside him, using his body to block Joe from the view of his teammates. Quietly, he asked, "Are you okay, Joe?"

"Yeah, there's just an emotional letdown after a game like I just pitched."

"Sure." His manager wasn't buying it. "If there's anything I can help you with, just let me know. You pitched a hell of a game today. You've been in four games now. Three starts. This was the best one yet. They're already talking about you in the office in St. Louis. I suspect they'll be moving you up to Memphis before the end of the summer. Let me know what I can do; if there's any way I can help you here. With anything at all."

Later, back at his apartment, Joe walked alone out into the humid Midwest night. He found a bench in a park, sat, and called Jessie. There was no answer. Next, he tried his house.

"Hi, Dad."

"Joe! It's really late here on the East Coast. Are you okay? How are you doing?"

"Great. I threw a shutout this afternoon. They're already talking of moving me up to Memphis."

"Wonderful. I'll let everyone here know."

Joe sat in silence. Joao sensed that there was more than baseball on his boy's mind. "What else is going on, son? Everything okay?"

Joe's voice caught as he opened up about what had happened with Jessie. "Dad? Jessie called earlier today. She lost the baby. I want to be there with her, I need to be with her, right now. But I can't. I have to stay here playing ball. Baseball matters, but it's really not that important when I think about things like this. I don't know what to do. I want to come home."

"Oh, Joe. That's terrible. Do you want me or your mom to go see her? Do you want me to come out there to be with you?"

"I don't know. She doesn't really know you, and Mom hates her because she got pregnant. I can't just up and leave the team here for a few days, can I?"

"I don't know. If you told them about Jessie, they might let you go from the team for a while. Maybe they'd let you take some personal time?"

"Maybe. Do you think I should ask Wilson?"

"I don't think so, Joe. It seems like it's all business, all the time with him. He's a good baseball guy, but I don't know if he would care about something like this."

"Yeah, that's what I thought, too. That's why I didn't call him."

"Okay, Joe. I tell you what. I'll tell your mom what's happened, but I'll keep her away from Jessie. And I'll get a message to Jessie somehow to let her know we talked and we care and are here if she needs anything. Maybe I'll go through the Arnolds. Isaac's little sister is Jessie's best friend, right?"

"Good idea. Violet can help her. Jessie told me she already knows about it. I'll call Isaac and let him know what's going on, too. Thanks, Dad."

"Stay in touch, son. We'll talk again tomorrow. We're thinking of you. I love you, boy."

As soon as he hung up, Joe called Isaac. When Isaac answered, Joe heard voices shouting in the background. "Joe! How's it going?" Isaac shouted to be heard over the background noise. "I'm out celebrating with a few of my teammates. We just won again. Four straight games now. We've got a great team! Having a great summer!"

"Great. Congratulations."

"How about you? You still killing it out there in the farm country?"

"Yeah. I threw a complete game shutout today. But that's not why I'm calling."

"Oh. Okay. What's up?"

"I talked to Jessie earlier today. She lost the baby, and I don't know what to do about it."

"Oh, shit! Geez, Joe. I'm so sorry. I know Violet's been with her the last few days, but she didn't tell me on the phone what was happening. After she told me you guys were pregnant and I let it get out, she doesn't always open up to me about things like this."

Isaac's tone changed, and the background noise faded as he stepped outside the bar where he was partying with his teammates to continue the conversation from the parking lot. He leaned his head on his forearm, resting against the brick wall of the building. "What can I do to help?"

"I don't know. I can't be there, and I don't know what I could do if I were. Could you maybe talk to Violet? Jessie says she already knows. Find out what's happening and see if she can look in on Jessie for me?"

"Like you said, I expect Violet already knows. You know how close she and Jessie are. But sure. I'll check with Violet. I'll tell her we talked and you're worried. I call and talk to my mom and dad, just about every day, so I can see what they can do too. You know how Jessie's life is. Her mom's probably off, away on business. But I'll make sure Jessie's got people around to look after her. To help."

"Thanks, Isaac."

"Of course, Buddy. That's why I'm here. I've got it for you."

Joe hung up and dialed Jessie again. Again, there was no answer. He walked alone, back to his apartment, and went to bed. Dawn was already approaching before he fell asleep.

The next day, when he got to the ballpark, his manager pulled him into his office. "Pack your things. You're moving up to Memphis."

CHAPTER FORTY

Lucas had always liked his world logical, clean, orderly, broken down into predictable factors. Due to Jessie, the school year had ended in chaos, leaving him unsettled and edgy. He was relieved that it was all behind him and he could now get his life back to normal.

He retreated with Jennifer to the beach every day for the first days after school ended, watching his little girls play in the shallow water. He read spy novels, one a day, sheltering in a make-believe world of international espionage. He liked that he could usually sort out the good guys from the bad.

One afternoon, reclining in a low beach chair, almost dozing in the sun, a book lying open on his belly, he was interrupted by a familiar voice.

"Hi, Coach. I knew I'd find you here. I thought I should tell you. Jessie lost the baby. It was just one of those things. Physically, she's recovering, but she's a real mess emotionally right now. Maybe she could do with a visit from you. She respects you and you're one of the few adults she listens to."

Lucas marked his place and set the book aside. "Have a seat, Violet."

Violet sat on the sand next to her coach.

Jennifer leaned toward Lucas. "Call her. Go to her house and visit her. She might need guidance from an adult friend right now. You've told me her mom's not always there for her."

Lucas mulled for a moment. "Where's her mom?"

"She was out of town on business when it happened. I took Jessie to the hospital. Her mom got there as soon as she could. She stayed home for the first few days after it happened, but she left again this morning on another business trip."

Lucas paused a moment. "I'm not her teacher or coach anymore. But there are still boundaries. I don't know. As a man, I'm not comfortable going to her house, not even if you or my wife were to come with me."

Jennifer interceded. "Violet, could you bring her by our house some evening?" Then she turned toward Lucas. "I'll be there with you, Lucas."

Violet stood. "Will you be home tonight?"

Lucas nodded, but was looking toward the water. He didn't like students dropping by his house. It didn't feel right, but if Jennifer said so...

He turned toward Violet, "No. I can't have you coming by my house either. I want to help her if I can, but I'm concerned about what would be appropriate."

Jennifer looked at Violet. "Could you stop by here out in the open at the beach tomorrow morning?"

"I expect we could do that," Violet replied, glancing from Lucas and Jennifer to their girls playing in the sand. "What about your girls? I don't think we want them involved in this."

"I agree. We can still keep an eye on them if you're here talking with us," Jennifer said.

"Ok. See you tomorrow morning." She walked back up the beach to the parking lot.

*****

The following morning, Lucas and Jennifer were back at their customary spot on the beach. The girls were splashing in the shallow water, dumping sand into a plastic pail, and turning it over to make towers for their fairy castle. Jessie and Violet found Lucas and Jennifer and set up beach chairs across from them.

"Violet told me what happened, Jessie. I'm so sorry. How are you doing?" Lucas said.

"Okay, I guess."

Lucas cocked his head to one side and thought, this is not the brash athlete I know.

With shoulders slumped and a tired expression on her face, she offered nothing more than direct answers to his questions.

"Beyond the physical side of things, how are you feeling?"

"Awful. I didn't want to come see you. Violet made me come, just like she made me meet with you at the end of the track season when this all started to blow up. The worst part, aside from the physical part, is that I've lost control of everything. I wasn't in control of the pregnancy. And then when that went away...I've always been in control, and now I'm not."

"Your body will recover. And, you should know this: your emotions will as well. I understand how tough this must be."

"No! You don't understand. You can't know. None of you can. You've got two healthy little girls," Jessie said, looking at the girls playing down at the edge of the water. "You can't possibly know what it's like to lose a baby." Anger filled her voice.

"Actually, we do," Jennifer interjected. "We have Sophie and Emma, but the first time I was pregnant, I lost the baby. We've been through this. We understand."

Jessie nodded, chastened. This was a revelation for her. Thoughts crowded her mind: I thought I was alone with this. No one could possibly understand the racing emotions I've been dealing with. Certainly, Mom doesn't. How could my coach, a man, know what it's like? But they've been through this? Maybe they do understand. And Violet gets it. I'm so thankful she's been through all this with me, every step of the way.

Lucas continued. "The thing is, while you were still a student, and I was your coach and teacher, I didn't think I could advise you on things like this. Now that you've graduated, the teacher-student barrier is gone. That line isn't there now. But as a man, I'm not sure I know what to say."

"You have no advice for me?" Jessie was almost pleading. "Just tell me what I should do to get past this."

"I wish I could. I don't have answers. I wish I could say or do something to help. I can't set things right for you. Maybe counseling? Your doctor or the hospital probably has people you can lean on with this."

"I'm not crazy. I don't need counseling!" Jessie blurted out.

 Lucas took a deep breath and continued, "Well then, all I can suggest is that every day, every hour takes you a bit further past all this. It will get better. Learn from all this and take steps to make sure nothing like all this happens again."

"Oh, I will. I'll be on the pill as soon as the doctor says I can."

"That's a start."

"And I'll be at UConn by the end of the summer. And now I'll be able to be on the track team. When I was pregnant, I didn't know... Maybe there's a silver lining to this cloud."

"And you don't know what would've happened to your scholarship if you couldn't run and jump there."

Jessie's eyes widened. It had occurred to her that she might not be on the track team while pregnant. Now it struck her for the first time that if she couldn't run track, her scholarship might have been in jeopardy. And with that, her college education. She sat in silence, considering the awful revelation of what might have been.

Lucas interrupted her reverie. "What about Joe? How's he handling all this?"

"Okay, I guess. I told him, and he seemed okay. He's somewhere in the Midwest playing baseball."

"Keep talking to him. He lost the baby, too. He's feeling that loss. I know I struggled when we lost our baby. He'll need you right now. You'll both need each other."

"That's right," Violet added. "He might not be feeling what you are physically. But you know deep down, he's really an emotional guy. He tries to be a man and hold everything in and not let anything show, but he must be hurting, too. Lean on each other."

"I'll check back with him," Jessie promised.

Jennifer spoke up. "Let me know if you need a woman to talk to, someone who's been through this. I'm here for you."

Jessie smiled, "Thanks. Maybe later."

"If you need advice on how to get ready for the UConn team, I'm here," Lucas said. "Once the doctor gives you the all-clear, I can help with any workouts they've sent you."

"You'll always be my coach," Jessie smiled at Lucas. "Thank you for what you've done for me while I was on the Rock Haven team." Sincerity almost crept into her voice.

"I've done what I could. But I'll defer to the knowledge of the UConn coaches now. I can help with your preparation, but then it's up to you and your new coaches. Most of all, it's up to you going forward."

That's the way I like it, Jessie thought. I'm back in control now.

CHAPTER FORTY-ONE

Isaac had been offered a rarity: an empty motel room on Cape Cod on a summer weekend. The motel was owned by people who enjoyed Cape League baseball, and when they had a last-minute cancellation, the room became available. They gave it to the team, and the team rewarded Isaac with the first crack at the room.

He called his family, inviting them to come to the Cape for a visit to watch him play. Just like that, his family was on their way. Sam and Evelyn took personal days from the packing plant; Violet got the day off from the restaurant.

The game had not gone the way Isaac hoped. Pressing to show off for his family, he went hitless, one of the few games all summer when he didn't get a hit.

After the game, standing with his family in the parking lot, sweaty and dirty but happy, he introduced Juan. "These are my parents, and this is my sister Violet."

"Call me Sam," said Dad, "and my wife Evelyn."

Juan shook their hands. "Pardon the dirt and sweat. It's great to meet you. Isaac's become a good friend these last few weeks."

A stranger, a gray-haired man, thickset with powerful forearms, joined them. "Hi, Juan," he began, clapping Juan on the shoulder.

Isaac suddenly recognized him from when Juan had pointed him out in the stands a week earlier: Juan's college coach.

"And you're Isaac Arnold?" the man asked. "Juan's told me a lot about you, and I've been to several of your games now and followed you in the box scores in the paper. I'm Jack Bradford, Juan's baseball coach at Northeastern."

Isaac and his family stood by, quietly listening, wondering where the conversation was headed. "These are my parents," Isaac said, providing introductions again. "And my sister, Violet."

Coach Bradford nodded to them and shook their hands. Then he turned back to Isaac. "Juan tells me you just graduated from high school at Rock Haven, up north of Boston."

"Yes," Isaac spoke, his mouth dry, nerves constricting his throat. He knew where this conversation could go. It could be what he had been hoping for ever since Joe's Cardinal scout set him up with the Cape League team. His voice came out barely more than a whisper.

"I checked out your high school stats too," Coach Bradford continued. "You had a great year. Hit over three hundred for the season?"

"Yeah. I was over three hundred in both of my last two years."

"And you're still hitting the heck out of the ball down here on the Cape. Close to four hundred against some pretty good college pitchers."

"No hits tonight."

"No, but I've seen what you can do. And you're a good defensive catcher, too. You threw that base stealer out in the third inning tonight and blocked a few balls in the dirt."

"Yeah. I did. Thanks."

Isaac's parents stood by, quiet, attentive. Violet also sensed where the conversation was headed, but she held her breath.

"Juan tells me you don't have plans for after the summer season here on the Cape."

"I'll probably be going to work in the fish packing plant down the street from my house back home. Either that or I'll get a job going out on one of the fishing boats."

"You're not going to college?"

"We don't have the money for college."

"How were your grades in high school?"

"Okay. Good, I guess. Mostly B's, with a few A's. I studied hard."

"I still have a bit of scholarship money available. I'll need to check out your grades, to be sure, but if you had a partial scholarship, would you play ball for Northeastern?"

Isaac looked at his parents. Evelyn beamed. Sam nodded. "We can make it work," Sam said. "With a partial scholarship, and maybe a loan, we can make it work."

Isaac almost shouted, "Absolutely! What do I have to do?"

"I've got an application right here, and the paperwork for the scholarship." He pulled a packet of paper out of a canvas briefcase and handed it to Isaac. "I'll be staying down here a couple of more days, and I'm coming to the game tomorrow evening. If you can get all the paperwork filled out before the game, I can meet with you and your parents then, before or after the game, and wrap this up. If you need more time, take it. But I'd like to tie this up soon. You'll need to send me some information from your high school: your transcript, that kind of thing. I'll take the papers back to Boston on Monday, and you'll be in."

Sam spoke. "I'll drop by the high school on Monday and have them send you the paperwork electronically. Will that do?"

"It should. I'll give you the information on where to send it. Here's my card." Bradford gave both Sam and Evelyn his business card and then gave Isaac one as well.

"We truly appreciate this, Mr. Bradford," said Evelyn. There were tears in her eyes. "No one in our family has ever gone to college before."

"He'll be an asset to our school and our team," stated Bradford. Then, turning back to Isaac, "I'll be in touch the rest of the summer. Have a good season, and you'll be coming to Northeastern a few days after the Cape League season ends. Congratulations and welcome. You're a Husky!"

Coach Bradford shook hands with Isaac and his parents and gave a quick pat on Juan's shoulder. Then he walked back to his car.

Isaac first, and then his parents, all turned to Juan. Isaac hugged him, thanking him.

"No problem," Juan said. "You're too good a ball player to be packing fish the rest of your life. I'm glad you'll be my teammate next fall."

"Nothing wrong with packing fish," Sam said, defensively.

"No, there isn't." Juan apologized. "My mom works in a factory outside Worcester. Nothing wrong with any sort of job. People do what they do. But I'm glad we've got a spot on our team for Isaac. You're going to Northeastern. I share an apartment with a couple of my teammates up in Boston. I'll see if there's room for you, too."

"We're all thrilled," Evelyn agreed.

"Go get cleaned up, boys," crowed Sam. "I'm taking everyone out to dinner to celebrate!"

CHAPTER FORTY-TWO

Jessie and Violet

Jessie and Violet leaned on the top of the chain-link fence that rimmed the track, using it the way ballet dancers use a barre to stretch and warm up. On the other side of the fence in the first row of the bleachers, Lucas sat with Jennifer. Sophie and Emma played in the sand of the long jump pit in the end zone, filling primary-colored plastic cups with sand and dumping the sand from the cups into a red and yellow plastic dump truck. Joggers and walkers circled the track in the summer evening heat, a slow parade of out-of-shape adults.

"Jog a couple of easy laps to warm up, then come by to check in and let me know how you're feeling," Lucas said, addressing Jessie. "Run with her if you'd like, Violet. I'm not allowed to coach you outside of the regular season, but I can coach Jessie, now that she's graduated, and I can't stop you from dropping by the track and running with her."

"Sure, Coach," Violet answered, suppressing a smile. She understood Lucas' compulsion to abide by the rules.

The two girls trotted away from the fence and began circling the track, appropriating the inside lanes, cruising past the plodding joggers and walkers. When they finished their two laps, they returned to Lucas and his wife.

"How are you feeling, Jessie?" he asked.

"Fine. No discomfort at all. It's been a couple of weeks. Dr. Goodman saw me yesterday morning, a follow-up visit after my time in the hospital. He says I'm okay to start running again."

"Good. Try some strides, not too much at first. See how you're feeling as you move along. You haven't run hard for almost a month, what with graduation and the pregnancy. Maybe four laps, accelerating off each turn for just a bit on each straightaway. You know the drill." It was a gentler, briefer version of the same workout Jessie had quit on when she had first discovered she was pregnant.

The girls turned and ran away from the fence, again taking the inside lanes, dodging the slow fitness pedestrians. Joggers and walkers began shifting out of the inside lanes to the perimeter of the track to give them room. Coming off the first turn, they converted into full sprint form, erect posture, arms pumping, knees lifting, legs reaching, pulling the track back beneath them. It was as though they were beings from another planet flying by the mere mortals who shuffled along on the outside lanes. Against the backdrop of the slogging pedestrians, their speed was stunning. The sprinters coasted down to an easier run as they neared the end of the straightaway and rounded the turn. They lifted and flew again on the next straightaway.

As they finished their second lap, Lucas could see that both girls were grinning, talking to each other, thrilled with the exhilaration of the speed, the sheer joy of running fast. They opened up and sprinted again on the far side of the field. Jennifer tapped Lucas on the arm, "Are they laughing while they run?"

He listened and heard the distant but distinct sound of children laughing. He looked at Sophie and Emma, but they were intent on their sand play. Still, the unmistakable sound of laughter came across the track from Jessie and Violet. "This is play for them," he explained to Jennifer. "It's fun for them to race like that. It's wonderful that Jessie is having fun for a change."

They began their fourth and final lap with a flat-out racing sprint, tearing past the joggers. The final sprint down the backside straightaway was more subdued, but still blazing fast. When they finished, they coasted over to Lucas. "What now, Coach?" Jessie asked.

"That's enough. Cool down a couple of laps and you're done. For today. You mentioned that the UConn coach simply wants you in shape and ready to start training when you arrive on campus. Let's see how you recover tomorrow. This is plenty for now to begin to get you ready."

"And to have me ready for fall practice," added Violet, grinning. "Thanks, Coach!"

*****

Driving home in Jessie's Miata after their workout, Violet turned to her friend. "You didn't talk at all to Coach's wife tonight. Have you talked with her about the miscarriage?"

Jessie focused on the road ahead, not looking at Violet. "No. I don't think I need to. That morning at the beach was enough. It got me over the hump of my problem. I can handle it from here."

"She's been through it. Coach's wife could give you advice and support. Turn to her if you need someone to talk to about it."

"Like I said, I can deal with it now without her help." There was an edge to Jessie's voice.

"How about Joe? How's he doing with this?"

"He must be fine. He calls at least once a day to check on me."

"What does he say? He's all alone out there in the west. Is he okay?"

"I guess so. I haven't really talked with him that much. I'm usually busy with something when he calls. I let most of his calls go to voicemail."

Violet shook her head. "C'mon Jessie. You don't have to carry all this alone. People are there for you. Coach's wife. Joe. Me. How about your mom?"

"We talk when she's home, but she still has a lot of business trips. And like you just said. I've got you. I appreciate what you're trying to do for me, but trust me. I'm fine."

Violet gave up. "Okay. Suit yourself. Just know people are there for you. Turn to them when things get hard."

"I said, I'm fine." Jessie's voice was hard, definitive.

Jessie pulled up at Violet's house and dropped her off without another word.

As she drove away, thoughts crowded her mind.

I wish they would all just leave me alone. Violet's okay, I guess. But mom's always looking at me when she's home and asking me how I feel. I want her off my back. And Joe, with all his calls. And his parents keep calling me, too. Really? I don't even know them. I'm not telling him how I feel about the miscarriage. He wouldn't understand. It's a woman thing. And that goes for Coach, too. I hardly know his wife. I can't talk to her about this. I'm fine.

CHAPTER FORTY-THREE

Patricia sat at a quiet corner table in Leonardo's, assessing Jessie across the table. Their meals sat freshly served in front of them, lasagna for Jessie, a chicken and mushroom concoction in a cream sauce over fettuccini for Patricia. They each had a glass of white wine.

Patricia reached across the table and rested her hand on Jessie's. "I'm glad we have a moment to catch up on things. How are you feeling, Jessie?"

"Fine. Since my follow-up with Dr. Goodman, I've been running with Violet every evening so far this week. My body's doing well."

"Emotionally, how are you?" Patricia frowned for a moment, finding herself truly concerned for Jessie's overall well-being.

"There are still moments. Probably hormones, I guess. Dr. Goodman says that's normal. But he says, physically, I'm fine."

"And you're okay to be working out?"

"Dr. Goodman gave me the go-ahead."

"Good. Have you talked again with Joe? How's he doing?"

"Yeah. He's doing well. They've moved him up to Memphis, which is a level higher than where he started. He's still winning games."

"I meant, how's he dealing with the loss of the baby?"

It was the most personal conversation Jessie could remember having with her mom. Now it almost felt intrusive, too prying. For a moment she stiffened, but she relaxed, smiled, and answered. "He's okay with it. He doesn't say much about it at all, so I'm thinking he's okay."

She looked at the plate of food and thought, C'mon, Mom! What do you really want from me? Now she cares about how Joe feels? She wanted me to break up with him. Now she's concerned about how he's doing? She wanted me to have an abortion. Then I lose my baby. And now she's concerned? First, she wants one thing, then another.

I don't know how to read her anymore.

Chapter Forty-four

Joe

The Cardinals booked Joe on a flight from Peoria to Memphis. A driver took the new black Ford truck Joe had bought in Peoria and drove it south for him. Wilson met Joe at the Memphis airport and took him to a garden apartment complex near the river where several of the Redbird players lived in furnished apartments owned by the Cardinals organization. The transition up to AAA had been swift and easy. A day after he arrived, Joe won a game, allowing only four hits and one run in six innings. Wilson sat in the stands, smug and satisfied with his protégé's progress.

Barry Carmichael, the Redbirds manager, was a former major league pitcher. He sat with Joe after the game. Carmichael's shaved head betrayed a hint of gray hair against polished dark skin. "Listen, Joe," Carmichael began. "I never had near the talent you've got. Even so, I made it through several seasons in the majors. I understand the game, and I know pitching. I'm here to help you develop to be ready for the next level."

"Great. If I have another game like today, I should keep progressing, don't you think?"

"Maybe. You pitched well today. But there's still room for you to grow, to learn. What do you think you need? What can I do to help you along? Is there a pitch you struggle with? How does your arm feel?"

"I think my slider's okay. And I've got a good fastball that I can make go in different directions. I depend on my slider and rarely throw a real curve, but I can if I need to. What do you think I need?"

"What I see is that your delivery looks the same no matter what pitch you're throwing. That's good. It means the batters don't know what to expect until it's too late and the pitch is on them. You don't tip off your pitches. I haven't seen your curve yet. Or a change up."

"I can control the slider better than the curve. And my fastball is good enough. Why bother with a curve or a changeup?"

"Let's work on your control of the curve. And a changeup means they can't sit on your fastball. If everything you throw is hard, the batters can time your pitches. Major leaguers can all hit the fastball, but a changeup keeps them off balance. Master the curve and the changeup, and you'll have four pitches to rely on. It'll make you a complete pitcher."

Joe nodded, absorbing the lesson. "Okay, before the next game, can we work on those a bit? You'll help me? Do I grip the changeup differently?"

Throwing on the second off day between starts, Joe worked on his curve and changeup with Carmichael right beside him.

After the off-day practice, Carmichael instructed Joe and the catcher, "Work those new pitches in just once or twice each inning in your next start. Your slider's still your best pitch, so depend on it whenever you need a sure out. But we're going to make you a much better pitcher, Joe. The hitters won't know what to expect when you master all the pitches."

He won again four days later. That night, he couldn't sleep. His arm ached, the elbow sore and numb. A day later, he felt fine and threw a light practice, working to make sure his motion on the curve and changeup was exactly like the delivery of his fastball and slider.

He won a third game three days later, still using his slider whenever he needed a sure out. Again, his elbow was sore for a day after the game.

It was still aching when he met Carmichael for his off-day throwing. Carmichael noticed a lack of velocity on his usual pitches. "How are you feeling today, Joe?"

"My arm's a little sore," Joe admitted.

"Where does it hurt?"

Joe pointed to the inside of the elbow.

"We're skipping today's workout," Carmichael said. "We'll see how you are in four days when you're scheduled for your next game."

The team trainer left two other players on the training table, icing their hamstrings. He pulled Joe aside, handing him an ice pack for the elbow. "How long has the elbow been hurting?" he asked.

"A few weeks, off and on. It got worse over the last few days since my last start."

"Can you back off the slider?"

"It's my best pitch."

The trainer put the ice aside and took Joe's arm, manipulating it, twisting it, kneading the bicep and the forearm, evaluating the damage. "Try to use the fastball more in your next game. Hold back on the slider. It might be a good thing to do anyway, since the other team will have scouted you and be looking for the slider. Depend on the fastball."

When the trainer left, Joe put the ice back on his elbow, pondering the trainer's advice. Pitch without my slider? I need my slider. It's my best pitch. What's going on?

Joe got shelled in the second inning of that next game. His fastball lacked its usual zip, and his arm hurt every time he tried to throw the slider. Carmichael pulled him from the game.

*****

The next day, the Cardinals had Joe in St. Louis with Wilson, meeting with Dr. Matthews, an orthopedic specialist. It had all happened so fast. Joe felt his world, his life, spinning out of control. After an MRI, the doctor confirmed, "There's a problem with your UCL. Your ulnar collateral ligament. How often have you been pitching?"

"A couple of games each week ever since March. And a bit of throwing between starts."

"Do you throw a lot of sliders?"

"It's my best pitch."

"Stand up. Now make the motion like you're throwing your slider."

Joe did and winced from the pain.

Matthews nodded. "Okay. See here." He pointed to the MRI image. "That's a small tear in the ligament on the inside of your elbow. That movement, every time you throw the slider, tears at it some more. It probably hurts on every pitch you throw, but the slider's the problem."

"It's my best pitch. I can't give up my slider." Joe looked at the blurry, grey, and white image. It made no sense to him. He couldn't see the tear the doctor was talking about. But he could feel it.

"What do you suggest we do?" Wilson asked the doctor. It was a question Wilson knew the answer to. He wanted Joe to hear it from the doctor.

"Shut down his throwing before he does more damage," Matthews said, addressing Wilson. Then, looking Joe in the eye. "If you keep pitching, the tear will only get worse. You're done for this season. I suggest we replace the ulnar collateral ligament with a graft."

Joe looked at Wilson, numb, his ears ringing. For a moment, he felt sick, nauseous, and dizzy. "I can't pitch?"

"Not until we fix this problem," said the doctor. Wilson nodded.

"It's called Tommy John surgery," explained Wilson. "It's named after the first pitcher they did the surgery on. Now it's as routine for pitchers as getting an oil change on your car. You'll be better than new after the surgery."

"How long will I be out? I want to pitch."

"You can't until we deal with this," said Wilson. "We'll know how long you'll be out after you have the surgery."

"Okay," Joe, still stunned, looked to the doctor. He tried to think, tried to make sense of it. *Pitching is what I do. It's my job. It's worth hundreds of thousands of dollars. And they won't let me pitch?*

"The surgery isn't that difficult," Dr. Matthews explained, blandly, no emotion clouding his words. "I've done it dozens of times. I make a small incision on your non-throwing arm, harvest a tendon from your right wrist, and tie it into the elbow on your left arm, your throwing arm, anchored to the upper humerus and the lower ulna. We'll anesthetize you, so you won't feel a thing. It's outpatient surgery, so if we get you in first thing in the morning, you could be out of the hospital later that day. I operate. Your arm will be in a sling, so you'll need a ride home from the hospital, and you won't be driving for a few days. Otherwise, it's actually pretty simple."

Joe fought back panic, holding in tears, thinking my whole life seems to be coming apart. "I don't understand all the medical stuff, but it doesn't sound simple. Cutting both my arms. And how long will I be out?"

"A year. Rehab and exercising can begin after a few weeks, maybe a month. You're from Boston? I'll connect you with a doctor I know in Boston to check on you throughout your recovery and decide when you're ready to start rehab. You can start some easy throwing after about six months. Even a bit longer before you can really pitch. You'll be good as new when I'm done."

"Maybe even better," Wilson added, resting a supportive hand on Joe's wide shoulder. "We'll work with the doctor to set you up with a schedule of exercises and weight training for rehab, and I'll take care of helping you begin your recovery. If all goes well, we might invite you to Spring Training next year, even though you'll still be a year away from playing ball. We can check you out then. You'll be doing some light throwing by spring."

The doctor shook Joe's hand and left him with Wilson.

"I'm done," said Joe glumly, slumping on the small chair in the examination room, looking at the wall, blank, aside from a medical diagram of a skeleton.

"No. Don't think like that. This is a setback, not the end. The Cardinals are invested in you. We know what you're capable of and we'll help get you rehabbed and back throwing. This doctor has done the procedure with several other pitchers in the Cardinals' organization. Two are on the major league roster right now. You'll be fine in a year. Stronger than ever."

"So, what do I do next?"

"We'll get you scheduled for the surgery as soon as possible. Probably just a day or two from now. Then I'll help you get back home to Boston to begin your rehab. I'll take care of all the travel arrangements for you. You'll be flying to Boston from here. I'll get you booked for a flight, take you to the airport, and stay in touch all the way. We'll have someone gather your things in Memphis and take your new truck with all your stuff up to Boston. You won't be driving for the first few days after the surgery, so let your dad know you're coming home and have him pick you up and drive you to Rock Haven from the airport."

"Do I have any say in all this?"

"Do you want to pitch again and play major league ball with the Cardinals?"

"Of course."

"Then this is the way to go about that."

*****

The operation was scheduled for early the following morning. That evening, Joe sat with Wilson in the hotel dining room. A Porterhouse steak and baked potato sat on a plate in front of Joe, untouched. "I'm not hungry," Joe finally said, pushing the plate away. "I can't eat, thinking about the surgery."

"It's really pretty routine," Wilson said, encouragingly. "Like the doctor said this afternoon, a lot of pitchers have this operation."

"It's not routine for me. A year with no throwing? Will I ever throw again?"

"Of course you will. You're still young. You'll be back in a year with your whole career ahead of you. What you need right now is to get some rest so you'll be ready for tomorrow. I'll meet you in the hotel lobby at six tomorrow morning, and we'll get this all taken care of."

*****

209

Joe spent the night alone in a suite of rooms in the hotel, unable to sleep, worrying about what would happen the next morning.

Though it was late, he called Jessie. Again, she didn't answer; he left a message. "Hey, Jessie. I hope you're doing okay. I miss you and love you. I need to let you know that the Cardinals have shut me down for the rest of the season. I'm having surgery on my elbow tomorrow morning. Give me a call. I really need to hear from you. Right now, I need you. I need to talk with you. I don't care how late it is. Call me."

Then he called his dad. His words poured out before his dad could say anything. "Hey, Dad, I'm in trouble. My arm's been hurting, and they're going to operate on it tomorrow morning here in St. Louis. Tommy John surgery. I'll be flying home a day or two later, and I'll need someone to come to Boston to pick me up."

"Oh, Joe. Do you need me to come out there and be with you?"

"No. I'm okay. You wouldn't get here till after the operation anyway. And the doctor says it's pretty routine. It might be routine for him, but it's my arm and it's not routine for me. I'm with Wilson. I'll let you know when my flight is coming to Boston, though. It'll be great to see you and everyone when I get home."

"Okay. I'll let your mom know, and we'll be thinking about you tomorrow morning, praying for you, praying everything goes well."

"Thanks. Right now, I just don't know what to think. My pitching arm is all I've got, and they're cutting that tomorrow. I'm a little scared. They say I'll be better than ever after this is over, and they'll take me to spring training next year to check me out."

"That's good."

"Have you heard from Jessie? I tried to call her, but she didn't pick up."

"Your mom and I have left messages with her and her mom. And we talk with the Arnolds about everything. Violet says she's doing okay."

"Good. I'll be able to see her when I get home."

"Okay, let me know when your flight is scheduled to get to Boston. I'll be there waiting for you at the airport."

After the call, he dialed Isaac. "Hey, Buddy," Isaac answered. "I've seen your stats. You still knocking them dead with the new team?"

"No. My arm's hurt. They're doing Tommy John surgery on it tomorrow. I'm coming home in a couple of days."

"Damn! First Jessie with the miscarriage and now this? How are you feeling about everything?"

"Not good. I guess I'll be fine after the surgery. At least that's what everyone is saying. But, yeah, after Jessie and our baby, and now this, I'm screwed. I tried to call her, but she's not answering my calls."

"Violet says she's doing okay. Physically, she's fine. She's running again, getting ready for college track. Otherwise, emotionally, she might still be a bit messed up. Violet says she is. It'll probably do both of you a lot of good to get back together once you're home."

"I hope so. They say I can start rehab a few weeks after the surgery. So physically, I might be okay too."

"I'll be in college in the fall, but I'll work out with you when I can. Get through the surgery and come on home. Everyone here will take care of you once you're here."

Chapter Forty-five

Joe

Joe sat with Wilson at the airport. Joe's head was down, staring at the floor between his feet. His right wrist was wrapped in bandages. His left arm was in a sling, bent at a ninety-degree angle, and bandaged under a soft cast. Both arms hurt. Though he hated taking medicine, he was on painkillers.

"The doctor says it went well," said Wilson, hoping to lift Joe's spirits. "Rest a couple of weeks, then start the rehab exercises he gave you. Those are really important for you to do regularly to get back to baseball."

"I will."

"Your dad's meeting you at the airport in Boston?"

"Yeah. I called him. He's taking a day off from work to come get me."

"That's good. You told your girlfriend what's going on?"

It touched Joe that Wilson remembered his girlfriend. He smiled. "I've called her but I haven't been able to reach her yet."

"How about your buddy? Your catcher, Isaac?"

"Yeah, we've talked. He's having a great summer down in the Cape League. And he got a scholarship to play next year for Northeastern."

"Great news! Good for him! I'll keep track of his progress. He might make it to pro ball too, if he keeps that up."

"Yeah, I hope so. He understood about me and what happened with my arm."

"Good. I got two first-class seats for you. They're next to each other, so you'll have plenty of room and nobody will be bumping into your arm. Sit so that your pitching arm, the left one, is over the open seat. Give it room. Prop it with one of those little pillows."

"Thanks."

His flight was called, and Joe stood, carrying his small carry-on bag with his right hand, the arm where the doctor had harvested the tendon. That wrist hurt, but not as badly as the left arm in the cast. Wilson reached up and rested a hand on his shoulder. "Be strong, Joe. Don't get discouraged. You're going to be fine. I'll stay in touch."

A flight attendant greeted him as he entered the plane from the jetway. "Oh my God! Joe Goncalves! It's so good to see you again!" It was Melissa. Smiling her sunny smile.

"Hey, it's Melissa, right? What are the chances you'd be on this flight?"

"Pretty good, actually. I do the Boston to St. Louis flights all the time."

She noticed the bandages and the cast. "Oh, Joe! What happened?"

"I had surgery on my throwing arm yesterday. I'm done for the season."

"Oh, geez! But you'll be back throwing again in a while, right?"

"That's what they say. I hope so."

Melissa noticed the line of passengers piling up behind Joe. She quickly checked his ticket and said, "You're in first class, Joe. Go on in and turn left. Take your seat. I've got to get back to work. But we'll talk more once we're in the air."

Mid-flight, Melissa found a free moment and stopped in the aisle, leaning on the back of the seat in front of Joe, being careful not to bump his sling. "I'm not supposed to sit with the passengers or interact with them like this. But let me ask. What happened?"

"I guess I threw my arm out. Too much pitching, too many sliders, and not enough rest. The doctor says I'll be out about a year, but I'll be stronger than ever once everything heals."

"Was everything going well before the injury?"

"Yeah. I did great at Peoria. That's single A, the Midwest League. I was still doing okay when they brought me up to Memphis, which is triple-A. Then my arm started hurting. They did the operation yesterday here in St. Louis. It's called Tommy John Surgery."

"How are you feeling today? Does it hurt?"

"A little," he said, reluctant to tell her how much it really hurt.

"Are people meeting you when we get to Boston? Your family? Your girlfriend? You mentioned in the interview on television that you've got a girlfriend back in Boston."

"My dad's picking me up. I can't drive with the sling on my arm. I haven't heard from my girlfriend, but I left her a message telling her what happened."

"Oh, Joe. Take it a day at a time. You'll be out of the sling in no time and working your way back. I just know it."

"Yeah. I hope so. The doctor says these next few days will be the worst. But I start rehab in a few weeks. Then, we'll see."

"Let me know how it goes. I'm rooting for you. I gave you my phone number the day we met. But here it is again, and my email address." She handed him a slip of paper.

"I'll let you know how I'm doing with the recovery. Thanks. Here's my number. And my email." Joe tore her paper in half, saving the top part with her information. He scrawled his number on the rest of her paper, his hand awkward with the cast.

Melissa stood back in the center of the aisle. "Now, I've got to get back to work. Good luck."

After she left, Joe pondered about Melissa. She seems to really care about what happened to me. I wish Jessie would call back. That's okay. Probably see her tomorrow. I'll be fine when I see Jessie again.

Melissa gave Joe a light pat on the back as he left the plane in Boston. "I'll stay in touch. Keep your chin up. You're going to be okay, Joe."

Again, just as he had the first time he met her, he thought, she's really nice to talk with, but I've already got a girlfriend.

Chapter Forty-six

Jessie and Joe

As soon as he got home to Rock Haven, Joe called Jessie.

Jessie's phone rang, and she glanced down. It was Joe. She remembered he had told her about the arm surgery. Would that have been yesterday? Crap! *What do I say to him?*

"Hey, Joe. What's up?"

"I'm home. I left you messages. You know I had surgery on my arm yesterday in St. Louis. I'm done for the season and now I'm home."

"That's a shame. How did the surgery go?"

"Okay, I guess. I start some exercises and rehab in a few weeks, and I'll work my way back. Can I see you?"

"Sure. I'm kind of busy today. Maybe tomorrow morning? Let's meet up at our spot in Herring Head Park at ten?"

"I was kind of hoping I could see you tonight. I've missed you and really need you right now."

"Like I said, I've got a lot going on. Tomorrow morning at ten. Okay?"

"Sure."

Before he could say more, Jessie hung up. Joe sat alone, still holding his phone, anxious. *What's with her? She knows I'm hurt. She was never like this before I left. What is happening with her?*

Jessie also fretted. How do I handle him? What do I say? He's hurting right now after his surgery. But I have to tell him. I've got tonight to figure out what I should say to him. How do I tell him? I'll be direct. Without the baby, there's no reason to marry him. And I'm off to UConn in a couple of weeks. He may be done as a baseball player if his arm is hurt. What has he really got if he can't play baseball? Maybe Mom is right. I can't marry him if he's never going to be anything more than a fisherman. I can have more in my life than that. I'll just tell him tomorrow morning, straight out. I can't say it's because he got hurt and won't ever amount to anything now. But I've got to break it off. I'll get right to the point and let him go.

*****

Joe walked up to Herring Head Park a little before ten, eager to be with Jessie, but concerned by her chilled tone on the call and the remoteness he'd felt on the few calls when he had been able to connect with her since she lost the baby. He went to their bench on Herring Head and waited. The park was deserted; everyone was off at work.

A few minutes later, Jessie drove up, parked on the street near their bench, and joined Joe, sitting beside him, next to his damaged arm. Awkwardly, he leaned over and hugged her. His cast was in the way, but still it felt good to be with her, his cast arm almost around her again, his right arm reaching across to her shoulder. She leaned into him briefly, indulging his hug, but didn't reciprocate. He tried to kiss her. She turned her head, accepting the kiss on her cheek.

"How are you feeling, Joe?" she asked, pulling away, leaning back to assess him.

"Okay. It's hard to sleep at night, with the cast and everything."

"Is there any pain?"

"A bit. Less now than yesterday. God, I've missed you. I really wish you could have come out to the Midwest with me."

"It sounds like you were doing fine without me there."

"Yeah. My pitching went okay, at least until I got hurt. But it would have been better if you were there with me. I felt very alone without you or my family, or all my friends here in Rock Haven."

"Well, I was still here. You called me. Just about every day. And it's just as well I was here. When I lost the baby, I was able to see my regular doctor, and I had my mom and Violet here with me."

"You're okay after losing the baby?"

"Yeah, I'm fine. I guess. I've started running again, getting ready to go to UConn."

"That's good. I really lost it when I found out our baby was gone. It hurt. I wanted so much to come home and be with you, but I couldn't. I worried about you. I really wanted to be here, but I couldn't get through on the phone. And I couldn't leave my team. I'm glad you're okay."

"Yeah, I'm recovering. I still have moments when I wish it all hadn't happened. The doctor says that's normal, those emotions."

"Well, anyway, after everything, I'm home now, and at least we're together again."

Jessie paused. It took her a moment to get ready to say what she knew she needed to say, the words she'd rehearsed in her mind so many times since she'd lost the baby.

"Joe, listen. We really had a good thing going last year. And the year before, too. You're a really special guy, and maybe I loved you. But if I hadn't gotten pregnant, we never would have talked about getting married. And now our lives are headed in such different directions. I leave for college in Connecticut in a couple of weeks, and you'll be here in Rock Haven, letting your arm heal. Without the baby, I don't think we should get married. We don't need to now. And if we're not getting married, it might be best if we just make it a clean break before I leave for college."

Joe leaned forward, his elbows, one of them wrapped in a cast, resting on his knees. He looked out over the glistening water of the harbor and said nothing. He had no words to sum up all he was feeling. The odor of low tide and the fish smell of the plant drifted up to him. The view was beautiful. Nothing else was.

"Joe?" Jessie queried. "You're okay with this, right?"

"No. When you kept not answering my calls, I guessed you might be thinking of doing this. But it still hits me hard. I don't know what to say." He fought for control, determined not to let her see him cry. His jaw was clenched, his brow furrowed.

"It's for the best, Joe. We had something really special, really good. But we never really had much except sex, did we?"

"I thought we did."

"Look at it this way, Joe. When your arm heals, you'll be playing major league baseball. You'll have all kinds of girls chasing you. You'll forget about me."

"I don't think so. No. I love you, Jessie. I don't want another girl."

"You'll find another. One who'll sincerely care about you and your baseball career. I'll never forget you, Joe, but it's time we both move on."

Jessie stood abruptly and walked away, back to her silver Miata. She got in, closing the door quietly, but with finality. Without looking back, she drove from the park, down the hill, and back across town to The Heights above Rock Haven.

Joe remained alone. His arm hurt. For a moment, he held it close to him, trying to ease the pain, but the ache continued, throbbing inside the soft cast.

Jessie's face was blank as she drove off. There. It's done. It's over. Now I can get on with my life. Joe was good while it lasted, but now I can move on. Maybe Mom's advice was right all along. There will be a great guy at UConn. He's probably there already, waiting for me. The new guy will have a great future to offer me. I can't wait to meet him.

Chapter Forty-seven

Joe shook his head, trying to make sense of it. Maybe I knew all along she was going to leave me. But now that it's happened, all I really feel is regret. And a sense of loss and emptiness. My girl is gone. My baby is gone. I gave up college to play pro ball, and now my arm hurts and I can't pitch.

He sat alone on their bench the rest of the morning, mulling it over, trying to decide what to do with the rest of his life. He needed someone to talk to. He called Isaac.

"Hey, Joe," Isaac answered. "How're you doing? You home yet?"

"Yeah, I got home late yesterday."

"How's the arm?"

"Getting better, I guess. It still hurts."

Sensing a reason for the call, Isaac probed. "How's everything else going? It's good to be back in Rock Haven, right?"

"Yeah, it's good to be home, but I just saw Jessie, and..." Joe paused, struggling for the right words. "...she's left me. Broke it off because the baby's gone, so she doesn't see a reason to get married."

"Damn that girl! She left you? No chance of getting her back?"

"I don't think so. Don't know what to do, where to go, where to start to fight to get her back. You know her. Once her mind's made up, that's it. I don't know what to do."

He continued, "For me, it was always about Jessie, and the baby, our family, and playing pro ball. That's how I saw my whole life developing. Now I've lost everything."

Isaac heard Joe quietly sniffling and realized his buddy was crying.

"Joe, listen. I'm down here moving into an apartment in Boston with my buddy Juan. He was my teammate on the Cape this summer, and he's at Northeastern. I'm coming home to Rock Haven late tonight. I'm going up to the school tomorrow morning. Coach Lancaster has the gym open for me to lift. I'll call him. Maybe you can come join me and meet us after I'm done. We can sort this all out with Coach. He always seems to know what to do about things."

"I can't lift right now. Not with my arm like this."

"No, but let's talk with Coach."

"I don't know."

"Sure. C'mon Joe. I can help. So can Coach."

"What time?"

"School isn't open for another week, but football practice began this week. Coach is at practice until noon. I go in about eleven for my workout. I'm meeting him at noon after I lift."

"I'll be there at noon."

Chapter Forty-eight

Joe walked home, fixed a sandwich for lunch, and napped through the afternoon on the living room sofa. He felt drained, exhausted, even though he had done nothing physically tiring since the surgery. *I'm empty. Maybe it's the painkillers. I've got to cut back on those. But my arm hurts. I can't spend the rest of my life lying here on the sofa. But what can I do? I can't do anything else.*

His mom and dad arrived in the late afternoon after walking back from work at the harbor. Joe stood up, fuzzy and flushed from sleeping in the hot living room.

Dad noticed his distress. "How're you doing, son?"

"Not good. I saw Jessie this morning. She broke up with me. We're not getting married." He looked from one parent to the other. His mother's eyebrows went up; his father's jaw dropped.

Helena quietly approached him and pulled him close to her. "Oh, Joe. It's no secret I didn't care for that girl. But I know how you felt about her. This is awful. As bad as losing the baby. Worse. Even more than your arm being hurt. I've got you."

Joe held onto his mom. For a moment, she felt him shake and snuffle like he was about to cry. Then he regained control.

Joao said, "I'm calling your grandpa. He'll help work this out. He always has answers, brings good advice. I'll have him join us tonight for dinner."

*****

Grandpa, Joao Senior, pulled his truck up to the house less than an hour later. Helena set out fish tacos. Joao Junior passed around cold bottles of Bud Light. They sat at the kitchen table.

"Catch me up on everything, Joe," Joao Senior said. "I heard your baseball was going great out West. And I heard about your arm surgery. And your dad filled me in about your girlfriend. Let me start by saying I was sorry to hear about the baby. And the breakup. Now, what's going on?"

Joe took a bite of his taco, paused, chewing and swallowing a spicy bite of fish before he replied. It gave him time to consider what to say to Grandpa. "Sounds like you know most of it. Baseball aside, it's been a hard time this summer, being alone out there. And now Jessie's broken up with me. I expected I'd have a great season, then I'd come home, and we'd get married in a few weeks."

Grandpa nodded. Then, looking into Joe's eyes, he instructed. "This isn't going to be what you want to hear, but if she left you that easily because the baby is gone? Count your blessings. The marriage wouldn't have lasted. It was only based on the baby, not on you and her. A marriage is a lifetime commitment, and people can't just walk away when times get tough. I can see you're hurting right now, but as time goes by, you'll see it as the best way for things to be."

Joe slumped, forearms on the table, surrounding his plate. "Sure. You're probably right, but right now, all I feel is that I've lost everything. I can't pitch, I'm not going to college, and my baby and my girlfriend... It's all gone. I'm tired of talking about it."

His parents sat back, letting Joao Senior sort it out with Joe.

Grandpa leaned towards Joe and said, "Listen to me, Joe. You've hit the bottom. Your dad says the Cardinals want you to start rehab in a few weeks. Tell me about that."

"I'll have exercises to do for flexibility, and then I'll start weight training. They gave me a whole list of things to do."

"So, you'll do them. They haven't given up on you. So, you can't give up on yourself. Let the arm heal and then do your exercises."

"I gave up Clemson for this. Everybody's already working or leaving for college. Jessie's off to UConn in a few days, I expect. Not that she matters now. Isaac's already down at Northeastern. I'll be here trying to figure out the rest of my life alone."

"Enough of that talk. This is not the time for a self-pity party. Look at it this way. If you'd gone to Clemson and hurt your arm, where would you be? The Cardinals paid for the surgery, right? I don't know if Clemson would have. Maybe yes, maybe no. You might have gotten injured anyway, and that would have been the end of it. And don't go saying you're alone with all this. You're not alone. You've got your family. You can stay in touch with Isaac and your other friends. Maybe take some classes this fall at Salem State. It's nearby and with your grades from high school, you can get in for a few classes. It would set you up for more things at other colleges and maybe a job someday, somewhere, if baseball doesn't work out for you. You've got all that money from the Cardinals. Go back to school and do the exercises the Cardinals gave you."

Joe lifted his head slightly and looked beyond his grandfather. He began to imagine the way forward. "Thanks, maybe I'll do that. But I've still lost Jessie and our baby. There's no answer for that, is there?"

"Ah, women." Joao Senior shook his head and laughed, clapping Joe on the shoulder.

Joe winced, feeling the clap in his elbow. "No," he said.

Grandpa noticed and pulled his hand back. Then he continued, "I don't have an answer for that one. I can give you this advice. A big, good-looking stud like you, with all that money, and a career as a professional athlete waiting for you? More girls than you can handle will be after you now that Jessie's gone. You'll get over her in time, but be careful with the other new girls. Watch them carefully. Don't get caught with the ones who only want to be with you because you've got money, or because you're famous, with the baseball career. Be careful even with the ones who want to be with you because they like the way you look. You're more than that. There's a good girl out there, and you'll find each other when the time is right."

Helena interrupted. "Go to Mass this weekend. Check out the girls in church. Maybe a nice Portuguese girl?"

"Ma! I'm not ready for that. Not yet. Mass, yes. Not a new girl."

Mom insisted. "Many pretty Portuguese girls at church. You'll see!"

Suddenly, Joe laughed. "Ma! A new girl will come along, but let me be the one to decide who it'll be."

He felt like his life was back to normal with Ma advising him to find a nice Portuguese girl. It was a start.

*****

That night, as Joe prepared for bed, his phone buzzed with a text message from Wilson:

> *Your truck and things should arrive late tomorrow afternoon.*

> *I've emailed you contact info on a Dr. Sprague.*
> *He works in Boston but has an office up near you in Peabody. He's a friend with Dr Matthews, and he'll check you out and clear you for rehab and exercises when you're ready. Call him tomorrow and set up an appointment next week.*

Finally! Something positive. Joe relaxed. Maybe he could start his recovery in only a few days.

Then his phone buzzed again with another text message. The number, also from St. Louis, was unfamiliar. He hesitated for a moment, then opened it:

> *Thunderstorm has me delayed here in Atlanta. I thought I'd check on you and your arm while I wait for takeoff. How ru doing? Is the arm better? Thinking of you—Melissa*

Joe smiled. He wasn't ready to reply yet. Maybe tomorrow. He thought about grandpa's advice about women. Still, it was comforting to know Melissa cared, even if all she knew about him was that he played baseball and had just had arm surgery.

CHAPTER FORTY-NINE

Joe

Joe woke refreshed the next morning. His arm felt better. He had instructions to change the bandages on his wrist every day. As he slowly removed the bandages from the right wrist, he saw a taut line with no sign of infection where the incision had been. His mind meandered from his injury to his new truck, loaded with his belongings, on its way from Memphis.

He rambled downstairs. It was quiet; his parents had left for work early. He fixed breakfast and ate alone in the kitchen, then called the doctor Wilson had recommended. He made an appointment for the next Monday morning. He sat quietly, waiting for noon to go meet Isaac and Coach Lancaster.

Still wearing the cast on his left arm, driving was difficult. He managed to coax and start his old, rusty truck that hadn't moved in two months, backed out of the driveway, and drove slowly through town and up to the high school. He would sell the old truck, a connection to his past life, once his new truck arrived from Memphis.

Coach Lancaster was waiting for him in his office. Isaac walked in, his cropped-short afro damp from a post-workout shower. Football players, still sweating from their practice, most of whom had played with Joe just a year before, watched the three of them through the office window, awed that a professional athlete was right there in the locker room with them.

"How's the arm, Joe?" Lancaster began.

"A bit better every day. I'm meeting a doctor in Peabody, Monday next week. I hope he clears me to start my rehab."

"Good. Once the doctor says it's okay, let me know, and I can get you in the weight room and give you access to anything here that might help."

"Great. Mostly for the first few weeks, I'll just be stretching and doing exercises. Weights will come later. I've looked over the plan they have for me. Here. Take a look." Joe handed a sheaf of stapled papers from the St. Louis doctor to Lancaster.

Coach Lancaster thumbed through the instructions and nodded. "Whatever you need, you've got it here. How's everything else going?"

Joe sat quietly. He snuck a look at Isaac.

"I told Coach about Jessie," Isaac said.

Joe nodded grimly. "Okay, then. It's out there. Jessie lost the baby, and yesterday she left me. I'm a mess."

Lancaster turned serious, his face stern, but his eyes soft. "I'm a high school phys ed teacher and a baseball and football coach, not a psychologist. Even so, I can tell you I've dealt with this before. Other guys have lost their girlfriends and come to me about it. Maybe not at the level you're dealing with, a pregnancy that went wrong and a girl you were ready to marry, who walked away. These things happen. Joe, everything you do is on a level beyond most other guys; your athletics, particularly your baseball, everything about you. All I can tell you is this. Your arm will heal, maybe stronger than before, if the rehab goes well. So will your heart once you put some distance between this moment with Jessie. Take it a day at a time with her. It will get better."

He paused, assessing Joe's reaction. Joe nodded. Coach went on, "You're not alone. I know your family. I expect they're there for you."

"They are," Joe interrupted.

"And you know I've got your back," Isaac interjected.

Joe nodded and reached out with his right hand to tap Isaac on his shoulder.

Coach Lancaster continued, "I'm always here too. You've got my personal phone number. Call me anytime if things get difficult."

"I'll call you. I'll stay in touch. Thanks, Coach, I'll let you know what the doctor says Monday."

"And when the doc says it's okay, you and I can go over your rehab plan again together. Hold on, Joe. Trust me. Everything is going to be okay."

They stood. Joe shook his coach's hand and left with Isaac for lunch at McDonald's. He had received a new message that his truck would arrive late that afternoon.

CHAPTER FIFTY

All across New England, the school year was starting. At Rock Haven High School, Lucas sat with Jonas in the auditorium, listening to inspirational words from the superintendent. They held paper cups with thin coffee, paper napkins, and sugar-coated donuts, their one free meal from the school department for the year.

Whispering while the superintendent talked, Jonas asked, "You ready? All recharged after summer?"

"Do I have a choice?" Lucas replied, suppressing a chuckle.

"No, I guess not," Jonas also laughed quietly. "What did you and Jennifer and your girls do this summer?"

"We spent it at the beach, mostly. Good, relaxed days for the most part. How about you?"

Jonas smiled, thinking about his summer. "My wife and I spent a couple of weeks with our kids and our grand-kids up at the lake in New Hampshire." His demeanor turned serious. "Have you heard anything from Jessie? How's she doing?"

"Not good. You know she lost the baby. But now she's off to UConn, so at least that's a positive thing."

Later, at lunch before they set up their classrooms, Harvey Lancaster pulled Lucas aside. "Joe and Isaac saw me a few days ago. I heard about Jessie and the baby. That's a shame. And they're not going to get married now."

Lucas smiled. "That's probably good news. It never would have lasted. Also, I suppose it's good that she can run for UConn. But yes, I have to say, it's too bad about the baby and breaking it off with Joe."

"Nah. He's lucky to have gotten away. She's a hell of a runner, but not much as a human being. He's better off without her."

"I agree," Jonas added.

"You're still coaching, Lucas?" interrupted Tibbetts. "I thought you would have learned from everything that happened last spring."

"Of course, I'm still coaching. Are you still teaching art after all your experiences with Gabe?"

"Sports are a waste of time and take too much of the school budget. We're here to help the kids learn. Not play."

"You wouldn't know the first thing about coaching," Lucas said, boiling, having had this dialogue with Tibbetts too many times.

"I don't have to. I know about education. And art," Tibbetts said as he began to walk away.

Still seething, Lucas turned Tibbetts to face him. "You have to get your two cents' worth in? How's your boy Gabriel doing?"

"I wouldn't know. I've spent most of the summer painting in Spain. I haven't seen him, but I expect he's off to college in Maine."

*****

It was the beginning of a new life for the graduated Rock Haven students. Most of the students had dispersed, leaving Joe behind in Rock Haven. Jessie was off to UConn. Isaac was at Northeastern in Boston. Gabe left for college in Maine. Barry got a job a few miles away in Newburyport. Violet and Marie remained as seniors at Rock Haven High School.

Chapter Fifty-one

Jessie

Jessie slouched in the passenger seat, checking messages on her phone, her long legs resting on the dashboard as her mother drove. The Lexus was packed with all of Jessie's clothes and an assortment of things for her dorm room. For miles, neither had spoken.

Finally, as they crossed the border into Connecticut, Patricia asked, "Are you excited to start at UConn?"

Jessie hung up her phone and sat up. "Sure. My next big adventure." She laughed with sarcasm. "They enrolled me in communications classes. Maybe when I graduate, I can become a sports broadcaster. That wouldn't be a bad job. But mostly, I'm looking forward to getting ready for the track season this winter."

"What would you major in? If not communications, what?"

"I'm not sure. I expect I can master any subject, except maybe something really technical like physics. But I need to think about what I'll do after college."

"If you could do anything, what would it be?"

"I don't know," Jessie answered, beginning to slouch again. "I guess sports broadcasting might be it. I'll figure it out over the next few years."

After a mile more of silent travel, Jessie asked, "What did you major in when you went to college?"

"Psychology."

"That prepared you for your sales job?"

"No. Not really. But I met your dad and fell in love, and then we got married."

"And we know how that worked out."

Patricia ignored the comment. "Well, I'm in love again and about to get married again. It'll be better this time."

"Let's hope so," Jessie replied with a sarcastic edge to her voice.

"You'll be able to get away over the Columbus Day weekend to come to DC for the wedding? I still want you to be my maid of honor."

"Of course, Mom. I was planning on it. I've got the dress and shoes packed in the back of the car. Let me ask you. If I meet someone here, can I bring him as my plus one?"

"Not that Goncalves boy? You did the right thing there. Yes, you can bring a new boy as your plus one. Just let me know, and I'll make sure to hold a room at the hotel for him. You and I will be about the only people who need to stay in a hotel. The guests will mostly be Michael's DC friends and people from his office there. I don't really have many friends from Rock Haven. It's going to be a really small wedding, seeing as it's the second time around for both of us. We would have gotten married in Rock Haven, but our life will be in DC once I sell the house."

"Fine. I'll let you know if I meet a nice boy here at UConn."

"When you do find a new boy, send me his name and I'll book a flight for both of you."

I'm sure I can find a good boy here at UConn, Jessie thought to herself. I've never had trouble finding a boyfriend. He's here somewhere. I know that. Maybe on the track team? This should be fun. Now that Joe's gone, I can have some new adventures!

Chapter Fifty-two

Isaac

Isaac settled into his apartment with Juan in the Back Bay of Boston. It was a seedy second-floor walk-up a few blocks south of the Northeastern Campus in a building filled with other students from the many Back Bay college campuses. He had enrolled in all his classes, focusing on introductory education. If things worked out, he would graduate, teach high school, and coach baseball. Just like Coach Lancaster.

Living in a city was an adjustment after the small-town life in Rock Haven. He felt claustrophobic, surrounded by strangers, the buildings looming, the constant traffic and noise. It took a few days before he began to relax and draw energy from the crowds.

He loved his classes and his new teammates. He couldn't wait for the fall baseball practices to start. The word from Juan was that the games would begin during spring break in Florida against college teams from the Carolinas and Florida. There was even a game scheduled with the Red Sox during their spring training.

He missed his old friends, most of all Marie, who was a senior now at Rock Haven High. And Joe, of course. But the summer on the Cape, away from home, had prepared him for independence. He checked in daily with his family and with Joe. There were regular weekly calls to Marie, long talks where they finally reconciled the trouble that followed her disclosure of Jessie's pregnancy to her friend the previous spring. He went home most weekends, did his laundry, ate dinner with his family, and spent the rest of his time with Marie. She and Rock Haven were his base.

CHAPTER FIFTY-THREE

The doctor from Boston cleared Joe to begin his exercise program and rehab. He was booked for three weeks at a facility in Peabody. The therapist, Stacy, a lean, fit, dark-haired woman, was supportive and encouraging, kneading his arm, stretching it to extend the range of motion, and apologizing whenever she saw Joe wince with pain. "Are you okay?"

"Yes, keep doing what you have to do. I want to get back to throwing as soon as possible, and if it hurts a bit right now, it's just something I need to work through."

With three weeks of therapy completed, Joe was ready to begin weight training. He had a list of exercises to do to continue PT. And he had the weight-lifting plan from the Cardinals. As he was leaving the medical rehab facility for the last time, Stacy pulled him aside. "You're going to be fine, Joe. I can't wait to see what you do when you're able to play baseball again. Here's my number. The regular scheduled therapy is done, but call me if you need anything more."

Her eyes met his expectantly. Her message was obvious.

Joe smiled and took the number. "I will," he said, but he was thinking of Grandpa Joao's words of caution about women, and of Melissa who texted him at least once a week. Joe replied every time.

In the metal-walled toolshed behind his house, he found the old bicycle he had ridden as a child until his early teens. He began riding every morning from his house to the high school, looking like a trained circus bear on the small, rusty bike. He could have driven in his new truck, and he knew he looked ridiculous on the bike. It was good exercise for his legs, and strong legs were important for having a good fastball. The way he saw things, the daily bike rides were part of his therapy. Steps on the road back to playing professional baseball.

With the money from his signing bonus, membership at any of the shiny fitness gyms in the nearby towns was possible, but they seemed to be filled with middle-aged women in pastel leotards doing aerobics, and narcissistic body-building young men, their perfectly tanned arms, oiled and decorative, but useless for real work or sports. He felt out of place, so he returned to his old, familiar workout room at the high school.

He met Coach Lancaster late every morning at the school. Lancaster let him into the weight room and designated a football player, one of Joe's old teammates, to spot him. Joe's workouts were hard on Mondays, Wednesdays, and Fridays, with light lifting and stretching on Tuesdays and Thursdays. He took the weekends off to rest. He began to feel his old strength returning. Progressively, he began increasing the weight he lifted. Cautiously, he went through the motion of throwing a baseball, striding forward from his set position and swinging his arm. He felt no pain and craved the feel of a ball in his hand.

It's working, he thought. I can't wait to start throwing again.

Chapter Fifty-Four

Jessie trotted along the track next to a lane filled with low hurdles, spaced for the hundred-meter women's race. She began doing drills to practice snapping her trail leg down quickly as she passed each hurdle. Two lanes over, Darren, a tall, lean Black man, with tight bunches of muscles prominent on his biceps and calves, ran a similar drill next to high hurdles spaced wider than Jessie's, for the men's one hundred-ten-meter hurdles race. Finishing the drills, Jessie and Darren moved over a lane and ran through their full hurdles races twice, focused on using the aggressive trail leg motion they had practiced. The indoor season was still weeks away, but they were ready for the short hurdle straight-aways of indoor track.

Walking together back from the track after practice, Darren asked, "Want to grab a bite to eat again tonight?"

"Sure," Jessie smiled, enjoying his deep voice and Jamaican accent, "and I want to ask you something."

Darren stopped and faced her. "What?" A brief smile of anticipation flickered across his perfectly symmetrical ebony face.

"Columbus Day weekend. Do you have plans?"

"I can't think of anything."

"My mom's getting remarried in DC that weekend. I'm the maid of honor. Would you come with me? It'll be fun."

"Why not? We've gone out a bit. Sure. How would we get there?"

"My mom says we can fly from Hartford to Dulles. She'll set you up with a hotel room while we're there, and pay for our flights."

"Sounds like fun. And we'd be back here right after the weekend for our classes and workouts?"

"Of course."

That evening, Jessie called her mom. "Hi, Mom. You said I could bring a boy to the wedding if I met someone nice here at UConn?"

"Yes. And, you met someone?"

"Yes. His name is Darren MacKenzie. Can you book our flights and hold a room for him in the hotel?"

"Darren MacKenzie?" Patricia jotted the name on a pad of paper. "Good. I'll take care of the arrangements. I have you all set in a room already, right next to mine. I'll book another room for your friend, Darren. I'll send you the flight arrangements as soon as I have you and your friend booked. I'll meet you at the airport and drive you and Darren to the hotel. Michael and I are so excited. It's only a couple of weeks away!"

Patricia hung up and sat back, smiling, thinking. MacKenzie. Perfect. Jessie's finally come to her senses after her fling with that Portuguese boy.

*****

Two weeks later, while waiting to board the plane in Hartford, Darren asked Jessie, "Have you flown much before now?"

"Only a bit. My mom took me to Disney when I was little and to Cancun for winter vacation a couple of years ago. And we went to Europe for a river cruise when I was in middle school. How about you?"

244

"Also, only a few flights. My family can't afford to fly places. But there's really no other way for me to get from Jamaica to Connecticut. A UConn booster pays for my flights at the start of the year, at Christmas, and again at the end of the year when I go home. So, this is a little new for me."

"A booster paying for your flights? Is that legal?"

"I don't know. But I need help getting here."

*****

Patricia was waiting when Jessie came out of the gate at Dulles airport. She embraced her maid of honor, happy, smiling, radiant, thrilled that all the wedding plans were working out perfectly. Then she saw the handsome Black athletic man waiting a step behind Jessie.

"Mom, this is my friend, Darren. He runs the hurdles at UConn. We've been seeing each other since the first week of practice."

Patricia put on her gracious face. "It's nice to meet you, Darren. Where are you from?"

"Jamaica. I've been at UConn two years. I plan to get a job in financial services in the States after I graduate."

Patricia noted the slight lilting accent that confirmed his Jamaican background. "You brought a suit for the wedding? And a necktie?"

"Of course."

That day, Patricia looked for an opportunity to confront Jessie about her choice of a new boyfriend, but due to the constant activities the day before the wedding, at the rehearsal, and the rehearsal dinner, she never had a chance to be alone with her. Jessie made sure of it.

245

She finally cornered Jessie as they were heading back to their hotel rooms.

"Darren seems nice. But let me put it out there. Being Black and foreign, what sort of a future does he offer you?"

"Mom, you're about to get married. I don't want to fight about it. Not now. I like Darren, and he likes me. He's a great hurdler and a top student. He'll graduate in a year or two and go into international trade or banking or something. He'll probably be very successful and make a lot of money. And you have to admit he's good-looking. What's not to like?"

"I always told you that you can grow up to be anything you want to be. Have everything you want if you work for it. You can date any man you want to. Why him? Is this what you really want?"

"Right now, yes. We like each other. Good night, Mom." Jessie turned away and walked down the hall to her room.

Frustrated, Patricia went to bed, trying to forget Jessie's situation and instead think about her wedding the next day.

Later, an hour after everybody had turned in, she heard voices through the connecting door. Maybe Jessie turned on the television, Patricia hoped. Then, even though she tried not to eavesdrop, it was clear from the accent of the male voice that Darren had joined Jessie.

*****

Jessie embraced Darren and said, "I'm so glad you were able to come to the wedding with me. Let's get some sleep. Tomorrow will be a big day."

Lying in bed with Darren, Jessie's mind wandered. Can Mom hear us through the door? I don't know and I don't care. Tonight, Darren is mine. Mom can have her day tomorrow.

Chapter Fifty-Five

Joe

The doctor in Boston had said Joe could begin light throwing five months after the surgery. The Cardinals planned to have Dr. Matthews check Joe's arm in St. Louis in March, a bit more than six months after the surgery. If he were healthy, they would have him work out with the Cardinals all spring and do some light throwing at their spring training facility in Florida.

At Christmas, it was still less than five months since the surgery, Joe noted, but he felt good and Isaac was home from college. Bundled against the New England cold, they carefully played catch between the street and the snow-banked curb in front of Joe's house. Joe felt great. They chatted as they threw, their conversation punctuated by the crack of the ball hitting their gloves, stiff and hard from the cold.

"You doing okay with Jessie being gone?" Isaac asked.

"Absolutely. I think of her once in a while, but less and less."

"That's good."

Isaac caught and tossed again. "Do you ever think about losing the baby?"

Joe tossed the ball back, gently and relaxed, striding into the throw but taking it easy on his arm. He was careful not to use any of the twisting motion he used for the slider or the curve. "Yes."

Joe continued. "If the baby had survived, it would almost be time for the birth. I think about that a little. Looking back on it, everything last spring and summer revolved around her. The pregnancy, her losing the baby, everything. I feel like I have more in my life now, with her gone. It's odd. I really have nothing right now. No girlfriend, no baby, no job, no school, but I feel better about things than I did at the end of the summer."

"It's your life now, not having to worry about Jessie. No burdens."

"You're right. Every decision I made back then fell apart. Taking the job with the Cardinals rather than going to college, Jessie and me planning to get married, all of it. And then she left for Connecticut. I don't even know if she came back to Rock Haven at Thanksgiving or now at Christmas."

"Violet told me Jessie's house is for sale."

Joe nodded. "I'd heard that, so I drove by there a week or so ago. I saw the For Sale sign. Not a smart time of year to try to sell a house, the dead of winter in New England. I heard her mom married her boss in D.C."

"How's the arm feel?" Isaac asked, noting how cautious Joe was with every throw. "You look like you're holding back a bit."

"Fine. No pain, nothing. I'm not going to push it for a while. Not yet. But I think I'm going to be okay."

"With Jessie, too?"

"Yeah. I'm okay with that."

"You got a new girl?"

"No. I know she's out there. The right one will be there when I'm ready."

Joe smiled to himself, thinking about his exchange of texts with Melissa, now several times a day. He thought about Melissa as much as he thought about rejoining the Cardinals.

The Cardinals want me to go through St. Louis on my way to Spring Training and get checked by the doctor there. Maybe I'll try to connect with Melissa while I'm in St. Louis. I'll take a couple of extra days and maybe see her before I go on to Florida. It's only a month away. Let's see how things go with her these next few weeks.

Isaac noticed the shift in Joe's demeanor and also smiled, but said nothing. He knew Joe and understood. Joe would let him in when he thought the time was right.

Chapter Fifty-six

Lucas

Following his habitual route, Lucas Knox ran at dawn on the day of Christmas Eve, as he always had, morning after morning, in all seasons and all weather. His feet knew the way after so many runs over the same streets. It was empty and silent; most of the town was already on vacation. A shallow dusting of dirty snow from the storm two days earlier coated the frozen roads.

The quiet allowed him time to think about the year that was ending. Overall, it had been a good year, he thought. At least until it all went to hell late in the spring and throughout the summer. Still, my track teams won last spring, and again with cross-country this fall. And I have a wonderful wife and a beautiful family. If everything is perfect, why do I still feel unsettled by what happened six months ago? I need to let it go, put it in the past.

Cutting through The Heights, he was, as always, overwhelmed by the wealth of the people who lived there. He surveyed glittering Christmas decorations above wide, snow-covered lawns, and oversized wreaths with bows in every window. One of the houses was dark. The driveway had been plowed but was covered with several inches of fresh snow. This house had no decorations, only a *For Sale* sign in the middle of the lawn. It occurred to him suddenly that this was Jessie's old house.

She's gone. Moved away. I haven't heard from her since she left for Connecticut. I've followed her results online, but not a word from her. I know she cleared six feet for the first time last week in a meet down there. I've got to let that go, too. Every Olympic-caliber athlete had a high school coach somewhere in their past. Jessie's moved on. No matter. As talented as she was, she turned out to be an awful lot of trouble for far too many people.

Cruising out of the wealth of The Heights, he turned downhill, back into town. His mind methodically traced his route.

I'll be running through the inner harbor neighborhoods in a couple of minutes. Their homes and their lives are nothing like what I just passed in the Heights. The people in The Heights have more money, but are they really better off than the families in the inner harbor? I live between the two neighborhoods. My income is adequate for this time in my life. Do the rich feel the same unease I'm feeling? Is money at the heart of my discontent? No. I have enough. It shouldn't matter which side of the town you live in, should it? But there are lines separating everyone, it would seem.

Maybe it has to do with race. Or opportunity. The rich always seem to get richer. Blacks, working class, and poor whites, immigrants? They all seem to live in the inner harbor. Do any minorities have homes in The Heights?

Turning for the final mile home, his thoughts turned to the day ahead. I'll probably bump into Jonas and his family at the Christmas Eve service tonight. He's undeniably my best friend at the school. He knows how tough it was for me deciding what to do about Jessie last spring. Everything was so orderly and predictable until all that blew up. I get along with all the teachers, really, except maybe Tibbetts, the art teacher, who thinks that anything other than art is a waste of time.

Lucas returned to the warmth of his home, dejected, depressed, wondering if any of what he did as a teacher and a coach mattered at all.

"Daddy, Santa's coming!" Sophie screamed, pointing at the stockings hanging on the fireplace. "Tonight! He'll be here tonight!"

Lucas grinned and picked up his youngest girl, hugging her, spinning so her feet swung out. In that moment, everything was right again.

"Daddy," she screamed again. "Don't drop me! And eww! You're all sweaty and smelly."

Lucas eased Sophie back to the floor. "Merry Christmas, little one."

*****

Jonas Brown pulled Lucas aside as they were leaving the church that evening. Jennifer herded the girls off to the car, all of them struggling to contain their excitement. "Merry Christmas, Lucas," Jonas said, wrapping his arm around his friend's shoulder, pulling him in for a manly embrace.

"Merry Christmas to you, too," said Lucas.

Jonas stepped back, assessing his morose friend. "You appear down, not like your usual self. It's Christmas Eve, and you've got the kids waiting for Santa. How can anything be getting you down?"

"It's the end of the year and I've been thinking a lot about all that happened this year," said Lucas, shuffling his feet in the slush in the parking lot. "Does what we do as teachers really matter?"

"You had a great year. The championship last spring, a good academic year at the high school. And, outside of school, too. Emma starting kindergarten. Sophie in pre-school."

"I suppose. But there was all the trouble last spring. Jessie, her pregnancy, losing the baby."

"She pulled you into all that. I know you truly care about your students, but when they screw up, you have to let it go. It's over.

You can't let that drag you down. Certainly not now on Christmas Eve."

"I know. But she had nowhere else to turn. Her mom's never there for her. Maybe Violet was trying to help, but Jessie needed an adult. Someone had to look out for her."

"Let me ask you a question," Jonas said, turning Lucas by the elbow so they faced each other. "Do you remember who was the MVP of last year's Super Bowl?"

"No."

"Do you remember who won the Oscar for Best Female Actor last year?"

"No."

"Can you tell me who won the Nobel Prize for Medicine?"

"No."

"They were all celebrities of the highest order less than a year ago, but you've forgotten them. Can you tell me the name of a teacher who mattered to you when you were a kid, and maybe still does?"

"Sure. Miss Hobbs, my seventh-grade math teacher. She was a great teacher."

"What made her great?"

"I don't know. She knew me and seemed to care about how I did in math."

"Do you see my point? You're a good teacher and a hell of a coach. You do make a difference. Move on and don't let Jessie's issues get to you. You did what you could."

Lucas nodded, absorbing Jonas's lesson. "I guess."

Jonas added, "Everyone needs to know that they've left their mark on the world. That the things they've done matter. Your biggest legacy is your family, Jennifer, and your little girls. But your students and what they'll accomplish after graduation are also part of your mark on the world."

"Thanks, Jonas. Merry Christmas!"

Lucas got in his car and reached to the back seat for his girls. "We've got to get home and get you two to bed. Santa's probably on his way already!"

Jennifer reached over and rested a supportive hand on Lucas' arm. She hadn't heard his conversation with Jonas, but she understood.

CHAPTER FIFTY-SEVEN

Joe

In early February, the Cardinals scheduled Joe for a flight to St. Louis to meet Dr. Matthews. Joe alerted Melissa, and she made sure to work his flight.

Wilson met Joe at the airport and accompanied him to the doctor's office. Dr. Matthews did a new MRI, compared it to the old one from before the surgery, and showed the two images to Joe and Wilson. Then he smiled and nodded.

"Things look good," he said. "Let's check your flexibility and strength."

He checked Joe, pushing and pulling and kneading his arm, and finally declared, "You should be able to begin throwing. No twisting motions for a while, so no sliders or curves. But work on your straight throws. Long toss and easy throwing from the mound with the fastball and changeup. If all goes well, you can begin to throw your breaking ball again in a month or so."

Joe didn't tell the doctor or Wilson that he'd been doing some easy throwing with Isaac for two months.

Dr. Matthews clapped Joe on the back and shook Wilson's hand as they left his office. "I'll be eager to see how you do with the comeback. I'll try to get to a game when they call you up to St. Louis."

Wilson, grinning, shook Joe's hand in the parking lot of the doctor's office. "You're on the way back, big guy! Spring training starts next week in Florida. I've got you on a flight next Monday, and I've

"

booked you a place near the ballpark in Jupiter. You said you wanted a couple of days here in St. Louis to visit friends?"

"Yes. Thanks."

"A girl?" Wilson understood his star.

"Yeah. I met her here last year."

"What happened to the Rock Haven girlfriend?"

"That's over. In the past. I'm moving on. She's off to college now."

"Okay. Well then. I'll meet you when you arrive in Florida."

*****

Leaning on the balcony railing, Joe looked out across the low surf at the sunrise. The ocean glare was intense, more than he was used to, even after years of staring into the summer sun as he set out on the fishing boats at dawn from Rock Haven with his father and uncles. Melissa joined him, taking his arm, gently stroking the scar on his elbow. They watched a line of pelicans, black dots against the light, passing above the water, dipping and lifting as they followed the shoreline wind.

"How's the arm, Joe?" she asked. It was a frequent question initiating a daily discussion.

"It's been feeling good. I'm still just throwing straight, long toss, and nothing but easy fastballs from the mound, no breaking stuff, working on my form and my follow-through. I'm still cautious about snapping off any sliders or curves. I worry about how that might feel and don't want to get hurt again. I remember the pain." For a moment, his brow furrowed with the memory.

Melissa stepped back and assessed Joe, looking him in the eyes. She continued touching the fading purple welt of the scar inside his left

258

elbow. "The doctor back in St. Louis said it was fine. He said it healed well, and it's solid. Right?"

"Yeah. He did some procedure where he could see what it looks like inside my arm. I don't really understand it, but I trust him. I've asked the coaches if they think we could start working my slider back in with my regular pitches. They told me, 'Not yet'. They've been with other guys recovering from Tommy John, so they'll know when the time is right."

"You're not going north when the team leaves in a few days?"

Joe frowned, suddenly despondent again. "No. I want to get rolling, but they say no. They'll keep me down here a month or so, doing my rehab work and light throwing every couple of days. If all goes well, I'll probably go back to Memphis again, sometime this summer. I don't know what the timeline would be for me getting up to St. Louis. Maybe late this season. Maybe not until next year. They don't want to rush me."

Melissa brightened, her smile lighting her face. She let go of Joe's arm and ran a hand through her light brown hair, catching the cool morning breeze, tasting salt. "Oh, Joe. Don't get discouraged. Think of how much you've done just in the few weeks since you came here after seeing the doctor in St. Louis. You're on the way back."

"It helps that you're here with me," he said. He wrapped a massive arm around her and pulled her to him. "I'd be facing this all alone if you hadn't flown down here."

"You're not all alone. You talk to your parents almost every night, and you've got Isaac, too. He texts you all the time."

"Yeah. And my coach back in Rock Haven stays in touch, too. They're always in my corner. But, they're not here. You've been a real help. You can't imagine how good it is to come home from the stadium every night and find you here. I need people to help me get through this. You're the best."

"Is it okay if I visit you again while you're still in Florida? I've got flights I need to work starting on Sunday. I've got to get back to St. Louis tomorrow and go back to work."

Joe grinned, teasing. "You enjoy waking up and seeing this view of the ocean. Hanging out on the beach while I'm off working at the ballpark. That's what you like."

She smiled back at Joe, leaned up, and kissed him. "Sure! That's why I want to come back and visit here. The beach. It's also not so bad waking up next to you in the morning."

"If they move me up to Memphis in a month or so, would you visit me there as well? There's no beach in Memphis."

"Of course I'd go to Memphis."

Joe smiled. He remembered Grandpa Joao's words of caution about women, but he also thought of how Melissa checked his scar every day and talked him through his recovery.

"That'll be the real test," he said. "Throwing the slider and the curve without pain. And then, I'm going to have to learn the mechanics all over again to make my delivery look the same on all my pitches: the fastball, the changeup, and the breaking balls. If the hitters pick up on a different motion on any of my pitches, if they know what pitch is coming, they'll crush it. I've got to relearn everything. I've still got a long way to go. They say the last thing to come back is my control. I can't be walking a lot of batters."

"I'll be there with you, here or in Memphis, while you work your way back. And, I'll be there when you come back to St. Louis."

Joe kissed her. "That's all good."

He looked out over the ocean, finding the calm he always felt with the sea in front of him. *I love the ocean. If I spend most of the rest of my life in St. Louis, will I be okay? Maybe with Melissa? And, I can always go back to Rock Haven in the off-season.*

"Could I ask you something?" Joe turned, facing Melissa.

"Of course. Anything, Joe."

"Where do you think we're going? We've known each other almost a year, and we've gone back and forth with the phone calls and text messages. But really, we've only been together off and on for a month or so. What happens now?"

Melissa leaned on the balcony railing for a moment, silent.

Turning back, face to face with Joe, she said. "I don't know. I guess we're both still figuring it out. What I'm sure of is this. The day we first met, when you were starting out with the Cardinals, I had a feeling about you. I felt it before you sat down across from me, and that little boy when we were waiting to board our flight in Boston. And I knew you were special as soon as we talked. I still have that feeling. I let things happen in their own time. With you and Jessie. With your arm and the surgery. Even now that we're together. I simply let it happen. All of it. If it's meant to be, I figured somehow it would work out for us. So far it has. How about you?"

"I stayed away from you at first. I had Jessie, and I wasn't going to get it started with another girl while I had her. But I always was thinking of you, even back then. And when it fell apart with her.... Well, you know that whole story."

"Yes. So, what do we do now?"

Joe smiled. "I guess we take it one day at a time and see how it goes. If it's meant to be, we'll know for sure at some point. So, let's keep on as we've been. Visit me while I'm here. Come see me when I'm in Memphis. And I'll be sure to see you whenever I'm in St. Louis."

"That works for me. Now for today…I bet you're hungry right now. You're always hungry."

Joe perked up. "You know me too well! Let's go get breakfast!"

Chapter Fifty-eight

Lucas, Isaac, and Violet

As he did every year, Lucas sat at graduation with Jennifer. Sitting behind them were Jonas Brown and Harvey Lancaster, also with their wives. The ceremony began and proceeded along the familiar path of all graduations. The same as a year before, with the graduations of Joe, Isaac, and Jessie. It was always the same, as far back as any of them could remember: a constant in their lives.

After it was over, Lucas, Lancaster, and Jonas wandered towards the parking lot across the lawn next to the stadium. Their wives followed, gathering their children, allowing their men time to talk about school.

"Mission accomplished," announced Lancaster. "Another crew of graduates launched out into the world."

"Do you think we'll ever see any of them again? Do we matter to them?" asked Lucas, repeating the question that had plagued him for nearly a year, ever since the troubles with Jessie.

"Some of them, probably yes," Jonas suggested. "There are always a few who come back to visit."

As if on cue, Isaac appeared from the crowd alongside Violet and Barry, who had graduated a year earlier. Marie, also newly graduated, was hanging on to Isaac's arm. Violet and Marie both still wore their red gowns, unzipped and flapping. They carried the mortar boards. Violet had gold cords draped around her neck, the tassels swinging knee high. The cords signified her ranking at the very top of her class.

"Hi, Coach," Isaac said, grinning as he approached Lancaster.

"Hi, Coach," Violet mimicked, facing Lucas.

Lucas laughed. "We were just saying, will we ever see them again, and here you all are."

Isaac continued, "With my baby sister graduating, and my girlfriend too, I had to come home. I'll be playing down on the Cape again this summer, but I have a few days off before we start."

Lancaster asked, "How was your year at Northeastern?"

"Great. I love my classes."

"Baseball went well, too?"

"Yeah. I had a good year, but I'm really working on my studies. That's what matters. I've decided I'm going into Secondary Ed after I graduate in a few more years. My plan is to come back here and teach and coach."

"You want my job?" Lancaster smiled. "You can have it. The team struggled this year without you and Joe."

"Speaking of Joe," Isaac turned serious. "I hear from him every few days. Does everyone know how he's doing?"

Lancaster nodded. "He sent me a message last week. He's got a lot going on. The Cardinals had him at their training facility in Florida, doing some light throwing all spring. They just moved him up to Memphis. He's working out there now. They think he might be ready to start real pitching again by later this summer."

"His arm is strong again," Isaac stated. "I lifted with him a bit this past winter. Have you heard how everything else is going?"

Lancaster laughed again. "Oh, yes, did he tell you about his new girlfriend?"

Now Isaac joined in the laughter. "The flight attendant from St. Louis?"

"That's the one. It's such a stereotype, right? The pro athlete who settles in with a flight attendant? Sounds like she's spending a lot of time in Memphis these days. She was vacationing in Florida earlier this spring, but she's followed Joe north to Memphis."

Isaac turned serious. "Sure. A stereotype. But he's really taken with her. And she with him."

Violet joined the conversation. "So, he seems to have gotten over Jessie."

"Oh, yes!" Lancaster and Isaac said together and laughed again.

"You know Joe," Isaac said. "He's probably sure he's in love. Again."

"Coach," Violet asked, changing the subject and turning to Lucas. With her graduation, the indistinct barrier that was always there between students and teachers, athletes and coaches was less clear. "Have you heard anything from Jessie?"

Lucas suddenly became serious. "I told you the little I know about her at practice a couple of weeks ago. Since then, I haven't heard a thing from her, not a word, not a text or anything. Not that she contacts me much anyway. But I follow the college track results. She's doing great down at UConn. Clearing six feet regularly and winning a lot of hurdles races. Aside from her athletic success, I don't know anything more."

"Maybe I'll bump into her at a meet next year. I'll be running for Simmons College. At least I plan to run right now. Simmons isn't exactly competing on the same level as UConn, but we might both be at some of the big invitational meets. I love track, but I'm on an academic scholarship to study nursing, and I might not have time to really focus on training for track."

"It's a shame if you can't continue competing at a high level since you won both the hundred and the two hundred at the New England's. But that's all right," confirmed Lucas. "Do what makes sense to you, what you need to do. I agree, nursing school is more important in the long run."

"I think I'd like to go into neonatal care or OBGYN nursing, or something similar. I think being with Jessie throughout her situation steered me in that direction."

Jonas finally joined the conversation, turning back to his fellow teachers. "Thinking back to all the trouble a year ago, last spring, we seem to know what everyone involved in that mess is up to now. Except Gabe Sloan. Tibbetts isn't here to tell us. I was the advisor for the yearbook, and Gabe contributed some of the portraits of the seniors. He dropped out of college, but he's got a photography studio downtown on Washington Street. He seems to be doing okay."

Lucas frowned for a moment. "Tibbetts never comes to any school functions unless it's an art show. You weren't expecting him here today for graduation, were you?"

"No, not really. But he might have the inside scoop on Gabe."

Violet offered, "All we know is this. Gabe opened a photography shop and studio down on Washington Street. It seems to be working for him. It appears he's not dealing drugs anymore. He's running a legitimate business and keeping his nose clean."

She continued. "It's not all good news about Gabe, though. There are rumors that photos he took of some senior girls weren't just portraits. For no extra charge, he would offer to take... how do I say this, questionable photos of some of the girls for them to give to their boyfriends."

"Yeah," Marie spoke up. "He asked me if I wanted to pose for him. I said, 'No'."

"If I see him, I'll kill him!" said Isaac.

"Let it go. I didn't pose for him."

Isaac shook his head dismissively, but he wasn't smiling.

Jonas said, "It's good that Gabe is doing okay. He finally seems to have turned things around. It seems that Gabe lives in an apartment above his store."

Jennifer joined the group, herding the little ones. Leaning toward Lucas, hugging him, she offered her insight. "It's really too bad about the Sloans getting divorced."

Lucas picked up Emma and hugged her, trying to shelter her from the dangers of the world. "A lot of marriages end that way. It's too common. Yes, it's a shame, and it must be hard on the two boys."

"Take care of our own families," suggested Jonas. "Raising our kids is the hardest job in the world! That's what matters. Life is too short to get wrapped up in all this drama."

CHAPTER FIFTY-NINE

Joe

Melissa was always there. Whenever there was a break in her flight schedule, she met Joe wherever he was. A couple of days here and there, a long weekend when she could. First in Florida, and later in Memphis. She met him in St. Louis the day he was promoted to the Cardinals near the end of the season in September. From then on, she only saw her roommates when the Cardinals were out of town.

*****

Joe returned to Rock Haven after the season. It had been a good year for him. His arm felt strong, and he began sifting his slider back into his complete arsenal of pitches. After two months pitching in Memphis, he was called up to St. Louis the first week in September. In the waning days of the season, he started four games, winning three of them. His arm withstood the workload with no pain.

When Joe returned to Rock Haven, he brought Melissa. Early November cold and a sudden flurry of snow left Rock Haven desolate. Inside his home, it was warm. His family sat at the kitchen table: his mom, dad, and Joao Senior. Joe stepped forward and put his hands on his mom's shoulders. Melissa stood behind him.

"Mom, Dad, Grandpa, this is my girlfriend, Melissa. I've told you all about her on the phone, but I figured it was time for you to meet her and for Melissa to see where I'm from. It's hard for her to imagine what it's like here without ever having visited Rock Haven."

"Well, young lady," Joao Senior began. "Now that you've had a look at Rock Haven, what do you think?"

"We just got here an hour ago. Joe gave me a quick tour, driving around town. I saw his high school and the ball field where he played. I can't say that I really got a feel for it, though. It was all under a bit of snow. We stopped for a few minutes up in that little park on the bluff. Joe said it's one of his favorite places in town. So, I can't really say I know the town yet. But I love the ocean."

His dad, Joao Junior, picked up. "What did you think of the fish packing plant? That's where we all work. There or out on the boats."

Melissa answered cautiously. "Again, I can't really say. We drove by on our way here. A lot of the boats were tied up at the dock."

"That's because today's Saturday. During the week, they'd all be out, even in this weather. Sometimes in the good weather, they're out on the weekend too."

"Where are you from?" Helena started. "Joe says he met you in St. Louis. Is that where you're from?"

"That's where I live now. I was raised in Iowa. My parents still live near Council Bluffs. It's not a big town, maybe a lot like Rock Haven."

"Really?" Helena's eyebrows raised. "Not much of a coastline in Iowa, not much of a fishing business."

Flustered, Melissa responded. "No, we're farmers in Iowa. But a small town is a small town, right? Anyway, I live in St. Louis now. That's where most of my flights are based."

Joe stepped back in. "Mom, Dad, Grandpa, Melissa and I really love each other. We're talking about maybe getting married a year from now. We want to take our time to be sure. But we want to get married. That's really why I brought her here. I want you all to get to know her."

There was a quiet moment in the kitchen. Joe's pronouncement was not a surprise. They had heard him talk about Melissa during most of his phone calls. Joao Senior stood and hugged first Joe and then Melissa. "Welcome to the family."

Dad stood and hugged Melissa as well. If Joao Senior accepted her, she was in. "You'd better get used to the cold, young lady. It's only November now. Wait till January if you really want to know what a New England winter's like."

"Oh, it gets really cold in Iowa, too. And we get a lot of snow. Maybe not like here, but I know a bit about winter."

"Come on then," instructed Helena. "If you're going to marry my boy, I need to teach you how to cook fish. When Joe told me you were coming to visit, I figured I'd make my famous Caldeirada. It's a fish stew. But you need to make it the right way. Cod, mussels, and do you know about saffron?"

"No, but I can learn."

"Okay. Let's get started. It doesn't take long to make it, but you want to let it simmer a couple of hours to get the flavor right." Helena led Melissa to the refrigerator in the garage to retrieve the fish, caught by her husband the day before.

CHAPTER SIXTY

The wedding was in Melissa's home town in Iowa two months later, just before spring training. It was a small ceremony in the church she had attended as a girl.

Joe flew Isaac and Marie, along with Violet and Barry to Council Bluffs for the wedding weekend. Joao Senior, Joao and Helena, and his uncles Gualter and Hermano, and their respective wives were on the same flight. Harvey Lancaster took a couple of days off from his teaching job to fly out as well.

Wilson sat alone in a back pew. Joe's new contract, negotiated by an agent he had met through a teammate, gave him more than enough money to fly them all in and put them up in a Best Western.

Melissa's parents were quietly overwhelmed by both the celebrity status of their new son-in-law and his boisterous Portuguese family. Melissa's sister was the maid of honor. A high school friend was a bridesmaid. Isaac was Joe's best man. Her brother stood alongside Isaac as an usher. Helena cried quietly with happiness during the ceremony. So did Joao Senior.

Her family filled one of the tables at the reception. The Rock Haven crowd filled two tables. A few dozen other friends, including several of Melissa's friends from high school and two of Melissa's flight attendant roommates, comprised the rest of the guests.

A day after the wedding, Joe and Melissa flew to Jupiter for what they called their first honeymoon. Once the season started, they made their home in Joe's townhouse in St. Louis.

Eight months later, when the season ended, Joe and Melissa took two weeks for their real honeymoon, first in the Azores and then in the Douro River Valley in Portugal.

A year later, a baby was born. It was a girl they named Helena.

CHAPTER SIXTY-ONE

Violet

By the spring of her freshman year at Simmons College, Violet faced a turning point. She was a star on the small track team at the college, but she realized she was more consumed by her studies than by her training. The workouts she had done the year before in high school had been more intense than her college training. She rarely had time for weight training. Her times in track meets suffered.

She saw Jessie once, at a big invitational meet. When she went over to talk to her, Jessie was briefly cordial, giving her old friend a quick hug. "How are you, Violet? You're on the track team at Simmons? Nice."

"Yes," Violet answered, pointing out the college name across her singlet. It seemed to her an obvious, inane question to ask if she was on the team. "How're you doing?"

"Great. I win a lot of hurdles races and almost always win the high jump. You?"

"I win a bit. I'm more interested in my nursing studies. To be honest, that takes more of my time and energy."

"Oh, I understand. I'm majoring in Communications. That's at least as important as my training."

The two old friends and teammates then stood looking at each other, realizing they had nothing more to say.

"Well, it's great to see you, Violet. I've got to get ready for the high jump. Have a good meet."

Jessie turned her back and walked away. Violet headed for the start of the long sprint.

Violet competed through the spring season. She realized that, along with her classroom time and studying, she would need time to spend in hospitals and doctors' offices, beginning her next year of college. She worried about how she would find time for running, too.

Mid-winter, her sophomore year, she quit the track team. The coach was disappointed, but not surprised.

*****

Months later, Violet cut along the edge of the Fenway from her dorm at Simmons College and found her way to the sidewalk restaurant on Boylston Street across from the Prudential tower. Isaac was already basking in the autumn sunshine at a table with Marie at his side. He stood and hugged his sister. Violet gave Marie an appraising look, wondering what she was doing in Boston. Shouldn't she be in her classes at Salem State?

Catching Violet's look, Marie explained. "I took the day off at Salem State. I only have one class on Friday morning, and it's early, so I caught the first train I could and walked over from the station." A duffel bag sat on the pavement under the table next to her feet.

"How are your classes?" Isaac asked, sitting down next to Marie, but addressing his sister. "You filled me in a bit when we talked on the phone last week. But tell me more. You quit the track team? I never expected that!"

"Fine," Violet answered. "My classes are fine. As a junior, I'm getting into the more advanced things. I miss track, the daily training, the fatigue even. But it was hard enough balancing my studies with my track training as a freshman. Last year, it got to be too much. It made sense this year to concentrate on academics. I'll be starting

276

rotations in hospitals and doctor offices in a few weeks. It was hard doing that just a bit last year. This year it'll be even more, and I wouldn't have had the time I need both to study and to run. If I can't do track right, I shouldn't do it at all. But I miss it."

"Your studies are going well?" Marie asked.

"Yes, I'm leaning more and more to going into OB/GYN when I graduate. That part of the medical business calls to me. Maybe it started when I was dealing with Jessie's situation back in high school. I like what I can do with the patients in that line of medical work. We'll see."

"Do you still see Barry?" Marie asked. "I see him around town a bit, but I think he's moved out on his own."

Violet paused for a moment. Of course, Isaac knew all about the status of her relationship with Barry. Marie was another story. It had been years since Marie had let Jessie's secret get out around the school. Over time, Violet had forgiven her. She knew that Isaac had. But there were still moments when she remembered. For Violet, sharing confidential things with Marie was still difficult. If her brother and Marie had patched things up, Violet knew she had to move on as well.

She thought about it. Maybe it's time for me to let Marie know where Barry and I are in our relationship. Isaac knows, and he's kept it to himself if Marie's asking me now. That's good.

"Yes. He's got his own place up in Newburyport. He's working in an auto repair shop up there; been at that shop since he finished his year of tech school. He loves it. I get home and see him almost every weekend. And when I can't, he comes down to visit me in Boston. So, yes, we're still seeing each other, and we talk all the time."

"How about you, big brother?" Violet said to Isaac. "When I told you I had to quit the track team. You mentioned a while back, you're not as much into baseball these days. You haven't quit the baseball team, have you?"

"No. I'm still playing. I have to be part of the team if I want to keep my scholarship. But I understand that I'm not good enough to go pro after I graduate. So, I'm like you, cutting back on your track workouts. I do what I need to do to stay on the team and contribute, but it's my studies that matter now. I'll be student teaching this year and, if I get certified, I'll be looking to get a teaching job somewhere next year that could allow me to coach baseball."

They sat together, enjoying the fading warmth of autumn, talking about school and old friends from Rock Haven. They knew their lives were in transition, their time in college a stop along the way. They shared a feeling that they were on the verge of better things.

CHAPTER SIXTY-TWO

When she was interviewed after winning the high jump at the NCAA championship meet during her junior year of college, ESPN noted Jessie's commanding presence and her stunning eyes. Their research showed that her major was Broadcast Journalism. ESPN contacted Jessie and asked to meet her for an interview. Her charisma overwhelmed the interviewers. They told her they'd wait a year for her to graduate, but that they were interested in hiring her.

Things are falling into place for me, she thought to herself. I'll graduate. Then the Olympics. Then a career with ESPN. Perfect!

The year flew by. Soon it was her senior year, then Christmas break. Jessie returned to her mom's house outside Washington, DC. Patricia insisted that Jessie accompany her to a party. "They're all Michael's friends. Very well off. The right sort of people. Some are lobbyists, some are actually involved in political work. Who knows? Maybe this is where you'll meet the sort of guy you should be settling down with."

"Sure, Mom. I'll tag along."

She kept quiet, but assumed they'd all be a bunch of old people with too much money and fancy attitudes. Not likely I'll meet anyone interesting there. Certainly not a man worth spending time with. A bunch of elderly, white, rich folks. I'll probably get a good meal and some good wine. That's about all. But, there's nowhere else to go. Nothing else to do. Nothing to lose. I'll go. Why not?

Jessie's hunch was right. Most of the people at the party were a generation older than her, some of them considerably more. She sat alone on a silk upholstered sofa nursing a glass of sparkling wine watching her mom work the room. It appeared that Patricia knew everyone there. Jessie couldn't wait to go home.

Then Jessie saw him. He was tall, his skin swarthy, his hair jet black and trimmed in short waves. He had dark piercing eyes. She was stunned. He might be the best looking guy I've ever met, she thought. And I've been with a few really nice guys.

The man looked her way and began to approach slowly, his eyes locked on hers.

When he reached her, he asked, "Who are you? How did you get here? Why are you here? I don't feel this is exactly your element. You're like a fish out of water."

Jessie stood. He's taller than me! That's a good start. I have no interest in short men.

"I'm Jessie," she said, trying to remain calm. "My mom and my stepfather brought me. Let me ask you the same question. Why are you here?"

"I'm Julio. My parents made me come, too. We might be the only people here less than a hundred years old."

Jessie laughed, took a quick sip of her wine and brushed her hair back. "You're right. Are you in college somewhere?"

"No. I graduated from the University of Texas a few years back and got my Masters in Political Science here in DC at Georgetown. Graduated there two years ago."

"Really. Are you working now?"

"Yes. I guess you could call it work. I got elected as a congressman from my home district back in Texas a month ago. I'm settling in and trying to figure out what my job really is."

"Really! A congressman. Very nice, Julio. And you have a place here in DC?"

"Yes. In Georgetown, since college. I like it, so I stayed there when I got elected. I go back to Texas as often as possible though, to meet my constituents. Being both there and here is part of the job, but it's a hard balance to maintain. I have a place that I call home in Texas as well. And my parents are still in Texas, too, of course, although they came to DC to stay with me for Christmas. How about you, Jessie?"

"I'm in my senior year at the University of Connecticut. I still have a bit of time until I have to get a job. I came home to see my mom for Christmas."

"I'm glad you did. We might never have met if you hadn't. What are you majoring in?"

"Broadcast Journalism. I'm on the Track team at UConn. ESPN has already talked to me about maybe working for them after graduation."

Julio sat down on the sofa. Jessie sat again, and shifted next to him, their knees touching. They talked. At the end of the evening, he asked her to go to dinner with him the next night. That led to a quiet afternoon at a winery outside DC the day after that.

They continued finding ways to meet when Jessie returned to Connecticut after the Christmas break. Sometimes, Jessie returned to DC, claiming it was to visit her mom. But she spent most of her time with Julio. Sometimes, Julio went to Connecticut though he might have gone back to Texas to meet donors and constituents.

Once, over her spring break, Julio took Jessie to Texas to see where he was from. She had missed meeting his parents at Christmas, so this was her introduction to them and to Texas. She stayed in the family guest house, placed between the main house and the golf course.

"What do you think of Texas now that you've been here?" Julio asked her on the plane ride back to DC.

"It's lovely."

Julio said nothing. He simply smiled and took her hand.

Chapter Sixty-three

Jessie

Shortly before her graduation, Jessie enjoyed three victories. The first was at the NCAA track championship. Though Jessie was eliminated in a heat of the hurdles, the high jump came down to two finalists: a tall, stilt-like Black girl from Louisiana and Jessie. They both missed their first jumps at six feet, one inch. On her second attempt, Jessie brushed the bar. It rattled on the stands for a moment but settled. It matched Jessie's best jump ever.

The Louisiana girl missed her next two attempts, leaving Jessie the winner.

Grinning, Jessie received her medal and jumped from the podium after the awards. In her mind, she was thinking, there you go, Bitch. You lose! Now we know who's the best jumper in the country. Go on back to Louisiana.

Realizing ESPN and the world were watching, Jessie chose to display grace in winning. Radiant, she hugged her rival, aware of the television cameras. Then, she joined the ESPN announcer for her interview. "You had a good day today," the interviewer started. "How do you feel?"

"Amazing. That Louisiana girl's a great competitor and a good friend. But I'm thrilled to have won today. Now, it's on to the Olympic Trials in a couple of weeks."

Before she left the stadium, an ESPN executive pulled her aside. "Our offer to have you come to work for us still stands. Are you still interested?"

"Of course."

"When do you graduate?"

"Next week, right before the Olympic Trials."

"Perfect. Can we meet while you're out there in Oregon for the Trials? We'd like to offer you a contract."

She signed with ESPN the day before her event at the Trials. That was her second victory. And then Julio proposed. It was a great spring. Did it matter that she didn't make the Olympic team?

Chapter Sixty-four

After graduation, Jessie found an apartment in Alexandria, just inside the beltway and at the edge of DC. Her job with ESPN required her to travel frequently, so her apartment was barely furnished with old furniture bought at thrift stores. Although it was spare, it assured her mom that she was okay. The reality was that when she was in DC, Jessie was usually at Julio's apartment in Georgetown.

Her mother's house was a few miles away outside the beltway. The kitchen in her mom's new home was far larger than their kitchen in Rock Haven. The whole house was big, with far more space than Michael and Patricia required for just the two of them. Jessie liked it because it afforded her the distance she still needed to feel comfortable talking with her mom.

One Saturday morning, Jessie sat in her usual spot across the kitchen counter from Patricia in the new home. Half-empty coffee mugs sat on the counter in front of them.

"Mom, you remember Julio Garcia, the guy I met at your Christmas party last year? The Congressman from Texas?"

"Yes," Patricia responded with hesitation. She still worried about her impetuous daughter. As she waited for Jessie to continue she thought to herself, *I never know where Jessie will go with her discussions of her boyfriends. I still hope she'll find a nice white boy and settle down.*

"We've been together for most of the time since then. When I'm traveling with ESPN, he meets me on the road as often as he can, given his schedule here in DC. I met his family in Texas a few months ago. He's asked me to marry him and I said 'yes'."

Patricia's eyes narrowed. "Well, thank you for letting me know. I would have liked to have been a part of that decision." She fidgeted with her mug of coffee.

"It's really my decision, Mom, not yours. I'm the one marrying Julio."

Patricia sighed. "You love him?"

"Of course. I wouldn't marry him if I didn't."

"Okay." She felt she was giving up too quickly, but knew Jessie wouldn't change her mind.

"Okay." Patricia repeated, her hands up. "It's just that there have been so many boys. There was that poor Portuguese fisherman back in Rock Haven. Then that Black boy from Jamaica, your freshman year at UConn. Then others, all of them not suitable for a woman like you. Now you want to marry a Mexican?"

"Mom! Really? I've known since middle school that I can have any boy or man that I want. I've usually picked really attractive, powerful, and wealthy guys. First of all, Joe Goncalves isn't a poor fisherman. He's now playing major league baseball and probably making more money than anybody we know. Darren? Yes, he was from Jamaica, but he's now working for a huge bank somewhere, I think New York City. I'm not sure where he is, or what he's doing; we've lost touch. My other boyfriends are all good people, too. And Julio? Yes, his family's heritage is from Mexico. But, he's in Congress, for God's sake. You don't think he's good enough for me? The voters back in his district think he's good enough to send to Congress. Most of my boyfriends have been headed for success, and they've all been really good-looking, too. Not that that really matters."

"I suppose. I just want you to be sure. Yes, you can get any boy you want. You can marry any of them. Why Julio?"

"I love him. Isn't that enough?"

Patricia gave up. "Of course. If you're happy, that's fine. I just wish you wouldn't settle for someone who's not right for you."

"I'm not settling, Mom. He's the one I want. We're planning to get married this summer."

"Okay. Okay. Just let me know when and where. I support you, whatever you decide to do."

"Of course, Mom. Can you help me stage the wedding somewhere here in DC?"

Resigned, Patricia said. "Sure. Where would you like to do it?"

"Julio goes to a church here. We could do the wedding there. And some of his donors have access to a nice place for the reception."

"Sounds like you already made all the decisions. Which church?"

"It's called the Cathedral of St. Matthew the Apostle. It's a gorgeous place near Dupont Circle. I've been there a few times with Julio."

"But we're not Catholic."

"Julio and his family are. That's where we'll have the wedding."

"So, what's left for me to do?"

"Invitations and all the details. Julio's too busy with his Congressional work. And his family's in Texas. Could you help me with everything?"

"I suppose you've already picked a date."

"Yes. July sixteenth. It's a Saturday."

"Fine. And you've already booked the church and the reception venue?"

Yes."

"We'll do what we can to keep it small and intimate," Patricia told Jessie. "But Michael's got a lot of business associates and friends. We can't snub any of them, so we have to invite all of them."

"Sure. But with Julio's family and their friends...and his donors and supporters...there'll likely be a bit more than two hundred people at the wedding. That's how many we'll have to invite. You never know how many will actually show up, but that's about as small as we can have it."

"With that many people, it will be pretty expensive. I'll have to run this by Michael."

"Mom. Don't worry. Julio's friend is donating the reception hall. And his donors are paying for the food. All you and I need to do is pay for the church and anything else you'd like to contribute."

"Any friends from UConn or Rock Haven you'd like to invite?"

"Oh, that's all set, Mom," Jessie answered. "Julio's big sister, Vanessa, will be my Matron of Honor. Her little daughter will be the flower girl. And two of my UConn teammates will be my bridesmaids. That covers it for me. I've lost touch with everybody back in Rock Haven. Haven't heard from any of them for a few years. So, no need to worry about inviting any of them."

"Even your friend, Violet?"

"Yes. Even Violet. I think she graduated from college somewhere in Boston, but that's all I know about her. When we moved here and I left for college, I left all of that behind. I've totally lost touch with Violet."

"Considering what she did for you with the trouble your senior year of high school, we should probably send her an invitation at least. She should know you're about to get married."

"Sure. Okay. But I doubt she can afford to come. I still have her parents' address."

CHAPTER SIXTY-FIVE

Violet

Violet, Barry, and her family were seated around the kitchen table in the Arnold home. Violet and Barry sat side by side, holding hands under the table.

"This came in the mail early this week," Evelyn Arnold said, handing a thick envelope to her daughter. "I shouldn't have opened it, but I did. It looked like it might have been more than the usual junk mail you still get here, now that you and Barry have your own place."

"Thanks, Mom," Violet said, deflecting the debate about her having moved in with Barry after she graduated. She opened the envelope and slid out a thick piece of embossed paper. As she read the words, her eyes popped open widely.

"Oh, my God! It's from Jessie. And she's getting married. We're invited," she said, looking at Barry.

"Really? I'm invited, too? It says you can bring a plus one?"

"It doesn't say I can't, and there's a box I can check when I RSVP".

"When is it?"

"Middle of July in DC. Let's go."

"Well, that's wonderful," said Evelyn. "Maybe she's finally settling down. After all these years. Jessie Brandt is finally settling. Can you imagine?"

Violet sat up a bit straighter. "Mom, Dad, there's something else I'd like to talk with you about."

She paused. Sam and Evelyn waited, anticipating the next moment.

"Barry and I want to get married."

Sam stood. Looking at Barry, he said, "Young man, aren't you supposed to come to me first, and ask permission to marry my daughter?"

Barry slumped in his chair. "I guess. Mr. Arnold, can I have your permission to marry your daughter Violet?"

Sam circled the table to Barry and pulled him to his feet.

Grinning, Sam finished. "Of course. We wondered when you two would get around to it. Of course, you can marry Violet. Welcome to our family!"

Violet simply smiled.

*****

Violet and Barry sat in a pew at the back of the richly decorated nave of the Cathedral. Mosaics and frescoes surrounded them. High above the crossing where a dome rose, a great circular opening glowed at the crown, flooding the interior with a soft light. A quiet hum rose from the hundreds of wedding guests. Violet and Barry knew no one.

After the service, they took an Uber to the reception. They left their gift, a wrapped box containing a pair of crystal candlesticks, on a table among other larger packages.

They found their table near the rear of the huge hall and sat down. Eventually, other people found seats at the table as well. Making small talk while they waited for Jessie and Julio to arrive, one of their table-mates, a heavy-set man with perfectly styled white hair, asked, "How do you two know Julio?"

292

"Oh, we don't," Violet replied. "I was Jessie's best friend in high school. I'm Violet and this is my friend Barry."

"What do you two do for work?"

"I'm a nurse at an OBGYN clinic back in Massachusetts."

"And I'm a mechanic," Barry replied, proudly, defiantly. "What about you?"

"I'm in real estate in Texas. I help fundraise for Julio."

"Good for you," said Violet.

The fundraiser turned away to talk with more important and affluent people.

They waited a few minutes more. Then Violet asked, "Have you had enough, Barry?"

"Sure. Let's go."

They took an Uber back to their hotel, checked out, and headed for the airport. They were home in time for dinner.

CHAPTER SIXTY-SIX

Two years later, Jessie sat holding Julio's hand in a doctor's office in downtown DC. The doctor leaned forward in his chair, his forearms resting on the leather-topped desk. He looked into Jessie's eyes first and then turned to Julio.

"I'm afraid I have some hard news to deliver for you both. Jessie, you've miscarried twice now. And you mentioned that years ago you also had a miscarriage. For whatever reason, it appears that your body doesn't tolerate pregnancy well. We can try a few things. In vitro fertilization, for example. But I suspect that it's a long shot for you to ever carry a pregnancy full-term. Getting pregnant isn't the issue here. It's carrying the baby full term that's the problem."

"There must be something you can do, doctor," Julio insisted. "We want a baby."

Jessie began to weep quietly. Julio shifted his chair closer to her and rested a comforting hand on her shoulder.

The doctor looked down, sympathetic and understanding of their feelings, but concise. "Sometimes this is just the way it is. It's nobody's fault, but there's not much we can do. I can give you some information about adoption. But I don't hold out much hope for a full-term pregnancy."

They talked with the doctor a few minutes more. He explained some of the possible medical reasons behind her inability to carry a pregnancy to full term. Jessie's mind was blank. She heard little the doctor said. Finally, loaded with pamphlets about adoption, Julio led Jessie, still weeping, from the office to the parking lot.

"Maybe we should think about adopting," he said as he dodged through DC traffic heading back to their townhouse. He looked straight ahead, avoiding eye contact with his distraught wife.

Jessie wiped her face with her palms. She blurted, "I don't know. Do you still love me, even if I can't give you children?"

"Of course. Sure, it would be a good image for me to be seen with you and some little ones. Voters would like that. But maybe I'm meant to be a champion for adoption. My constituents might like that too."

"But you still love me? That's what matters the most. It's all that matters if I can't have children."

"Always. I'll always love you."

"How? Why? If I can't give you children."

"I love you for who you are. For what you are. There's more to you than bearing a baby. We can adopt and you can love and mother our baby that way. We can deal with this."

Jessie slumped in the car, still sobbing. Julio reached to her and held her hand most of the rest of the way home, only letting go when the DC traffic required him to do so.

EPILOGUE

Rock Haven

The ten-year reunion organizers planned the gathering for November to allow their star classmate, Joe Goncalves, a few weeks to complete his eighth season with the Cardinals. He was no stranger to many of his former classmates since he had bought a house in The Heights and now wintered there with his family during the off-season. Sometimes, even in the summer, Melissa would stay there with their two little girls. People saw her taking the girls to the beach in the morning. The babies accompanied her on her errands, riding with her when she went grocery shopping. Everybody in town knew Joe Goncalves and his young family. Despite their loyalty to the Red Sox, they all followed the pitching career of their famous son, Joe Goncalves.

Joe had offered to buy a second house a few doors away from his home in The Heights for his parents and another one for Joao Senior, but they all turned him down.

"I've already got a perfectly fine home," explained Joao Senior. "I've lived here for years. Why would I want to move up there on the hill with all those rich people?"

The class invited a few of their favorite teachers to attend the reunion. Jonas Brown, the class advisor from ten years ago, came alone; his wife had passed away two years earlier, a year after he had retired. They invited their two championship coaches too: Lucas Knox and Harvey Lancaster. Jennifer sat with Lucas. Lancaster's wife had decided to skip the evening, knowing few of the former

297

students. The teachers, feeling old and a bit out of place, sat together at a table on the side of the room.

Most of the former students mingled with drinks at the bar or clustered in the middle of the ballroom dance floor at the country club. A disc jockey played ten-year-old rock hits. The students gave Joe space, deferring to his celebrity status. It was uncomfortable for him to have old teammates and friends acting so unnaturally around him. As he saw it, he was still just Joe Goncalves, a classmate, not a famous athlete.

Midway through the evening, Joe brought Melissa over to chat with Coach Lancaster. Isaac tagged along with his wife, Marie. Isaac was now quite familiar with the three older teachers. He was teaching physical education at the Rock Haven middle school and coaching football and baseball at the high school as Lancaster's assistant. Violet, even though she had graduated a year later than the reunion class, was there too, with her new husband, Barry, a member of the class. The group of six crowded around Jonas, Lucas, and Lancaster. The three teachers and Jennifer stood.

Joe beamed and hugged Coach Lancaster. He shook hands with Lucas and Jonas, clasping their hands between his massive palms. He began, "It's good to be home. I'm away too much during the summer. Have you all met my wife, Melissa? Harvey, you know her. I introduced her to you right after our wedding."

 "It's nice to meet you," said Jonas, speaking for the group. "Yes, we've seen Melissa around town."

Lancaster turned from Melissa to Joe. "We watched you on television a couple of weeks ago. The National League playoffs? You had a great game."

"Yeah, thanks. I won my game, but we got eliminated the next day. All-in-all, I had a good season. I was the Cardinals' third starter. I'll take sixteen wins this year. Maybe I'll be better next season...Maybe win a few more."

Lancaster beamed. His protégé had made it. "You spend all winter here?" he noted. "Even with the New England weather? You're still welcome to work out at the school."

"Thanks," Joe replied, smiling graciously. "I'm all set. I lift at home when I can, in my home gym. Isaac spots me when he's around and able. I do lighter weights without a spotter on other days. Light workouts are what I need this time of the year, enough to stay fit, but taking some time to rest. The season's a grind. I grew up here, so I don't mind the cold and snow. The winter weather's not so bad. And I go to spring training in Florida in the middle of February. Melissa and the kids come with me."

"We live in St. Louis most of the rest of the year," Melissa explained. "I bring the little ones to Massachusetts for a few weeks in the middle of the summer when Joe has a long road trip. It's good at that time of the year to get away from the Midwest heat. I spend time at the beach with the girls, which is something we can't do in St. Louis. It's so great to visit with Joe's family. His parents love playing with their grandkids."

Joe nodded and continued. "We'll have to make a decision in a year or two, when the kids are old enough to start school, where we'll want to live year-round. The schools are better here than in St. Louis, and that really matters to both of us. I also like Rock Haven, so I can be with my family. Have them here with my girls. Maybe we'll settle here."

"We've started talking about it," confirmed Melissa. "I love it here. I can go back to St. Louis in the summer, during the season. But I don't have family in St. Louis. So, living here seems like the way to go. I also try to get back to my family in Iowa a few times a year."

Lucas changed the conversation. "How about you, Violet? We all know about Isaac and Marie and their young one, since Isaac's teaching with us. Isaac has told me you're a nurse somewhere. But we've fallen out of touch. How are you doing?"

"I'm well! I'm with an OB/GYN practice in Newburyport. I'm still taking classes, and I'll be certified as a nurse practitioner in one more year. I find it rewarding to deliver babies, help new mothers. I found my calling."

"Do you or Barry still do any running?"

"Not like the old days. We live in Newburyport and both work there, but there's no time to really train."

"We both jog a few days a week after work, and run an occasional 5K race," explained Barry. "That's enough to keep us fit and have some fun."

"But we're not really competitive anymore," Violet confessed.

"Any kids?" asked Lucas.

Violet paused, then answered, her face deadpan, suppressing a smile. "No. Not yet. We haven't had the time for kids, what with our work and all. Anyway, we've barely been married two years."

Lucas sensed from Violet's demeanor that there might be more to that story, but thought it better not to ask.

Joe took a final sip of beer, set his empty glass on a nearby table, and said, "I'm heading to the bar for another beer. Anybody else need one?" Seeing that Violet's hands were empty, he asked again. "Violet, you want a beer?"

"No," she broke into a full smile. Barry grinned next to her.

The group watched her, noting her empty iced tea glass on the table next to her. "Whoa!" said Isaac. "Little sister, are you...?"

"Yes. We're expecting our first baby next spring."

Isaac stepped to his sister and hugged her. Barry continued smiling but said nothing.

"This is a beautiful moment," said Lucas. "I'm so happy for both of you. And thrilled to be here to be a part of it."

Violet and Barry's moment ended abruptly. It was as though an electric charge went through the entire room. The ballroom suddenly went silent. Everybody sensed the change and turned towards the double doors from the ballroom to the lobby. The DJ stopped the music, watching.

Jessie stood there, posing in the doorway, her feet set apart, one hand on her hip, her presence, as always, demanding everyone's focus. While most of her classmates were dressed in casual attire, Jessie wore a low-cut red dress that accented her still-lean, tall frame. The hem stopped at mid-thigh, highlighting her long legs. Her blonde hair was perfectly styled, flowing to her shoulders. She paused, surveying the room, then strode, heels clicking, across the crowded dance floor, cutting through her old classmates, ignoring them, until she reached Violet, Joe, and Lucas, the people she had come to see. Everyone watched her.

"Hi, how's everybody doing?" she announced, surveying the group. She turned to Violet, pulled her in, and hugged her briefly, tiny pats with both hands on the back of her shoulders. "How are you, Violet? It's been ages. I'm so sorry we didn't get to talk at my wedding a few years ago. It was a crazy day. A lot of people there. Thank you for the candlesticks."

Violet assessed her old friend, looking to see if she'd changed. Everything seemed the same. For Jessie, it was as though time stood still. "We're fine," Violet confirmed. "We're doing well."

No need to tell Jessie the news of her pregnancy. That omission was noted by the group.

"We? Oh, I see you and Barry are still an item."

"Of course." Violet smiled and hugged Barry quickly.

Lucas took charge, stepping forward to hug Jessie. Jessie didn't react, her arms at her side. Lucas said, "Nobody had heard from you, Jessie. We didn't know if you were coming. I'm glad you made it."

"My life's a little busy. I never seem to know from week to week where I'll need to be."

"You married a politician. Right?" asked Lucas. "I've tried to follow what you've been up to. Everyone seems to know a bit about you, but none of the details."

"Yes, Julio Garcia, a congressman from our district in Texas. We spend most of our time either in DC or back home in Texas."

"How long have you been married?" asked Violet. Having been at the wedding, she knew the answer, but it seemed like as good a way as any to continue the conversation.

"Almost five years. I met Julio my senior year of college at a Christmas party in DC. We got married a year later."

"Any children?" Violet continued, asking about Jessie's status while not confessing her newly announced pregnancy to her old friend.

"No. Not yet. We're trying. It would be good for Julio's image to be seen with me and a couple of kids, but so far, no."

Violet nodded. "That's too bad."

"Are you working, Violet?" asked Jessie, changing the subject.

"Yes, I'm with an OB/GYN practice in Newburyport."

"Wonderful. I expect you're good with that sort of work."

"I love it."

"Are you still running?" asked Lucas, facing Jessie.

"Running competitively? No. I've moved on from that. I did okay in the NCAA championship my last two years at UConn. All-American. Then I went to the Olympic Trials after my senior year and finished fifth in the high jump. Fifth! They only take three to the Olympics, and I was fifth. It didn't make any sense to keep on training and jumping if I couldn't make the Olympic team."

Violet, taken aback, shook her head. "What? Really? You were that close to going to the Olympics, and you just walked away from it? After all the years of training?"

"It had become a hassle. And then with Julio... It's not like I walked away completely. I did some work on Track and Field broadcasts on ESPN right after graduation. But then, getting ready for my wedding down in DC and getting settled there and in Texas. There was no time, so I left ESPN. And, no. I'm not really running. I still do an occasional 5K for charity with Julio. We like to support the right causes. Julio and I laugh 'cause I usually beat him. We run together, and then I out-kick him at the end. My body still knows how to race. We joke about it."

Gabe appeared, pushing his way into the middle of the small group. "Hi, Jessie. How're you doing?"

Jessie looked down at him. "Fine, and you?"

"Great. I have a photography business downtown. I'm doing really well. I took a group photo of our class an hour ago, before you came. Could I get a shot of you to Photoshop into it?"

"Sure. When I'm done talking here." Jessie turned away from Gabe, her shoulder cutting him from the group. She wanted to interact with the rest of her old friends, not Gabe. She turned to Joe. Joe looked down, avoiding eye contact.

"How about you, Joe?" she asked. "I hear you're doing well." She started to lean in for a hug, but Joe pulled back, taking Melissa's hand.

"Yes. This is my wife, Melissa. And Melissa, this was my high school girlfriend, Jessie."

Melissa wasn't smiling. Early in their relationship, Joe had explained about Jessie.

Jessie nodded to Joe's wife dismissively, then turned back to Joe. "You're still pitching for the Cardinals?"

"Yes. Have you seen any of our games on television?"

"No. I don't really have time to follow baseball. And when I do, it's the Astros. I like to know what Julio's constituents are talking about, and that's the 'Stros. But football is what I usually watch. It's the game everybody loves in Texas."

The DJ started again with the loud music. People began dancing again, oblivious to the awkward conversation between the coaches and the former classmates and friends at the periphery of the room.

"Shake it up, baby! Twist and shout!" Dancers shouted along with McCartney, waving their arms in the air above their heads.

Against the noisy backdrop of the rock, the conversation between Jessie and the group stalled. There was a moment when nobody said anything. Everyone seemed to have said all they had to say to convince their classmates how successful they really were, now as adults.

Jessie looked around the group, starting with Lucas. Ignoring Melissa. Focusing briefly on Joe. She ended, looking Violet in the eyes. For a brief moment she reached to her, touching Violet's arm, the contact perhaps a plea for a renewed connection. Violet looked back, her face placid. Violet was content with the life she now lived without the ongoing calamity that was Jessie.

"I think I'll head out," Jessie shrugged. "I wanted to come see everybody again, and now I've done that. I've got an early flight tomorrow morning, back to DC, so I've got to go get some sleep." She cut back across the crowded ballroom floor to the doorway, ignoring the rest of her old classmates.

Gabe never got her picture.

Violet shook her head, perturbed. "That's it? She blows in and blows out. Never stayed long enough to talk with anyone but us? Why did she even come?"

Isaac laughed for a moment. "So? She's gone again. She never even said hi to me. Never seemed to know I was here."

Marie put her arm around his waist. "You hoped she would?"

"Nah. Life goes on without Jessie Brandt."

Joe and Melissa, Isaac with Marie, Violet and Barry, and Gabe drifted away, leaving the teachers alone.

The music continued. People danced. Small groups broke off the dance floor, settling into old patterns of classmates who had once been close. The teachers sat back at their table. Lucas swirled his empty wine glass as he looked at his long-time friends.

"I still wonder if we made a difference with any of them when they were in school," Lucas said. "Maybe I always will."

"I believe we did," said Lancaster. "Would they have all come back tonight if we hadn't? They all seemed to turn out okay. Even Gabe."

"They all came back to their roots tonight," added Jonas. "And here we are asking, did we make a difference? We must have. Everything evens out over time. We're all here in the same room tonight for some reason. Yes, we made a difference."

Lucas smiled. Jennifer squeezed his hand.

ACKNOWLEDGEMENTS

Nobody can handle life's challenges alone. That point resonates throughout much of *Crossing the Lines*. Writing and publishing this book is an example of that premise.

I sought advice on much of the story from teachers and others involved in education. I drew on my coaching experience for the track and field segments and gathered feedback on some of those segments from former coaches and competitors.

I was aided in the writing itself by suggestions from most of my colleagues in my two critique groups, the Silver Quill Writers and the Williamsburg critique group. My beta readers, Ellen Smith, Rick Bayko, Mike St. Laurent, and Archibald Campbell, offered their wisdom. The book is better because of their thoughts.

Finally, my publisher, ML Brei of Meripoint Books, has been a pleasure to work with. Dividing my original manuscript into two books, *Crossing the Lines* and *Seeking Wealth*, has made both books better.

Lastly, my wife, Debbie, has been with me throughout this project. I doubt that this would ever have been finished without her support.

About the Author

Peter Stipe has enjoyed a long and varied career that has included fourteen years in education as a public high school history teacher and track coach. He has also worked for many years in Management in Human Resource Development and Training for a variety of businesses. He has worked with Employment Boards for both the state of Massachusetts and the state of Rhode Island, addressing job creation and job skills development on Federal initiatives. He has a Bachelor of Arts degree in History from Boston University and a Master of Arts in Education from Tufts.

A competitive long-distance runner for many years, he has completed numerous marathons with six finishes in the top fifty places in the Boston Marathon and participation in the 1972 U.S. Olympic Trials.

A New Englander for most of his life, he now lives with his wife in Williamsburg.

www.ingramcontent.com/pod-product-compliance
Lightning Source LLC
Chambersburg PA
CBHW040856010826
48978CB00013BA/1039